I0667120

THE LOST

By
Edward F. McKeown

AN IMPRINT OF COPPER DOG PUBLISHING, LLC

The Maauro Chronicles: The Lost

Moondream Press
An Imprint of Copper Dog Publishing LLC
537 Leader Circle
Louisville, CO 80027
www.copperdogpublishing.com

Ordering Information:
Special discounts are available on quantity purchases by corporations, associations, and others. For details, contact the publisher at the address above.
Printed in the United States of America

Credits:
Author: Edward F. McKeown
Managing Editor: Michael H. Hanson
Creative Director: Helen H. Harrison
Editor: Laura Jean Stroupe
Proofreader: Julie Harrison Saunders
Proofreader: Catherine Van Sciver
Cover Art: iStockphoto: Tithi Luadthong Art

ISBN:
978-1-943690-14-5 (Paperback)
978-1-943690-15-2 (Kindle)

Library of Congress Control Number: 2017941757

Fiction: Science Fiction

DEDICATION

This book is dedicated to my friend,
Sifu Chris Facente,
and all the gang at
Mint Hill Kung Fu School
of Lai Tung Pai.

All the Best,
Sifu Ed

The Lost

The lost are never forgotten,
So anchored in our memory,
Sweet miracles once begotten,
That fate led on some dark journey.

The lost are more than life's echoes
Or ache forever lingering,
They are the truth lost in the throes
Of destiny's malingering.

The lost are beacons yet unseen,
Pale torches burning in the night
And all the blackness in between
Stars beckoning like candlelight.

I'll seek you always and an age
However far
Nothing will bar
My lonely love and righteous rage.

—Michael H. Hanson

CONTENTS

CHAPTER 1

OVERHEAD, A DARK-GRAY CONFED CRUISER ROARED defiance of gravity as it gradually climbed into the great bowl of the sky. The vibrations penetrated the plas-steel windows of our office. *Unusual to see such a large vessel in atmosphere,* I thought, as I looked toward the bay where our own small ship, *Stardust*, sat. From the third story tower that housed Lost Planet Expeditions it was only possible to see *Stardust's* slender atmospheric nose. All about her, dozens of ships sat, or were being serviced all the way to the horizon of Star City's main spaceport.

The window also reflected my face back at me. I wasn't bad looking for a dark-haired, brown-eyed human male in his mid-twenties. My age, even more than with most spacers, was an approximation and compromise. Almost thirty-two galactic-standard years had passed since my birth, but I had only lived twenty-six of them. Most of two had been spent in cold sleep when I fled my homeworld of Retief. Five more years passed when *Stardust* ventured inside the gravity well of the ancient Infestor Artifact ship, only days had passed for us, but the universe had moved on.

Movement interrupted my reverie. From the city side of the field a slender figure approached. To most eyes Maauro would seem to be a girl in her late teens or early twenties, about five-feet-four. Black hair tumbled to her waist and bounced in a pony tail gathered with a yellow silk bow. She appeared to be wearing a dark jump suit with orange panels, but that was an illusion. The suit was merely the outer casing of her armor, textured to look like clothing.

The eyes were the big giveaway. Maauro's eyes were almost three times as big as a standard humans'. She had patterned herself on a game simulation in my computer after I found her, stranded for 50,000 years on a wrecked asteroid base. She claimed she could not change her basic matrix without undue risk. I thought she had just grown used to her new face. I couldn't blame her for that. Her appearance was one of the first choices she'd ever made for herself.

"Watching your mechanical girlfriend?" a throaty voice sounded in my ear. I turned from the window to face Jaelle Tekala. She smiled to take the sting out of the comment, though with fangs resting on her full lower lip the effect was still alarming. The Nekoan was a creature of the sun—golden skin, yellow eyes. Her hair was a leonine pile topped by two large cat-like ears. Her ancestors had been omnivorous creatures resembling a Terran lion. The human mind wanted a pattern, so it said cat. Jaelle's small features made her surprisingly human in appearance, which worked out well for me. Our consortship was only six months old, though we had been a couple since the bad old days on Kandalor.

"Jaelle, you know I love you," I replied, looking her straight in the eyes, she stood only slightly shorter than my own six-foot height.

"Yes, me and her."

"Different ways."

She yawned. "What a discriminating anatomy you have, male-of-mine."

"My anatomy's irrelevant when it comes to Maauro." I sighed inside. Jaelle was my lover. Maauro, whose gender was an appearance she had elected for herself, was ...well, what was Maauro? A combat android and quantum computer from a long vanished alien race? The only self-aware artificial intelligence known to exist? She was also the closest friend I had ever had. Maauro knew me as no other being did, including secrets and flaws I had not fully shared with Jaelle.

Jaelle gestured with her delicate and pointed chin. "Here comes Dusko."

A tall, angular shape followed Maauro toward us. The Dua-Denlenn, with his pointed ears and pupilless blue eyes, looked like a woodland elf gone bad.

"Yeah," I replied. I'd forgiven the fourth member of our team, former Guild crime lord, for his persecution of me when I had been a broken spacer doing odd jobs around Kandalor. He'd joined us as a prisoner, betrayed the Guild to stay alive and had won grudging acceptance from the rest of us.

Jaelle left my side to drop into a chair and stretch her long, leather-clad and booted legs out on the table. I walked over to the small kitchen and fished out soft drinks and fruit juices for everyone.

The door slid open. Maauro entered with Dusko on her heels.

"Hello, Wrik," Maauro said in a high voice that complimented her appearance. Her face held its usual gentle, contemplative look, but I always felt there was an extra degree of animation in it when she looked at me. I couldn't stop my answering grin and I slid one of the soft drinks she enjoyed in front of her as she sat opposite Jaelle. Maauro turned all things she ingested to energy, but nevertheless favored anything sweet.

"Good morning, Jaelle," she added.

"Hello, Kit-sister," Jaelle returned with her pet name for Maauro.

Dusko and I exchanged nods, and I let him get his own drink and join us at the table.

"I am glad you were all able to come this morning," Maauro said.

"What was it you wanted to talk about?" I asked.

"About the next mission of Lost Planet Expeditions," she said.

"Does there need to be a next one?" Jaelle said, her face revealing little. "We're well set after Confed paid us off on the Predictor matter.

Not to mention the profits I make with our legitimate shipping interests."

I shifted uncomfortably. Even in our office, protected by Maauro's best cyber-defenses, the open mention of our last mission with its potential to start an interstellar war was unsettling. We had destroyed the Ribisan Predictor technology, ending a threat to Confed's peace, a peace that, with the waning of Earth's influence in the Confederacy, seemed increasingly chancy.

"Wealth was not the objective of our agency," Maauro countered.

"For you perhaps," Jaelle returned. I suspected Dusko agreed with her, but was cautious of appearing to oppose Maauro. "For those of us mortals of flesh and blood, it's nice stuff to have, along with security and comfort."

"True," she acknowledged, "but when we founded Lost Planet after escaping from the Infestor Artifact, we wanted to make some greater use of our talents than mere commerce."

"Truth be told," I said, "it was greater use of your talents, Maauro."

She shook her head and the glossy black hair bounced. "No, we are a team; a whole that is greater than the sum of its parts. Each of us at one time has been the factor that saved the others and the mission. Wrik, I wish you could come to believe this as I do."

"Keep on him, Kit-sister," Jaelle said, quietly but with force. "We'll make him believe it someday."

I looked away. There were failures in my past that had never removed their claws from me. Perhaps they never would.

"That said," Jaelle continued. "I do not see why we should concentrate on espionage for the Confederacy as opposed to commerce."

"Trade is second nature to you, Jaelle," Maauro said, "and fulfilling."

"But not to you, Kit-sister."

"No. For all that it pleases me to see you succeed, Jaelle. I'm even pleased for you, Dusko, so long as your violations of the law remain minor and result in no injury to innocents."

Dusko raised his glass in mock salute. "It is useful to keep our contacts in the Guild and other such organizations active," he said, his face blank as usual, but his voice betraying a touch of anxiety.

"You haven't brought this up casually," Jaelle said, her cat-irised eyes narrowing.

"You are correct. Late last night a message reached me from Candace Deveraux."

We groaned. Deveraux was the Confederate spymaster and our secret employer. Unable to seize Maauro, whose deadliness belied her small frame, she'd settled for extracting a promise to work for Confed Intelligence. In return, we received Confed commissions and Maauro was recognized as a citizen in data hidden in many places.

"Espionage," Jaelle said the word as a curse.

"Not this time," Maauro said. "Though the contact comes through her, this is more in the nature of what we planned for Lost Planet, something of a rescue or recovery mission."

Jaelle's frown lessened. "What are the details?"

"We'll find out this afternoon at 1300 hours. A visitor will attend us and brief us on this prospective mission. Candace says this one is our option as to whether to accept or not."

"Now that's the most unusual thing I've heard this morning," Dusko said, then sipped his drink.

"Is she coming?" I ask,

"No," Maauro replied, "which I regard as unusual. She hinted she would see us another time."

"Odd," Dusko said.

"I wish for us to have some time to talk before this person arrives," Maauro began. "We have been through many dangers before. I want to be sure everyone is willing to face more, before we entertain the client. Between recovering from our last mission and celebrating Wrik and Jaelle's consortship, it has been quite a while since we were last active."

She looked at me and I at her and Jaelle.

"Lost Planet was my idea as well," I said. "I don't see a reason to change."

Dusko surprised me by speaking next. "I'm as happy attending to my own affairs and supporting what we do here. However I know the Guild would make short work of me if Maauro's protection is lifted. In return I do what you need of me."

We all looked at Jaelle as the silence lengthened. "I'll hear what this mission is before I commit," Jaelle finally said.

I felt a sinking sensation in my stomach. I couldn't be sure if it was because I felt Jaelle might not come with us, or because she would. I rarely felt fear for Maauro's safety, never for Dusko's, but since I had found Jaelle, I lived in terror of something happening to her, or of her drifting out of my life. Nekoans were independent creatures and Jaelle was an off-the-charts rebel, even by her people's standards.

"That is fair," Maauro conceded. "It might even be reasonable to have someone here full time to run the trade business and its employees. Though, if you become much more successful, our cover business may displace our true function."

Jaelle's expression told me that she'd entertained similar thoughts.

"Why don't we have some lunch while we wait for our mystery visitor," I said. "There are some frozen lunches from Asteroid Asia in the fridge."

We ate and talked of the adventures we'd survived and what the future might hold and it became even more apparent to me that a split was coming. Jaelle's interests lay with us, but not in the dangerous business that Maauro favored. Why should that be surprising? Jaelle took second place to no one in courage, least of all me. But she was neither as close to Maauro as I was, nor as dependent as Dusko. She'd been raised in a trading family before her father's involvement with the Guild caused an irretrievable break. Nenan Tekala sold us out to his partners in the Guild on Kandalor. The resulting ambush cost me my small ship, *Sinner,* and Maauro her original left arm. It also cost Jaelle's father his daughter's respect and allegiance. We'd made good the losses later, but only after many bad days.

An aircar slid into view through the window, followed by two more. They landed in a triangular formation in front of our office and a mix of humans and others spilled out. Diverse as they were in appearance, their brisk and efficient movements practically screamed security.

I popped up our outside cameras and focused one on the biggest vehicle.

A woman got out. She stood tall and straight for all that her banner of hair, long as Maauro's, alternated bands of silver and black. Her face was striking, beautifully symmetrical, with ivory skin, yet it was a mature beauty.

"Oh my God," I managed. "That's Captain Shasti Rainhell!"

CHAPTER 2

"IT HAS BEEN A LONG TIME SINCE SHASTI RAINHELL HAS COMMANDED *a starship," I reply to my biological companions as I study Wrik's astonished face. "She now commands the Olympian Security Section on her homeworld. Her husband, Mikhail Vaughn is the current president, but many suspect her of being the true power on that world."*

"You don't understand, Maauro," Jaelle finally says. "That's a living legend walking toward us. She and her ship saved my kind and the Skurlock from the Evolvers. Hers was the first Confed vessel to find the old Concordiat."

"She must be a hundred years old!" Wrik adds. I note the wonder and enthusiasm in his voice and face, how it makes him look younger than his twenty-six elapsed years. I know he has studied the voyages of Rainhell and Fenaday. A model of their blood-red ship sits behind us on the shelf. Wrik built it on one voyage.

"As best it can be determined," I reply, "she is ninety-four years from the date that she was decanted in the eugenics laboratory where she was created."

"Gives you something in common," Dusko says dryly.

"In a way," I reply. "We were both designed for conflict by our creators, she from genetic material and I from silicon and ceramics and armor. Both of us have also slipped the hands of our makers. It will be interesting to meet her. Wrik, why don't you go down and greet our potential client?"

Wrik nods eagerly and heads for the door. While we were conversing in the slow time of biological life, I extended my cybernetic net to embrace the area behind our office building. I detect and infiltrate, on a basic level, the Confed security force surrounding Rainhell. I could intrude further, but only at the risk of leaving some indication or having to spend a considerable amount of time to erase my tracks by reprogramming the network.

Beyond the immediate area I check my traps and regular intrusion paths. I detect only a SWAT detachment nearby in an airvan, a standard precaution that does not concern me. No Guild or other intelligence forces are targeting us within the range of my detection. I complete my multi-level scan and surveillance before Wrik reaches the door. I would not have allowed him to proceed further without confirming his safety.

I walked to the elevator, trying to compose myself so I didn't look like a schoolboy, but it was hard to control my feelings about meeting a childhood hero. The elevator doors dinged and opened and there she stood. To my surprise, she was alone.

My first impression of Shasti Rainhell was of a much younger woman, her face was unlined, her body powerful and athletic, though silver shone in bands in her hair. The eyes, jade green, were not those of a young woman, and had seen much.

"You're Wrik Trigardt," she said, her voice musical and higher than I expected. I gazed up at her, fully nine inches taller than me, which made me feel even more like a child. She stepped out of the elevator with none of the slowness or infirmity of age. I felt a stab of jealously at the inhuman perfection of her; it retreated quickly as I remembered that her life had not always been a happy one.

Despite myself, I threw a salute at her. "At your service, Captain Rainhell." I shouldn't have been surprised that she knew who I was. She'd have been briefed on everything Candace knew or suspected before coming here.

She gave a slight smile. "It has been a while since I was called that. For now young man, Shasti, will do. My visit today is unofficial."

"Yes, Ma'am." I couldn't bring myself to use her first name. "If you'll follow me, I'll take you to meet the rest of Lost Planet."

She nodded. For all the noise she made as we walked over the stone flooring I could have been alone. How did she move so quietly?

I opened the door to find all three of my companions standing respectfully. Rainhell swept past me to stand opposite, Maauro. The two looked steadily at each other.

Rainhell gave a short laugh. "Our designers had similar tastes. Apparently they liked pale skin, black hair and green eyes, albeit our shades are different. Mine liked height though."

Maauro cocked her head, as if unsure what to make of the comment. "Alas, neither my coloration nor appearance are factory original. My form is something I chose shortly after I was found. I was originally forty percent larger as well."

"More proof of your superiority then," Rainhell said. "I certainly couldn't be reduced by forty percent of my mass and still function."

She gazed at the others. "Jaelle Tekala. I always enjoy meeting Nekoans; one of my best friends was Teleera D'abo, the first of your people I met."

"Yes, Madame Rainhell," Jaelle said, "I know. D'abo is a name greatly honored among my people." For the first time in my experience with her, Jaelle looked overwhelmed.

When Rainhell's eyes swept over Dusko, they were chilled. "You are the Dua-Denlenn, Dusko." There was no mistaking the menace in her voice. "I have had many experiences with your people and few of them have survived those."

CHAPTER 2

Dusko turned to Maauro. "She does indeed resemble you." Turning back to Rainhell he replied. "I know of no feud or quarrel that lies between us. Nor would I be fool enough to risk any such. As for the rest, Maauro guarantees my good behavior on similar terms to what I imagine you would employ."

Rainhell's eyes returned to Maauro. "Even after all I have seen in a long life, it's remarkable to converse with a being from when my species— and I do consider myself a human—lived in caves. Still more amazing to me is that you, too, are artificial in nature. Your creation makes my own look like a child's experiment."

"Shall we sit?" I said.

We did, though Jaelle immediately got up to bring more drinks and some cookies and chocolates into the room.

"Ah," Rainhell said. "Can it be that you knew it was me coming?" She reached out and took a number of chocolates.

"Happy accident," I said. "Maauro is fond of them too."

Surprise registered for a moment on her face. "How remarkable, it never occurred to me that you might eat."

"I enjoy the ritual of meals with my network," Maauro said. "I can convert anything to energy, but food is so slow and limited. When I dine on nuclear materials or other forms of high energy, I do so alone." She took a cookie and nibbled on it delicately with teeth that I knew could turn into serrated cutting edges capable of shearing bone.

"Is Captain Fenaday with you?" I asked, unable to restrain myself.

She smiled warmly at the mention of her old friend and lover's name. "No, Robert seldom leaves New Eire anymore. While his health remains excellent for one hundred and five, he is a standard human and age has bit harder on him than on me. One consolation of being cobbled together from good genes, I was built to last." Her eyes had been drifting through the room studying the pictures, paintings, souvenirs and trade items scattered about. They froze when she looked at the shelf where the model I'd made of her ship sat. She rose and walked over to it. I followed.

"*The Sidhe,*" she said, in a soft voice, "my ship."

"Wrik made it," Maauro said.

Shasti turned to me. Did I imagine a slight brightness to her eyes? "You have captured every detail; it is like seeing her from a distance."

I could not control blushing like a twelve year old. "Must seem rather silly," I managed. "Not like I don't have my own ship but..."

"I'm honored," she stated simply.

I felt like someone had pinned a medal on me.

"Maauro helped." I added, unsure of what to say.

She shrugged. "I made a very small nuclear reactor for it."

"Oh," Shasti said, "a small nuclear reactor. Is that all?"

"Wrik rather jealously guarded the rest of the work for himself."

"Most spacers have some hobby to while away the days in transit. I paint," Shasti said to me. She put a hand to the blood-red hull then sighed. "If I still had her and more freedom, I might not be here looking for your help, but be off on a voyage myself."

"Do you want to tell us what brings you to Lost Planet?" I added.

We walked side by side back to the table. "Your advertisement fits my mission well." Shasti began as she slid back into her seat.

"Lost Planet Expeditions," Jaelle quoted, "we find the lost."

"Yes," Shasti said and there was no mistaking the grimness in her now. "I need you to find those who are lost. Lost beyond my tracking, beyond even the formidable assets I have begged, borrowed or outright stolen.

"First you must know some background. Genetic engineering was banned on Olympia after Robert and I brought down Pard's government. But many cling to the old Mandelian Selective method of combining the best genes in natural parents, and that is still allowed.

"My daughter, Melisande, married Kasten, who also came from Engineered Stock. They have a son, Maximillian. He's one of the few third-generation, fully engineered humans and is descended from Vaughn, the highest legitimate Engineered created, and me, the X factor of the Black Labs.

"Maximillian is my youngest grandchild. If he still lives, he's seventeen years old. Unlike most of the family, Maximillian showed no interest in politics and power. He quarreled with his father over college and career choices. Maximillian favors academics. He wanted none of the life that his father, his grandfather, or I had. I supported him in this, to his father's disgust. In many ways I have had more to do with raising him than his parents. I think I am closer to him than any being other than his Uncle Robert.

"There is no way to completely evaluate his capabilities. Maximillian is large and physically capable, like most of us from Engineered stock. His mind is sharp. So at a young age, he was allowed by his parents to go off-planet to Earth to study with Professor Bexlaw. Bexlaw is one of the leading xenoarcheologists and an expert on the Lost Colony."

"The Lost Colony?" Jaelle and Dusko both said.

"Late in the 21st century," Shasti said, "a small group of human rebels escaped the tyranny that followed the Resource Wars on Earth. Legend has it that they refurbished an experimental ship with an alien hyperdrive found on Titan just before civilization collapsed. They escaped the Sol System and no one knows where they went, but there have been, over the centuries, sightings of the ship, the *New Hope* and rumors of a human colony."

"I've heard something about this," I said, hesitantly, "but I thought it was a tale for children."

Shasti nodded. "There have been other tales of lost colonies as well, but the *New Hope* was the first expedition to leave Sol System and the tale has never faded. There is also historical evidence establishing that they did lift off. But with an alien hyperdrive and no knowledge of which of the many hyperspace entrances near Sol they used, finding them would be wild luck, until recently."

All of us leaned forward, even Maauro. "Ten years ago, a lifeboat from the *New Hope,* was found in a system far out on the edge of Confed space. There were two bodies aboard, both mummified."

"There is no public record of such an event," Maauro stated.

"Correct. One of the bodies was a human; one was a new, alien species. The Interstellar Ministry classified the discovery and the lifeboat, bodies, all tapes and data disappeared out of Confed Navy hands. The rationale was that our meetings with new alien species have been a mix of blessings and disasters. No one knew which way this would break for the Confederacy. The ISM was still dealing with having encountered the Solari and the Drisnians. They didn't want a possible panic over another species."

"A lifeboat could only travel in the same system and even then two or three AUs at best," I said. "Then the colony would be—"

"Nowhere near that system," Shasti interrupted. "Confed Navy searched it. We do not know how the lifeboat got there. There was evidence of an attack on it, with burns on the hull; its electronic systems virally destroyed. It's believed the two aboard died almost immediately on launching, as there was untouched food, water and air aboard. The only message was scrawled on actual paper, crude handmade paper with a pencil. It said, "Help, Seddon," in an old Terran language from before Standard. The last word may be incomplete and meant nothing to any linguistic analysis.

"Somehow Professor Bexlaw learned of the lifeboat; I assume someone sold him the information. Xenoarcheologists have traded on questionable markets before and Bexlaw was the leading authority on the Lost Colony and a bit of a madman. I'd have had him killed if I realized what was to follow. He gained financing for a small ship, the *Isadora,* and crew, padding that out with his graduate students."

"Which included Maximillian?" I said

She nodded. "That expedition lifted off two years ago in a small ship before I learned of it. Even his parents were left in the dark. Bexlaw knew that if his information and destination were known, he'd be stopped, possibly imprisoned. So he filed false flight plans and did not convey back any of what he found. That ship is now missing, presumed lost as it has exceeded its life-support capacity. My grandson is either dead on that ship, or lost on some world that it touched.

"Despite all I could do with my own resources, and I have called in every favor ever owed me, I can find no trace of Maximillian. Confed

Intelligence has been very obliging. Not always willingly, but between Robert and me, we know of too many skeletons that they would rather remain buried.

"I was stalemated until I heard of something remarkable, deadly, incredibly intelligent and unprecedented," she turned to face Maauro. "You. All else has failed, but you are a quantum computer with the versatility of a living being. Maybe you will find clues where the rest of us have not.

"While it is not sensible to believe that Maximillian can be found, it was not sensible to believe that Robert Fenaday would find his wife's lost ship and rescue her after all those years. I have seen the living example of what one person can do who will not be stopped. I will not have it said that I did less for my grandson than Robert did for his wife.

"That is my mission. Will you accept it?"

CHAPTER 3

WE SPOKE WITH CAPTAIN RAINHELL FOR ANOTHER HOUR, REVIEWING the information that she had with her. She was disappointed not to receive an immediate response, but understanding when I said that I wanted to review the matter privately with my colleagues before giving her a decision. For myself the decision is easy and immediate. Two years ago I broke free of my programming as M-7, as a machine made for a merciless war. After that I decided I would use my powers to save life and to aid those in distress. Conflict seems my destiny and I could not deny that I seem to reach my ultimate potential by it. Perhaps it is also true that my appreciation for beauty and gentleness was heightened by my proximity to battle, a paradox of existence I cannot fully understand.

However, I knew that Wrik and Jaelle would need time. The disruption in our network caused by their differing needs and wants is deepening. It is beyond my power to aid in this. Indeed I fear I am its root cause.

Dusko and I work on stores and other matters related to current refit and upgrade going on the Stardust. If we are to voyage, the former Guild blockade runner will sport new and more effective armaments and electronics. Some of these have been obtained through Dusko's contacts and I suspect Candace might be unhappy to learn of them. So the work of arranging for payments and installation is tedious and careful and consumes most of the rest of the day. Wrik and Jaelle are busy with their own business and perhaps each other. I am careful to avoid surveilling either, though I do detect Wrik leaving the office earlier than usual.

Dusko and I say goodnight. He has not commented further on the mission, knowing that his going or staying will be determined by Wrik and Jaelle's vote.

I am leaving the office when I detect Jaelle waiting outside. I open the door and nod to her.

"Hello, Maauro."

"I am surprised you have not gone home. Wrik left an hour ago."

"I wanted to talk with you. Walk with me, Kit-sister."

I fall in behind her and we take the staircase to the roof. This surprises me. With the sun down, it is cool already, and Jaelle, who dislikes the cold, wears only a light jacket. But she does not hesitate and we walk onto the railed rooftop and its steady breeze. Jaelle turns up her collar and we move to a spot protected from the wind. Star City and the port glitter with lights. Before the Confederacy moved the capitol to this world, it was known as Harun II. Hardly anyone remembers that name now. The world had no native sapient life, just a decent biosphere that, *with minimal terraforming, made it an ideal capitol for the expanding Confederacy of twenty-three member species, wary of being governed from Earth.*

Overhead, two small moons roll through the sky. The galactic core shines brightly and ships add their lights as they climb through the darkening sky.

I wait patiently for Jaelle to begin. I know this conversation is apt to be unpleasant and use those weapons I am least comfortable with: words and emotions.

"I am not going on the expedition," Jaelle says.

"I feared that might be the case," I reply. "Your lack of enthusiasm was apparent, even to me."

"Enthusiasm," she replies flatly, "for voyages off the charts, into dangers we can't imagine, searching for people who are likely dead? No. I have built a business and its succeeding. I want a life, Maauro. I told you about my dreams that night on Cimer. They don't include constant risk of death and disaster. There's more. Fertility in my species is limited to our early life. I'm well into my fertile time and nearly thirty years old. I don't know how long this mission could last and I am not putting kits on hold for an unknown period."

"I understand," I reply. "Have you told Wrik yet?"

"No, Kit-sister. I want to settle some things between us. That's why we are here."

"It seems clear to me that Wrik will remain here with you," I say. "He has already wondered how he could be away from you while you are pregnant, not to mention that time he would miss with what he refers to as his future stepchildren."

Jaelle makes a gesture I recognize as equivalent to a sigh. "Ah, Maauro, therein lies part of the problem. Those are human feelings about it. Nekoan males have little to do with the raising of kits, our marriages are contractual affairs usually of short duration compared to what humans attempt. I will likely bring some females from my mother's line to help me with the kits. Kits are raised in the matrilineal family until adulthood when they formally become part of the patrilineal family, as I did with my rat-catcher of a father. It's very different from humans.

"While I want Wrik to enjoy and play with them, it would be bizarre in my culture for him to be around me that much during pregnancy. The only thing more useless than a Nekoan male around childbirth would be a human male."

"You have not explained this to him?"

"We have touched on the issue. Sometimes it's my culture that causes the confusion, sometimes his and sometimes both. In this case it rather sneaked up on me. My fault, not to take seriously his desire to be involved more in the process."

CHAPTER 3

"*Why have you chosen to tell me first?*" *I say.* "*This is against what I understand of biological relations.*"

"*Because you are wrong. Wrik is going with you.*"

"*I do not agree.*"

"*That's because you don't know what you are talking about!*" *she snaps.*

There is a long silence.

"*Maauro,*" *she says more calmly, managing a smile that even to my eyes is forced.* "*Wrik will go with you for several reasons. The most important of which is that if he does not go, he will pine and fret every second you are away. He will blame himself for anything that happens to you. He will miss you every damn day and I will have little joy of having him stay with me.*

"*You're right. Given a choice, he would stay with me. But the truth is he wants to go and he wants to go to be with you. I am not going to give him that choice because I don't want what I will win out of it.*"

"*I do not begin to understand,*" *I reply. I feel heat rising in me as every resource I have kicks into overdrive to deal with this network aberration.*

"*A part of him will always belong to you,*" *she says.* "*I had thought that I would have to share him with a human female, as he must share me with a Nekoan mate. I was prepared for that, sexual possessiveness is not part of Nekoan culture, even something of a minor sin. But I did not realize how much of his soul I must share with you.*"

"*Did you not think he would love the human woman he might father children with?*" *I am not dizzy, not capable of it, but the overdrive and conflicts running over my quantum pathways induce an analogue of that feeling.*

"*My bad, this time. I sometimes see Wrik as a Nekoan without a tail. I didn't realize that was something underlying his refusal to consider children with his own kind. You have to remember Wrik is the first human I ever met. I didn't plan to fall in love with him. I didn't realize how hard this would be.*"

"*You have regrets?*" *I ask. I am upset and barely able to keep my thoughts ordered. I think many hundreds of times faster than a biological, but not when emotion-laden information is to be processed.*

She looks away. "*There's another reason I'm not going. It will be easier, given how Wrik feels about my need for a Nekoan partner, if he's gone while I contract for my children. I plan a short term contract; odds are good my partner will be gone by the time you return.*"

She has both avoided my question and dragged me over more quaking ground. "*Will he?*" *I counter.* "*Are you now so sure that you do not wish a male entirely of your own?*"

Jaelle gives a short harsh laugh. "*On that you may rely, Kit-sister. I want no Nekoan male lording over me and mine. Too many still act as if it was the old days when they actually owned us. We females came* up with marriage contracts when we acquired political power. The males thought it was a great deal, with them no longer responsible for our upkeep. Took them a few generations to realize it was the basis of independence for us."

I walk over to the railing, placing my hands on it, staring at the spaceport beyond.

"Maauro," Jaelle says. "Have I ... are you all right?"

"No, I am not all right," I return. "I am confused. My network is stressed with new factors reordering things without either my permission or consultation. My actions, even when well-intended, have consequences that multiply out of my control."

"Welcome to the world of the living. I told you once that I would never again deny you were a living being. I didn't say it would always be fun or fair."

"I have tried to regulate my relationship with you to minimize disruptions between you and Wrik. I have disastrously failed."

To my bewilderment, Jaelle walks up behind me and places her arms around me pressing me back to her. Her chin rests on the back of my head. "No, Maauro. It's not your fault, certainly less you than Wrik and I, who were born biological and maybe should have known better. The bitter irony is the Wrik I fell for, is the one you helped rebuild after he ran away from the battle he still won't tell me about. He can't help but love you for what you did for him."

"I do not believe I will ever succeed in balancing my relationship with you."

"Stop expecting order and balance in the universe, Kit-sister, it's all about random collisions out here, stars and people both. We are not meant to be perfect."

"I am upset that you do not like me. That you are angry with me."

"I'm angry with the situation, not with you."

"How can that possibly make sense when I am the cause of the situation?"

"It just does," she kisses the back of my head. "I'm sorry it hurts sometimes. You just promise to bring both of you back. That will suffice for now."

"Thank you," I manage to her departing back. I am not sure I could move if I needed to. I stand at the rail, slowly cooling down, both literally and metaphorically. I remain there, the wind blows and toward the early morning hours, rain falls. These things affect me no more than the spacecraft standing exposed on the tarmac in front of me. There is no reason for me to remain, yet really no reason for me to be anywhere else. I spend some nights with Wrik and Jaelle, but clearly this is inappropriate tonight. I have other acquaintances, but none I can call friends.

On a world one hundred and five light years from here, I had made friends with three teens. I had believed they had accepted me as another *youth, but the girl had almost immediately realized my true nature. She and the two boys had, in the reflexively conspiratorial fashion of human teens, kept my secret. Yet it was dangerous for them to know me and my time on Stauver had been brief, if happy. I found myself missing their simple friendship, the unquestioning nature of their acceptance. Things in my network are far more complicated. I began to wonder for the first time if I should consider adding to my network, yet would that not only give more chances for endless complications?*

The sun comes up. I do not move. Some firebirds and a floating jelly plant settle near me, taking me for mere statuary, if they make any note of me at all. I am in a peculiar state, lacking volition to move. I find myself examining and reevaluating the time since Wrik found me. I still hesitate to examine the memories that I gathered while in touch with the Ribisan Predictor. That unfortunate silicon being, more dead then alive, had tried to persuade me to incorporate what was left of him in my being, liberating him from the massive computer sarcophagus the Ribisans were using to try and preserve his ability to see the futures of the multi-verse. I had no way of knowing which of the future tracks I was on, if I had, in fact, seen this one at all.

A door opens behind me and I know relief. Something will now happen to end this fugue state that has imprisoned me. I sense it is Wrik before I even turn. The birds and the jelly plant take to the air, their own rest disturbed.

Wrik's face is drawn and I know that I am not the only one who had a difficult night. He walks up to me and leans on the rail, looking at the port. Vehicles come and go and some people walk in secured areas. In the far distance, a ship rumbles and lifts off. We watch it in silence, as I do not dare to speak.

"Jaelle's not coming on the mission," Wrik says.

"That is not a surprise," I say carefully.

"No, I guess not."

"Wrik? I fear to ask but I must know if Jaelle is still networked to us."

He sighs. "Yes. In fact she got rather hot when I asked if she was ending our consortship, accused me of questioning her loyalty. She doesn't always see staying together as quite the same as being together."

"I do not understand."

"Me neither. As near as I can tell for her, it's like an orbit, we can be at aphelion or perihelion, but so long as the orbit remains, she is ok with it. In fact while pregnant she expects there to be a lot of distance. A human woman would regard that as betrayal."

"That's a relief…in a way. I must merely accept that our relationship survives." He sighs then adds. "She says that she'll go to Earth with us if we go there."

"Earth?" I question.

"It's where Bexlaw launched from. It seems as good a spot as any to start. We can at least select from the hyperspace routes out of Sol System."

"Very well," I said. The logic is questionable but I do not feel inclined to debate. It's no worse than any idea I had.

"That's good news. She has trade she can do on Earth and we won't have the time dilation of the voyage from Star Central to Earth to separate us."

I had not considered that. Wrik is cleverer than I this morning. I must get hold of myself and begin functioning properly again.

"We should inform Director Rainhell," I begin, "that we will undertake her mission."

"Yes," Wrik replied. "However, I think I will let Jaelle set the prices."

I give a slight smile. "What? Abandoning commerce?"

"In this case," he smiles back. "I can't see myself bargaining with Shasti Rainhell."

I straighten up from the rail. The universe has slid back into recognizable order for me. My network continues, even if bent in ways I did not anticipate. We have a mission and I have a purpose. It is time to move.

CHAPTER 4

WE RETURN TO THE OFFICE. DUSKO AND JAELLE ARE THERE. IT IS quiet, but not tense, decisions having already been made. There is much to be done before we can pull out of all our arrangements and undertake the mission. Even more because Jaelle will continue to actively run our trade business. Hours are spent on this, and lunch is eaten at desks.

Before I planned to make our call to Rainhell, a signal impinges on my awareness of the Star Central's network. It is a message in a microburst. What is remarkable is that there is a piece of Infestor code in it. The piece of code, I conclude, is gibberish, though I recognize its source. The code was in use on the asteroid belt base where I languished for 50,000 years. Someone has used this, knowing that I would immediately detect it. While I no longer must follow the programmed imperatives of my existence as an M-7 combatant, the message commands my attention.

I isolate the message and extract it from the network, back tracing it and eliminating all signs of it that I can access. I open the microburst; it contains a message from Candace Deveraux. "Meet me at the Denlenn contemplation garden near their trade building at 2030 hours. Bring Wrik if you must, but no one else. Do not be detected or followed. CD."

This is a startling development. One of the senior officers of Confed Intelligence has taken extraordinary means to meet us surreptitiously. I consider the possible meanings of this. One thing is clear to me: not everyone wants us to search for Maximillian.

I turn to Jaelle. "I find that I must do some work related to our commission," I say. "I will not be able to help you with the cargo selection for our voyage."

She frowns. "I suspected something might come up. Let me guess, you'll need Wrik's help."

"Correct. May we leave the financial arrangements with Rainhell to you?"

"Looks like a late night at the office for me," she said. "Is anything dangerous going on?"

"I do not yet know."

"Be careful, Kit-sister."

I hurry downstairs to find Wrik and advise him of Candace's contact. "Not a lot of time," he replies. "Especially if we want to get there and check the place out before she arrives."

"Correct. I suggest we arm ourselves and set out now."

Wrik obtains a stunner. I leave my armspac behind; the weapon is too large to escape notice. I will rely on my onboard weaponry. I meet

Wrik out front when he brings up a nondescript aircar we keep for such eventualities. Traffic will slow us and I estimate an hour to reach the gardens. We set off for our destination with the car on automatic within the city's zone control. I find it annoyingly slow, but I do enjoy the view of Star City.

Wrik also looks out the window. "Such a new city, I can't believe they couldn't come up with a better name for it."

"It does seem generic," I agree.

"There's your answer, the name didn't belong to anyone and didn't seem to favor anyone so, Star City for the city and Star Central for the planet."

We settle in and enjoy the sights until the aircar slides between two large towers that glow like huge emeralds set on their ends. We are near the Denlenn embassy and the structures began to reflect their esthetic, lower buildings with more natural materials and the emphasis on beauty over practicality that threads through their culture. We settle on the roadway and automatics guide us to a large vehicle parking lot near the luminescent gardens. Even late in the evening, they are an attraction and Star City never truly sleeps. Several of the species residing here prefer the lower light of the evenings.

We park the car. Wrik clips a com and earpiece to his jacket. Mine are built in.

"Any idea what we're looking for?" he asks.

"No. Stroll the grounds. Look for suspicious activity. Candace will be here soon."

An hour of walking the gardens, with its miniature waterfalls, fountains, shimmerwillows and moonflowers, had shown nothing other than the usual couples out for a romantic walk and parties of Denlenns admiring the beauty of the place. Wrik and I meet up near the pagoda-like structure near the entrance. Though no one has staked out our meeting place, I remain wary.

"Wrik, precede me into the garden. Remain alert."

He gives me a curious look but asks no questions, walking ahead to pass under the ornate wooden gate and back into the gardens beyond to await Candace.

I fade back to a corner across the plaza fronting the gardens and freeze into a silent immobility that no living being can duplicate, in a darkened nook. For added protection, I transform all my outer surfaces to a matte black.

Visitors and passersby stroll by me, some going into the gardens and others wandering out of my sight. No one notices me. If they did, I would likely be taken for some part of the garden decorations. I fully extend my sensors and enter the surveillance cameras and other sensors in the area. It takes only a few seconds to spot Candace Deveraux. She alights from an aircab, well short of the gardens. Her movements are alert and wary. I realize that she is alone; no security detail is in the immediate area.

Candace is a senior intelligence officer, not an agent. These actions tell me that she wishes her movements and contacts to be unknown to her own service. This implies that she is either in some disfavor in her organization, or worse, that she has a rival for control of that organization and that their interests do not align. Given our recent contact, this further implies a threat to Lost Planet.

After she examines the area, she walks toward our rendezvous. Five minutes later Candace walks past me, meters away, but she does not spot my dark form in its sheltered alcove. My precautions prove a sound investment. Candace is being followed, despite her own efforts. A female Dua-Denlenn trails her at a respectful distance. My sensors detect a particle beam weapon, a knife and—what concerns me more—a hypo-spray. The latter could be used to introduce a number of difficult to detect poisons.

I consider my tactical options. I return to my normal coloring, though I tone down the red panels on my jumpsuit and step out of the alcove into the light. My form-fitting coveralls are common among young people and I should remain unnoticed as I stalk my quarry.

Candace pauses before walking under the gate, scanning her back trail. The Dua-Denlenn has paused, pretending to examine merchandise in a nearby storefront. The window allows her to surreptitiously watch Candace without being in direct line of sight. I notice that the Dua-Denlenn has removed a hat and reversed her jacket since I first detected her, small changes but effective at throwing off an observer.

As Candace turns back toward the garden arch, the Dua-Denlenn moves, she is scanning the area and this decides me. She is considering how many potential witnesses there are as a prelude to an attack. I close in, also wary of pedestrians, both for fear of collateral damage and witnesses. The Dua-Denlenn pauses at the gate to the vast garden beyond. Her eyes slide over me as she scans around, then they snap back to me in alarm. I am recognized, or she would not have grabbed for her particle beam weapon.

I accelerate to combat speed; close the distance between us before her biological reflexes can even allow her to touch her weapon. Then I am holding her gun arm in my right hand.

"If you struggle or cry out," I say softly, "I will severely injure you."

Her pupilless eyes stare into mine and she remains very still then slowly nods.

I look around. A couple pass by twenty meters away, but they are engrossed in each other. A Morok with a briefcase notices us, but as no struggle has ensued, he elects to mind his own business.

I relieve the Dua-Denlenn of her weapons and then walk her over to a nearby banister on a little-used side staircase. Checking to see that no one is watching, I take the banister and bend the metal around the Dua-Denlenn's wrist. She gasps in shock as I tie her to the staircase.

"Unless you wish to gnaw off your hand," I advise. "You will remain here until I return for you. You seem to know what I am. Realize the impossibility of escaping me. Your continued survival will depend on your level of cooperation."

Internally, I open a channel to Dusko and advise him of where we are and what has transpired. "Obtain a stunner. Come here and I will release the prisoner to you for interrogation."

"Do you care how?" he asks.

"I do not, but Wrik will, so confine your effort to bribes or intimidation. She is one of your kind."

"Excellent," he replies, "one can rent one of my people, but we are difficult to buy."

I ignore my bound prisoner and make my way to the gate. I pretended not to discover the female Dua-Denlenn's hidden communication device in the hope that she will use it, allowing me to hack into whatever network she contacts. However, she makes no effort to do so, either wise to my stratagem or too cowed to attempt it.

While the grounds are large and broken up by groves, hedges and small ponds, I quickly locate Wrik and Candace. They are sitting in a miniature wooden temple by a mirrored pond.

"Where have you been?" Candace demands as I sit on a stone bench near them.

"Eliminating the person sent to kill you," I reply.

"What?" they both say, peering nervously into the darkness.

"The area is now secure," I say. I quickly inform them of the events of the last few minutes. "Dusko is en route to pick her up. Given the circumspect nature of our meeting, I assume you wish us to handle the interrogation and detention of this individual. Clearly your position is in considerable jeopardy."

"God," Candace muttered. "How much do you know, Maauro?"

"Only what is obvious. You slipped away from your security detail, which means you cannot trust it. You contact us in person, meaning your communications are monitored and this risky adventure is the most secure means available to you. You have been a great power in the intelligence community, meaning that parties of greater power outside your organization are constraining you."

"How do you know outside?" she demanded.

"If it was inside," I say impatiently, "you would either be replaced or neutralized by now. You have enough organizational power to avoid that presently."

She sits back crossing her arms over her ample chest. "Your analysis is flawless."

CHAPTER 4

"I am a battle computer. Politics is simply war by other means and office politics are not different in any meaningful way."

"It doesn't take Maauro's powers," Wrik adds, *"to tell that someone isn't happy with the fact that you brought us in to help Director Rainhell. Which of her significant field of enemies is it?"*

"It's not quite that limited," Candace said. *"Yes, Rainhell is the focus but there is more moving in all of this."*

She looks at both of us. *"I don't know where you four disappeared to in the six years between when we met on Kandalor and when you set up shop here. I doubt you'll tell me, but it's no secret that these six years have been rough on Earth and our allies in the original Confederacy."*

"With twenty-three species now in the Confederacy it's not as cohesive as it was. We have separatist movements among various races including our own."

I nod. *"Your Confederacy has expanded too quickly. Some of the species that entered did so less than willingly: the Voit-Veru, the Solari. Others, such as the Ribisans and Dua-Denlenn never truly integrated. Surely you see that you are entering a period of insurrections and probably civil war."*

Wrik looks shocked at my analysis, but Candace nods grimly. *"The Confederacy was a human construct and we basically ran it. Population, technology and our talent for war-time organization made it so. But that edge has dissipated over the decades and Earth's influence has waned since the Confed capitol was moved here to Star Cental."*

"Which, of course," I add, *"is the reason it was done."*

"The Solari and the Voit-Veru have made common cause," Candace adds *"and they have allies beyond that. Some of the neutrals don't mind seeing Earth's power diminish. They think we had too much to say before.*

"The Voit-Veru are the largest government we ever tried to absorb and they have proved pretty indigestible. Given their secret alliance with the old Eugenics masters of Olympia and how Fenaday and Rainhell exposed it and got them invaded, they have grudges. The party that fell from power after the invasion has gradually worked its way back up. Power is still clan-based with them and there was no way to get rid of them without destroying the clan entirely. So it was only a matter of time.

"The current head of the Interstellar Ministry is a Voit-Veru named Asuju Aporek, of the same clan that lost power when Fenaday and Rainhell attacked Mounus IV to rescue Lisa Fenaday. He is no fan of humans, or of Olympians like Rainhell, blaming them for decades of bad times for the Voit-Veru. He's been working with every anti-human faction in the Confederacy."

"Where is he?" Wrik asks.

"Ironically, based on Earth itself, in the capitol of Globalis; he spends half his time there and then half here on Star Central. All of it aimed at advancing the anti-human coalition's interests."

"Odd that he is based on Earth," Wrik adds.

Candace shrugs. *"The ISM HQ used to be there and there are still a lot of operations. Aporek is clever. He doesn't cast himself as anti-human, or anti-Denlenn, just a reformer interested in more 'equity.' Since it's an historical fact that humans had a special status under the old Confederacy, there are even liberal humans that back him. Fools,"* she said bitterly.

"You do not object to the human domination of the Confederacy?" I ask.

"If humans hadn't organized the war effort against the Conchirri, the galaxy would be one vast burp, Honey. Despite the fact the old Confederacy outnumbered the Conchirri, they were losing until we took over. The Denlenn were too concerned about honor to fight effectively; the Dua-Denlenn have no honor. The Enshari were useless as were the Frokossi. The Moroks and Okarans were good fighters if you could get them going in the right direction, but logistics and war-fighting, that was all us.

"But gratitude is a temporary coin. And beyond that, I'm a human and power is a zero sum game. I liked things as they were and as they will be again. If in the process of finding Rainhell's lost grandkid we find enough stuff on Aporek to bring him down.—"

"What has one to do with the other?" Wrik began.

"You suspect that Aporek arranged for the information to be sold to professor Bexlaw, precipitating this event," I answer, *"possibly even intervening further to waylay or otherwise discommode the professor's expedition."*

Candace nods. *"Smart killer-robot, though it's equally probable that someone below him, trying to curry favor started the chain of events. Whether he approved it or not, the die is presently cast. So I'm glad that you've taken Director Rainhell's commission."*

"The odds of success are not impressive," I reply.

Candace shrugs. *"Confed is glad to be able to bank a favor with her. We have had a long relationship."*

"Isn't it a bit bizarre to be working with her, when your grandfather recruited her?" Wrik asked

Candace smiles. *"Weirder than hell. The old boy always said she was the most dangerous of God's creations and to keep her on Confed's side at all costs. She could have taken his place if she wanted to, probably would have, had she not fallen in love with Mikhail Vaughn. As it is, she wields influence across more worlds than one would suspect. Worst part is how little she's aged from his old holos of her. Bitch."*

"Well Maauro holds the record for gracious aging," Wrik said.

"Thank you, Wrik."

"So what to do we do next?" Wrik asked.

CHAPTER 4

"We have to get Maauro access to the lifeboat and the bodies. Maybe she can find something that the previous analysis didn't turn up. That means a journey to Earth. It would be the logical place to start in any event. The professor's expedition launched from there."

"We'd worked that out, but where are those items?"

"Oh that," Candace said, with a lazy smile. "That's easy. They're in a secured ISM base somewhere on Earth."

We called Shasti in the morning to accept her commission. Her operatives met us the next day with all the information that she'd gleaned from her intelligence networks and the equivalent of a blank check. They also took the Dua-Denlenn female we had captured off our hands. Dusko had learned little from her with either threats or bribery, and both Maauro and I had forbade sterner measures. She was likely low-level Guild and had been hired indirectly.

There was no bargaining with Shasti. Her backer's assets were essentially unlimited and she accepted Jaelle's first offer. While the rest of us prepared the *Stardust* for its trip to Sol System, loading every nook and cranny with the highest-value natural products that would command the greatest prices, Maauro absorbed all the information known on the Lost Colony and the previous searches.

Maauro was done first. "The information," she said, while we gathered for a late lunch at the office, "while voluminous, does not support any conclusions or directions. Much of what was gathered is unverifiable and unreliable.

"We know that the *New Hope* was a small vessel, abandoned on Iriomoto island, where a nation called Japan had a military base. The stardrive was carried in by an old submarine and the rebels and scientists lifted off on January 19, 2092, local calendar. The base was subsequently destroyed in a nuclear attack."

"No point to landing there," Dusko said, around a mouthful of sandwich.

"We will land in London. Confed Intel has offices there, it is near Globalis, in what was once Geneva, and it makes sense as a trade destination. We will ostensibly be there on Jaelle's behest with a load of cargo."

"Thin cover," Wrik says.

Maauro nodded. "Lost Planet is not a secret organization and likely Rainhell's mission here did not escape ISM attention. Candace believes her part in aiding Rainhell may be suspected, but not known. She is quite sure that the ISM does not know who, or what, I am as she has kept that information close. The Guild personnel who came into contact with me are dead, or have no incentive to talk to the ISM. Even if the ISM tried to move against us legally, our business is legitimate. The worst thing that would happen is that my existence and secret citizenship in the

Confederacy becomes known. I am prepared for that eventuality. It is inevitable."

"So," Jaelle said. "Earth, here we come."

CHAPTER 5

STARDUST POPPED BACK INTO EXISTENCE IN SOL SYSTEM. After we shook off the effects of hyperdrive, I pushed the engines to maximum. A nice perk of working for Candace, fuel cost wasn't an issue.

The trip took a week. Despite the tensions of the impending separation, the flight was pleasant. Jaelle and I made love, laughed, enjoyed long massages and banked time for the year or better apart. It was the spacer's way. The ship was its own little universe; it required tranquility, being too small for anything else. In the way of those who traveled space, we'd boxed up any issues until we were planetside again.

Something had happened between Jaelle and Maauro and it wasn't something I understood, nor would either of them discuss it with me. Maauro seemed uncertain around Jaelle. Had she not been Maauro, I'd have said that she was afraid of Jaelle. She was exquisitely polite to the Nekoan. As for Jaelle, the resentment she'd expressed was gone, or buried, as if it never existed. In fact, she seemed oddly affectionate toward Maauro, playing with her hair, braiding it as if she were a child.

I quickly ceased questioning it, merely glad for the peace it brought. I didn't believe the issues of our little troika were resolved, but for now things were better. It was enough.

We watched Earth as it grew in the screens, or at least I did. For the others, Earth was simply another world. For me it was the home of my species. So I spent a fair amount of time alone in contemplation of the blue and white world ahead. I wondered if I would feel a sense of home when we finned down among its nine billion people. That feeling had left me when I fled Retief and I had not found it since.

Earth had survived the Conchirri war, generations ago, without being directly assailed. One Conchirri raid reached the outer system but was defeated there. Yet the blue marble had been scarred by its own children in nuclear wars. The scars had faded over the generations and nothing could be seen from space. I wondered about what Maauro had said about a period of civil wars coming. I hoped it wasn't true, but it was a slim hope.

On the seventh day, we entered the London Control Area and headed down. Our cargo would find lucrative markets there, as would the cargo in our second ship, following a week behind. The chartered vessel would bear Jaelle and any cargo she collected back to Star Central and the life she would live without me. Candace was waiting for us in the world below where the mission would really begin.

CHAPTER 5

We gathered for landing on the bridge, though the ship would be taken down by Gatwick's landing system. I was too much of a flyer to have my hands more than inches from the controls as my ship headed into a gravity well.

"What sort of security are we going to put out on landing?" Dusko asked. "You want me to break out the crab-robots?"

"Just two," I said. "I'm glad we replaced the ones we lost on the Artifact, but I don't see anyone moving against us in a secured port. Still, since you'll be onboard when we're off, you can keep watch using them and the ship's security system."

"Do I get a stunner?"

I thought about it. I'd never given Dusko clearance for the arms locker, a last holdover from our previous enmity, and Jaelle and Maauro had left it that way.

"I'll reprogram the arms room locker," I said. "From now on you'll have the same access that everyone else does."

He looked at me and merely nodded. Jaelle and Maauro continued watching the world come up.

"Atmospheric entry at 0930 ship time," Maauro said.

"Lunch in London," Jaelle said. "I want to see the Winter Garden and the Tower."

Down we came toward a vast city with a river cutting through it. We landed perfectly in the most crowded spacefield I had ever seen—ships as far as the eye could see. Our section was devoted to smaller ships. At 150 meters in height, *Stardust* was far from the largest but was one of the more colorful. When horizontal, her upper half was dark green and her lower half gold. Sitting on her tailfins with their large cylinder-like impellers, we looked like an old style rocket ship. *Stardust* had been a military courier meant for small and unimproved fields. She was atmospheric and sleek.

Beyond the spacefield lay cities filled with humanity. I found it a little overwhelming. I'd never seen so many humans in one place before. I couldn't see the ancient bridge, the huge Ferris Wheel or the dozen other famous sites, but I knew they were there.

"Look at the city," I managed, "so huge, so full and so ancient. This area has been inhabited for more than 5,000 years."

"Very different from where you grew up I imagine," Jaelle said.

I nodded. As usual any reference to my past raised a ghost of pain, this time muted by the excitement of seeing the homeworld of my species.

A crew of robots, led by a human and a port official, were already on their way to us as a ramp extended to our amidships section. They moved quickly on Old Earth. Our manifest and records had been transmitted before landing, but there were still formalities to be followed and a port official needed to make sure everything matched up.

CHAPTER 5

"Time for Port Inspection," I said.

"I'll remain in my quarters," Maauro said.

"Don't bother," I said. "The official will want to see every crewman and check your records are in order. It's probably a good idea to put your goggles on; we'll pass you off as light-sensitive."

"Pity," Jaelle said, "you do have pretty eyes, Kit-sister."

Maauro smiled, but refrained from entering into any verbal play. She fished a set of dark goggles out of a pouch on her coverall. The dark goggles effectively concealed her overlarge eyes. She would adjust her eyesight to see perfectly out of them.

I secured my board and drives and met the customs inspector down in the main hold. She was a pleasant-looking woman, brisk and efficient. I had to listen carefully to pierce her accent. Walking around the ship, she inspected our cargo and crew, asking routine, but probing questions. She did seem interested in Maauro, but she was the most unusual member of our crew, with her human mutation story.

The Customs Officer looked askance at our armaments and the crab-robots in the hold. The mini-tank machines were much smaller and more modern than the trio we'd lost on the Artifact, but no less deadly for all that their weapons were in storage.

"Three combat robots and a communications laser that has a hundred times the power it needs," she observed. "What sort of ports do you put into?"

"Too many that aren't as nice as Earth, or Star Central," I said. Jaelle smiled an enigmatic but toothy smile.

The Customs Officer shrugged. "Alright, you do have the correct permits. You can power up your bots, but no weapons. We don't even go for stunners around here, so don't go shooting up the port and keep everything under lock and key. Sign here."

I initialed.

"Cheers," she said, and with a breezy wave was off.

Jaelle handled the stevedore crew, who quickly off-loaded our cargo. The high-value items went directly to their new owners. Other materials were cached at warehouses to be called for later.

Maauro called me from the bridge. "Wrik, I've received a message. We have a meeting in two hours."

"Ok," I said, "I'll get ready."

Jaelle walked over to me. Behind her, the last robot loader was leaving with a cargo box, followed by its controller. What we had packed up between us had also been unpacked with the cargo. Still, she only leaned in to kiss me. "Be careful around Candace. Never trust her. Stay close to Maauro."

"I will," I replied. "Good luck with gathering a new cargo for Star Central."

She smiled. "No problem. Plenty of sexy things to take back from Earth itself. But Wrik, don't count me gone as yet. I don't know what Candace plans, but you'll need help getting to where they've hidden the lifeboat and corpses. Call me before you do anything dangerous."

"I will."

Jaelle smiled and walked out the hatch, into the slowly setting light of Sol.

Maauro appeared at the hatchway, as if she had waited for Jaelle to exit.

"A blue van will pull up to our bay in twenty minutes," she said without preamble. "It will say Leonard's Commissary on it. We get in the back."

"Candace isn't wasting any time."

"I do not believe it is on her side. The van will doubtless spend considerable time making sure it is not followed before we rendezvous with Candace."

I grimaced. "Better pee before going."

"I understand that is always considered good advice."

We went down to the base of the ship. I didn't take a weapon, unless you counted Maauro, the most dangerous fighting machine ever made. The crab-robots sat quiescent, watching the ship and looking like their namesakes with their splinter-gray camouflage. I could see some Moroks at another freighter looking over curiously, but evidently they had no desire to see the crabs closer. We walked out of their sight around one of the ship's impellers.

A blue airvan rolled up slowly and paused next to us. The rear doors opened and with a look around to make sure we weren't obviously being watched, we scrambled in. The van sped off. We found seats on the hard benches in the back of the windowless van, sandwiched between stacks of precooked meals in trays. We couldn't see the driver through the small one way window at the back of the cab. The van rolled on, changing directions and then, after it had cleared the secured area of the port, it began to vary heights. As a pilot, I wasn't much prone to motion-sickness but I was also used to being able to see. It became wearisome after a while.

I was glad enough when, after about an hour, we settled somewhere. We waited in silence for a while before the doors finally opened. A pudgy, middle-aged man stood there. "Out you come," he said.

We obliged, finding ourselves in an underground parking garage. He pointed to a large, dark aircar parked in the opposite aisle. It blinked lights at us briefly and we walked over. A man got out, looking in all directions and opened the door for us.

Candace sat inside, her buxom form covered in a conservative business suit. We slipped in next to her. The beaming smile in her attractive, dark-skinned face did not reach the chocolate-brown eyes.

"Good to see you," she said.

"The area is secure," Maauro said. "I have done a cybernetic scan to supplement your own efforts."

"Thanks. I find that quite comforting,"

"You should," Maauro said.

"Uneventful landing?" Candace asked.

"No complaints. Couldn't see anything unusual in how we were treated."

"Good." She leaned forward and opened a small cabinet. "Drink, Wrik?"

"Sure. I understand that something called a gin and tonic is a local favorite."

"What about you, Maauro? I may have some motor oil here somewhere."

I looked at her, wondering why she needled Maauro. It occurred to me that she was afraid of the android and that Candace couldn't stand being afraid of something. So she poked at Maauro to prove something to herself.

"Gin and tonic will be fine," Maauro said.

From the expression on Candace's face, she hadn't expected that and wasn't sure if Maauro was exhibiting a sense of humor or quite what.

Candace whipped up two G&Ts and followed with a scotch on the rocks for herself. We sipped our drinks in silence for a few seconds.

"You said that the ISM has the bodies and the lifeboat," Maauro began. "Have you confirmed the location and that they are still there?"

"Yes," Candace replied. "Aporek tried to get them moved off-world a year ago but we forestalled that."

Maauro sipped her drink and it struck me that she had never looked more human.

"But I couldn't stop him from removing everything from Globalis to a remote ISM facility."

"Where?" Maauro asked, swirling her glass so that the ice clinked. I wondered where she'd learned that gesture then realized I'd been doing so. I smiled to myself and took a sip from the drink before setting it aside. Maauro was often a mirror for habits I did not know I had.

"There is an old base in the Pacific. Ironically it dates from the time of the original expedition. Amami Island was an old United Nations Ocean Patrol Base before the last of the Resource Wars brought down the World Government and began the Tyranny. It's been used by the ISM for decades."

"Odd," I mused. "Why would the ISM want such a place?"

"They claim it's for training, storage and quarantine. It also allows them landing rights on a base exclusively used by their personnel. Why wouldn't they want it? Half the time he lands on Earth, Aporek comes in through there. He's had the base expanded and refurbished, even touts the expansion as proof that he's not anti-human."

Candace passed a chip to Maauro, who touched it only briefly to transfer the information. "That is all the data we have on the base."

"I congratulate you on the completeness of your intelligence," Maauro said. "Your information is excellent and recent, according to the time stamps. Let's hope Aporek does not have similar files on your operation."

"Amen," Candace said, draining her Scotch.

"How do you propose to get us access to the evidence stored there?" I asked.

"Don't look at me, Honey. You brought the quantum computer. I was hoping she had some ideas."

Maauro nodded. "I have a plan. We will need an automated fishing trawler and some reliable operatives, ISM uniforms, the most recent codes—"

"Already?" I said.

Maauro looked at me. "The logistics of the plan are simple. The execution will be complex." From inside her jacket, Maauro pulled a chip and handed it to Candace, who popped it in a scanner and examined it for a few minutes.

"I'll be damned," Candace said finally. "This might just work."

CHAPTER 6

I ACTIVATE FROM SLEEP MODE AND IMMEDIATELY SCAN THE AREA WITH *my sensors and cybersystems. There is no immediate threat, nor any nearby biologicals. The crate I am in is the rear of a warehouse, behind some other stacks. This is inconvenient. Slowly I break my way into the adjacent two crates, pushing their contents behind me, until I reach an area from where I can safely emerge into the warehouse. I must hope that we can complete our assignments before anyone looks at the damaged crates, or that they assume it is due to an unloading accident.*

The security systems I feared are not present inside the warehouse. I had already passed through multiple layers of security before coming here. Given that the crate I was in came from a secure Confed facility, I was spared the physical search that would have penetrated the fake packing that made me look like a collection of high-pressure piping and servos. As I straighten up, I shake off that camouflage and repattern my outer casing to look like an Interstellar Ministry First Lieutenant's uniform, complete with hat and crossed belts. As I stand, I begin to infiltrate the base's primary AI with the codes that Candace provided. Even with my skills, I could not defeat the military security without being detected by the base's defensive software. With the codes provided, it is simplicity itself to upload the false history for my persona, Lieutenant Ilsana, assigned to base logistics. Her assignment will be to meet and admit Wrik, posing as Second Lieutenant Alec Latham, nine hours from now, who is to pick up a classified cargo container and remove it from the base. The container will hold me, again in an inactive state, with the samples and records that we will obtain here.

I walk out of the cargo area. Security systems detect me as I exit the warehouse, but with the false history I provided the base AI, it logs me as base staff having entered there hours before.

As I walk on, it occurs to me that I have one great advantage over a biological life form with time to kill: I can walk the halls and corridors of the base with complete assurance, as if I walked them every day, using the downloaded maps in my brain. I do not have a billet to return to, but I can pass time in the cafeteria and the base library. If needs be, I can simply stand still in some little-used base section for hours.

Two enlisted men pass me and snap off crisp salutes, which I return. As I walk on, I notice that both men turn to give me a speculative look——apparently I do credit to the severe dark gray uniform I am wearing. I find this amusing.

CHAPTER 6

"I'll be damned," Candace had said, but I was the one who felt he was standing in hell as I exited the ISM Transport for the base on Amami Island in the Pacific Ocean. Once again, I wore a Confederate uniform I wasn't entitled to, only this time it was the gray and red of the ISM. Humidity struck right behind the heat. Despite my summer-weight uniform, cap and sunglasses, I was sweating in a few steps. The other occupants had trooped off the transport ahead of me. Most of them had been enlisted, or civilians, and hadn't bothered an officer, especially after I pulled my cap's visor down over my eyes. Silence was always good protection.

I continued to lag behind the others as they walked over to a bored-looking guard standing in a gatepost. She at least had a fan as she scanned our ID and laconically asked questions. I saw a line of drone helicopters sitting on the blazing coral of the airfield. One of them was warming up and lifted into the bright, blue sky. It carried a torpedo behind the chin turret. Overhead another transport circled upward. Higher up, a bright circle showed from the engine of some spacecraft climbing for altitude over the broad green ocean.

I tried to keep my breathing level as I handed her my card. She barely looked up at me. If she saw me sweating, she'd put it down to the Pacific summer. The card cleared and the base AI upgraded my order and authorizations. I was careful not to blow out my breath in relief. Maauro was inside and operating or my falsified orders would have caused an alert.

I walked in and checked my personal com with its copy of the base map. I knew there would be no message from Maauro, but I checked the time. If she was on schedule, Maauro would be on her way to the cafeteria where I'd meet her. Leaving the environs of the airbase, I hopped on a bus heading for the main building. I studied the structure, over seven hundred years old. The building had vast white wings that tilted upward, looking like a crown on the glass and steel body. It was an ostentatious place, built with pride by the forces that had once patrolled the seven seas before war brought on a dark age.

The bus pulled up and we hurried from its air-conditioned comfort to that of the main building. I traded salutes with other ISM personnel as I walked toward the cafeteria. I grounded my equipment at some lockers provided just outside. Fortunately, having landed at a secure base, there were no additional stations in the common areas for me to pass.

I walked into the officer's cafeteria, which buzzed with idle conversation. I picked up a tray, grabbed a drink and some food, hardly caring what I took. I scanned the room and saw Maauro seated alone at the back. I walked up to her—she looked up at me. I put the tray down and snapped a salute.

"May I join you, Lieutenant Ilsana?" I asked. Maauro's gold bar ranked my silver one and merited a salute.

CHAPTER 6

"Yes, Lt. Latham. By all means," she indicated a seat next to her.

I slid next to her so I could watch the rest of the room. "We secure?"

"Yes," she replied. "There are no scanners in here. No one is close enough to hear us if we keep our voices down. I will notice anyone trying to lip-read, which is impossible with me as my lips are not making the motions congruent with my words."

"Another nice trick," I said in admiration.

"Thank you. We will need all our tricks to get out of here intact."

"So far so good," I said, taking a long sip of the lemonade I had picked up.

"You should eat some of the food too," she said.

"Not hungry,"

"That is tension," she said, spooning up some of her own chocolate pudding. "Press yourself. It may be a long period until your next meal."

"Yeah." I forked up some roast beef, just to avoid an argument, as she was probably right anyway.

"I have located the secured sections where the lifeboat and bodies are kept," she added.

"How tough?"

"The lifeboat is merely secured in a storage area. It has not been visited since it was unloaded there. Getting access to the bodies will be the trick, so we will attempt the lifeboat first."

"What about files on the base AI?"

"I have downloaded those that are present, my authorization codes from Candace have proved most effective, but it seems there are unnetworked computers in each section that may have files in autistic mode. I will have to access those directly."

"Interesting, someone wants those two to rest in peace," I said.

"We will not disturb them long," she replied.

We finished our food and went out, picking up my gear along the way.

It was a long walk to the storage areas in the sprawling base, but fortunately there was a covered and air-conditioned path from the main to the outer buildings. We walked up to the door of the section we wanted. There was a reception area with a mix of enlisted and civilian personnel. An officer was looking at a monitor with one of the staff when he noticed us. Since Maauro ranked him, he saluted. "What can I do for you? We don't get many visitors over here."

"Lts. Ilsana and Latham," Maauro said. "We have orders to inspect the storage arrangements on Room 33A."

"The old lifeboat? Is there a problem?" he asked with a trace of anxiety.

"No," she replied. "Just routine."

CHAPTER 6

"You know what is in there?" I asked.

The officer shrugged. "Just what it says on the manifest, one old Model Three, 21st Century lifeboat they found in a dockyard on the periphery. It's supposed to go to a museum someday, I hear."

"Yeah," I reply. "Same thing they told us. They probably want to make sure the parts don't get lost."

Maauro handed over the chip with our orders. He ran it into the computer and it cleared once again, thanks to Candace's codes and Maauro's hacking.

"OK," the officer said. "Akina, take these two down to 33A. Here's your code key." He handed Maauro a small box with a tag dangling from it.

One of the civilians, a pretty Asian girl, nodded. "Sure thing." She gave me a friendly smile and waved. We walked past two Moroks who were grumbling about something on one of the monitors.

Akina seemed inclined to chat as we walked back. I related the cover story of my journey here. Fortunately we reached 33A before she asked me what I was doing later.

"No need to walk us in or wait for us," Maauro said. "We'll check in at the front when we are done." Akina nodded and with a last, somewhat wistful, smile at me, headed back the way we'd come.

The door opened to the code key and we entered the storage room. In the center of the windowless room sat the partially stripped lifeboat. Looking at it, I wasn't sure that lifeboat was the right term. The vessel was nothing like the rounded types we used today and it resembled an aerospace craft meant for maneuvering in atmosphere. Tables stood about the room, filled with plastic tubs and plastic wrapped parts. A fine covering of dust confirmed what we'd been told. No one had been in to look at the craft in a long while.

"Keep watch by the door," Maauro ordered. She moved quickly around the room sampling and recording with her onboard instruments. The samples disappeared into her body for storage and later analysis. She hooked into the stand-alone computer in the room through her finger filaments, copying all the information.

Maauro disappeared into the shuttle itself. I watched the hallway outside through the sliver I'd left in the doorwayway. Once I heard footsteps and froze, but they did not come closer.

"God," I muttered. "Is she rebuilding the damn thing?"

When I thought I couldn't stand it anymore, she finally reappeared. Maauro made a circuit around the room and seemed to be spraying something from her finger. It took her two minutes to work her way back to me.

"Dust," she said in answer to my unspoken question. "I covered our footprints with it. They will find no evidence that we moved beyond the doorway. "

We slipped out, resealing the door behind us, "now for the bodies. They're in high security storage in the middle of the base, lower down."

Ten minutes later we again approached a reception area, but the tone was totally different. This area was devoid of civilians. A metal desk stood at the junction of four corridors, manned by a first lieutenant, behind him stood two unsmiling guards with sidearms. Several techs sat watching screens, inputting information and handling communications. The officer looked up as we walked up. As he ranked me, I saluted, which he tossed back crisply.

"Lieutenants Ilsana and Latham," Maauro said. "We're to inspect and examine the bodies in Section X-1a chambers 8 and 9."

"Our orders." She handed him a chip. He put it to his screen and studied the download.

"News to me," he said. "Nothing on my schedule."

The officer's computer spits out an inquiry to one of the bases intermodal AI's. I intercept it and reroute it to me, then respond. This is more of a struggle than I anticipate, despite the codes Candace provided me with. Security in the network is robust, especially as I must remain undetected. The officer starts to frown at the delayed response, but I then get a confirmation to appear on his screen.

"Cleared," he says. "It says here you are to perform some noninvasive scans."

"Correct," I reply. I lift a suitcase full of instruments that Wrik brought in on the transport.

"Open the case, please."

"As you wish." I place it in front of him and open it. He removes each item and looks it over, asking me about one scanner he does not recognize.

"Alright," he finally says. "Corporal of the Guard will take you there and wait with you—"

"Recheck those orders," I interrupt. "We are not to be observed while conducting our inspections and tests."

"I can't see why," he returned, his face showing clear disapproval. "I'm in charge of security here."

"And I'm responsible for carrying out my orders as given," I reply. "Mine came from ISM Regional on Saturn. You want to query them, go ahead, but you're holding us up for minimum of four hours and we have transports to catch."

He grimaced. "Present your case on leaving and my man will wait directly outside."

"No problem," I say.

The corporal is a Drisnian, a slender, blue-skinned humanoid with gray hair. He doesn't speak as he walks us down the right hand corridor. The place is quiet and empty of traffic. We pass a few rooms where workers in lab coats go about their business, but no one pays us any attention.

This time, the corporal opens the large windowless steel door, retaining the key. He leans in and switches on lights. "The door will open from the inside," he says in the lisping way his kind manage Standard. The door seals, I examine it and satisfy myself that its thickness is ear proof, even against a Drisnian with their excellent hearing.

From inside my body, I pull a wedge that I prepared and stick it in the door. It will not reopen now. I look at the security cameras and note that they are off. I set cybertraps to prevent them from being turned back on. I place the instrument case on the table. They are not necessary, my onboard equipment is vastly better. I wave Wrik to follow me.

The room is chill, with metal tables and drains for autopsying bodies, along with body scanners. At the far end is the morgue proper with its slide-in containers for the corpses. We come to the ones we want and I open the one containing the human.

Maauro slides open the container and it pulls out easily. The frozen body is inside a plaststeel inner container which folds away and retracts at her touch. It reveals a young man, little more than a boy, mercifully his eyes are closed. He lies naked, but a small box at his feet contains his clothes, which Maauro pulls out and examines before replacing.

I look at the unknown boy and feel a pang of sadness. The body has the sunken, waxy look of death. Who was he? Who missed him when he went into space and didn't come back? What dreams had been his? The body shows damage and the marks of an autopsy.

Our files said the boy had been found years ago in the frozen lifeboat, but how long he had lain dead in the boat wasn't known. The lifeboat had been original equipment on the *New Hope* when she launched centuries ago, so that told us nothing. There was no way to tell when she'd been launched from the starship.

Maauro moved her hands over him, her finger filaments out. I looked away. I knew she would take samples from the interior, but didn't want to know the details. A few minutes later she pulled up the plast-steel sections. "Now for the unknown alien."

We slid the dead boy back into the wall. I placed a hand on the outer door and said a silent prayer for him. Perhaps it was foolish. But he'd been a human and deserved some remembrance, some sign that he was more than a curiosity.

Maauro opened the container with the alien corpse in it. My first impression was of a delicate creature about the size of Maauro. The bone structure was light and fine, the skin had an almost velvety look of dark-green, the eyes were large and a dark purple with small whites, the hair on the head had a feathery look. I saw no obvious sign of gender, but that didn't mean much. Like so many of the lifeforms we'd encountered it was bipedal and humanoid.

"Those look like burns," I said, pointing to the chest.

"They are," Maauro said. "Blast damage as well. This being was caught in an explosion."

Maauro extended her finger filaments into the alien's mouth and nose. As the alien didn't engage my sympathy as much as the boy, I watched with greater equanimity. She spent a few minutes examining the body and looked only briefly at the clothes, which were similar to those of the boy. They had clearly traveled together.

After a few minutes, she quickly repacked the body and slid it into the wall. Maauro walked over to the stand-alone computer and infiltrated it, taking only seconds to copy the records. "I have recorded all I can here. Analysis will take longer but does not need to be done here. Time to leave."

"I'll add this to the long list of places I'm glad to leave and never see again."

I pick up the case as Maauro opened the door. The corporal stood facing the door and I wondered if he'd been staring at it for the half-hour we'd been inside. He took us back to the front desk, where we were examined with a portable scanner and had our case checked again. The scanner didn't so much as bleep as it moved over Maauro, doubtless she was controlling it. Sometimes her ability to influence electronic equipment seemed damn near magical. I was glad the Confederacy had never had to face either her Creators or their enemies, the Infestors. Their technological heights were still out of sight of our abilities.

We walked away, but I didn't like the way the lieutenant's eyes stayed fastened to our backs. I wondered if he had, in fact, queried our orders again. We took the elevator back up. I slipped into the base gym and ditched my instrument case in a locker there. We didn't need anything but the clothes on our backs until our transport left. It felt good to be unencumbered.

I rejoined Maauro outside the gym. "Where should we go?" I asked. "We've got hours until the plane leaves."

"There is a library two levels down," she said.

I frowned. "I'd rather be outside."

"What explanation would we have for standing out in the heat and humidity? It is near to evening, but still quite warm. We can hardly sit under a palm tree in uniform. No, in the library we can remain still and quiet for hours and not be observed."

It was hard to argue with her. So I followed her down two levels. The library was more of a quiet area. There were some actual books and magazines lying about, along with tablets and alcoves for those who wanted to study in private. Screens were all over, but set so no one could see the materials. Maauro and I picked up tablets and dialed up local news, finding a quiet corner to sit in. Occasionally someone would consult the library officer in hushed tones. One older civilian sat in a corner with a heavy bound book in his hands. He practically fondled the pages as he turned them.

We'd sat for an hour, Maauro regularly changing the material on her tablet, me staring at it without reading, when she reached over and touched my arm. She rose and I quickly followed her out. As soon as we exited, she turned left and headed for a staircase.

"A security alert has been called in the base; I picked it up from the base AI. The officer on the desk did requery our orders. The base AI has your and my orders of transit on and off the base, but those do not reference checking the secured rooms as we did."

"Why not?" I asked.

"If I had included it in our transit orders, then it would have sent an automatic alert to HQ in Globalis. No, inserting the inspection in our orders had to be done locally, from inside their security. So far, all they have is that we are authorized to be here, but that we have two mismatching sets of orders. The alert is low-level, just to locate us and reconfirm our orders."

"How long until they figure it out?"

"Assuming they do not find us, then about three and a half hours minimum likely closer to four. I routed our transit orders from the Saturn regional office. A transmission will take that long at light speed, with some highly variable time to check the databases and respond. I cannot break into those highly secure communication nets without causing an alarm."

"Not enough time for us to get to the transport."

"No. Even if we did, the transport could be recalled and we would have to seize it. But then where would we land? Worse, we would not get to the transport. Even a low-level alert will stop us from setting foot on the airbase."

Ahead, two ISM troopers wearing sidearms stepped into the hallway, fortunately looking the other way. Maauro instantly pushed me into a side corridor and pointed at a spiral metal staircase. I went down it as quickly and silently as I could. We spent the next few minutes avoiding ISM security and checkpoints, always heading downward.

"This is not good," Maauro said. "The longer they do not detect us the more likely a full security alert or shutdown will be called. Add to that we have been forced deeper into the base. There are too many levels between us and the surface. You may have been right. We should have gone outside."

"You hide a pin in a drawer of pins," I said, shaking my head. "We'd have been spotted on the surface already. If we'd tried to leave the base, we'd have to have passed a checkpoint.

"Got any ideas?" I added, trying to keep desperation out of my voice.
"Yes."

We dodge to the lower levels. While base security remains unsure if there is an actual threat, they proceed cautiously, but rapidly, and in a very effective manner. We are sealed off from the upper levels of the base.

An idea forms in my mind. It is not a pleasant alternative, but we may have no other effective option. I look about and grab up some suitable pieces of metal and plastic pressing them into my malleable ceramic armor. Once inside, my factories reduce them to raw material suitable for my plan.

Wrik stands back from me, the process of necessity raises heat. "Maauro, you'll set off the fire alarms in a minute."

I offer what I calculate is a reassuring smile. "While the base security systems are well shielded, the fire alarms are merely commercial and I can blind them easily."

"Whenever you start eating the local scenery, it means you have a plan," *he says eagerly.*

"Yes."

Wrik follows me as we drop level after level. I cause a surveillance camera to loop as we pass it. It will be detected eventually, but perhaps not for a critical interval.

We reach an area of the base with an underwater lock. It has not been used in some time and there are no suits or other equipment nearby. The ancient UNOP insignia is still on the door, a dolphin leaping across a triangle.

"What is this place?" *Wrik asks, looking at the dank walls and wan light bulbs with concern.*

"It's an airlock dating from when this was an Ocean Patrol base," *I reply.* "Seldom used and only maintained occasionally to prevent flooding. There are no electronic systems even."

"Nor any diving equipment," *he notes*

Using my osmotic process I extrude an oxygen cylinder from my mid section followed by flexible tubing and a face mask which I quickly give to Wrik. "Put it on while it is still malleable," *I order.* "It will better conform to your face."

He does so. After a minute I allow him to take it off.

"Underwater escape?" *he mutters.*

"Yes."

"Maauro, I can't swim out to where Jaelle's got the trawler. We'd planned on stealing a boat if we had to escape that way."

"Impractical with an alert on. In any event you will not need to swim. I will hold you. We will only need to stay underwater until we clear the immediate high-security area."

"How deep are we?"

"We are twenty meters down. We will not stay that deep for long, though you may feel discomfort."

"It's hard to believe that you can swim given that you... ah...you know being made of metals and..."

"Wrik I am quite aware that I weigh much more than I appear to and I have no sensibilities about weight."

A look of relief steals over his face.

"How fast can you go?" he adds.

"Carrying you, I can make about 40kph. Faster than that and you might be injured, or your mask's seal might not be able to handle it. My main concern is drawing an attack where you would be very vulnerable to an underwater explosion."

"Well if one chance is all you have," he said, running a shaky hand over his face, *"then that's what you have to do."* He quickly strips out of his clothes.

I adjust the straps and secure the tank to Wrik's back. The half-bowl mask seals over his face. I still have doubts about the mask's seal, so I manufacture a mouth tube and rework the mask. *"If it floods,"* I reassure, *"then you will still be able to breathe through your mouth."*

"Yeah," he said, jaw knotting. *"Let's get this over with before the search gets down this far."*

I turn to the airlock. The inner door has thick grease on the valves and opens, though it would not have been easy for a human. I examine the inner mechanisms where maintenance was less even. I am satisfied that if I need to, I can tear the outer door off when the chamber floods. I open the outer valves and the chamber begins to fill. The yellow light comes off to be replaced by an icy-blue one.

I open the valve on Wrik's oxygen cylinder. It contains only twenty minutes of air, the best I could do with the material to hand. Then I turn to the wheel-like outer door lock. This time it creaks and threatens to bind, but I force it, stripping the internal mechanism. Darkness yawns beyond the outer door.

CHAPTER 7

COLD WATER LAPPED AROUND MY LEGS. SOMEHOW I expected the Pacific to be warm. The darkness and blue light disturbed me as well. I tried to keep my breathing slow and shallow as the water reached my chest, bringing pressure with it, but my heart hammered. I'd never been a good swimmer and always had a horror of sunken ships and drowning in dark water. The tube inside my face mask rested against my lips but I found the smell of the plastic nauseating and didn't take it in my mouth as the face seal seemed fine. The water closed over my head.

"Lean forward and crouch," Maauro said. Her voice, modulated for the water suffered only a little distortion. I felt her behind me, taking my upper arms in her hands. Then we were out of the airlock, Maauro kicking far faster than a human swimmer could. I looked down and saw she'd flattened her feet into flippers. She sounded more like an engine than a swimmer. We tilted upward and I knew we were shallowing as the stabbing pain in my ears eased.

I felt like I was strapped to a torpedo as we picked up speed and the water lightened. I knew that, left to herself, Maauro would have gone deeper to avoid being detected by a satellite or aircraft and swam far faster.

I'm holding her back. Nothing new about that, I thought bitterly. I was determined not to complain about the increasing pressure on my chest and face as we plowed forward, or about the pain in my arms from where she gripped me, particularly on the left side where her grip was not as finely tuned in her replacement arm.

I looked around without moving my head. The mask seal would be stronger for being pressed straight back on my face. All I could see below was darkness and a few small fish; the bottom had dropped away. Above, it was lighter but not bright, our escape had been planned for evening and the sun was doubtless near the horizon.

God," I thought, *"don't let us have to do this in darkness.*

We slowed and Maauro let go of me with her right arm. I felt her press something into my right ear.

"Can you hear me?" Her voice sounded tinny in the little speaker.

"Yes," I don't know how she heard me, but I'd long since ceased to be amazed at her abilities. "Why have we slowed down?"

"We are approaching the security curtain; the base's electronics are optimized at this point. Once beyond this half a kilometer wide zone, I can speed up again, but for now, even with my best ECM and water refraction camouflage I must slow and act more like a fish. So, expect random vector and speed changes as we work our way forward. I must be wary of sonar and use this earpiece to speak to you."

"You probably make a better sonar return than a fish," I said.

"Less than you think. My ceramic alloy body was made to avoid detection by more sophisticated devices than these. Plus your biological body muffles the signal as well."

I could not turn my head far enough to see her. "How are you staying afloat? I don't hear your legs cycling."

"I have generated two black airbags out of my back. They offset our lack of buoyancy."

I felt surges as Maauro, trying to be a fish, darted around. We proceeded for what I knew was only minutes, but felt far longer.

"Trouble," Maauro said. "An anti-submarine drone has been rerouted to check on us by the base AI."

"They're onto us?"

"No, this is a precaution by the AI due to the heightened alert. We have been identified merely as a curiosity, not a threat."

"What can we do?" I asked, heart pounding. I felt helpless.

"Nothing until it gets closer. The unit is an unmanned mini-copter carrying a torpedo. I can try for a cyber-hack, but I have no long-distance weaponry. If it gets closer, there are ways I can deal with it. All of them have their drawbacks."

"Can you outrun it?

"Not carrying you."

I swallowed. "Maauro, I haven't been counting the minutes—"

"I have," she replied. "I have added a line to your cylinder. I am breaking oxygen out of seawater and adding it. Remain as quiet as you can, as it is not a lot of additional air and the power cost is severe."

We continue our fish-like course.

"The ASW chopper is overhead and scanning us," she adds. "It has not received an attack command but clearly we look odd to it."

"If it drops a torpedo—," I began grimly.

"Quiet, Wrik. I will deal with it. Now."

I consider my options, the most certain one would be to leave Wrik treading water, zip at full speed to the surface, which would take me high enough to either tear the chopper to pieces, or hit it with my plasma torch. However, this attack would alert the base AI and it would respond with other units and signal its biological masters. I scan and infiltrate. The targeting computer is too well protected to hack without again alerting the base AI. If it is like most combat systems it will go autistic immediately if it detects a hack, then open fire. I infiltrate a maintenance subroutine for the mini-chopper's fuel system. By manipulating the servos I can bring the unit down by cutting off its fuel.

Inspiration seizes me. I do not want the chopper to come down while investigating us. Instead I begin to vary the fuel intake. The engine runs rough and the chopper dips, then seeks to open its fuel system up to regain power. Again I cause fluctuation. After a few seconds, I detect a biological controller entering into the loop. He detects the engine malfunction and hits override ordering the unit to return to base. Another will be sent out to replace it.

We will not be here. As soon as the unit's active scanning ceases, I accelerate to the best speed I can with Wrik. It is fortunate that many larger fish are swift. We exit the control area of the security curtain and I increase speed still further. I must also cut off Wrik's new oxygen supply, hoping that what remains will suffice.

I reach out with sensors that have no analogue in Confederation technology and thus should not be detected. The trawler is twenty kilometers away at the far edge of its planned rendezvous with us. We'd hoped not to need this contingency but planned for several ways of exiting the base. Twenty kilometers was as close as we dared bring the trawler and Wrik's air supply cannot last that long.

I put on the maximum speed I dare. I hear grunts of pain through the connections between us but I cannot slow. Still this concerns me as they grow more frequent.

A metallic tang of blood is in the water, I slow instantly, realizing that my left-handed grip has torn his skin. We surface.

We come up in a valley between huge black waves. I start to tear my mask free then stop as the wave knocks us under.

"Do not remove your mask," Maauro shouted. "Now that we are on the surface, I can replace the air in your tank."

I almost disregarded her until another wave smacked me.

Maauro floated next to me. The two black airbags she mentioned projected from her back like dark angel wings. She struggled with the piping to my air tank.

The sky above was purple, the sun must be setting, but in the trough of the waves I couldn't see it. I struggled with panic, then felt cool air blow on my face, with my mask on and oxygen back in the tank I could breathe even in the rough water.

"Get behind me," Maauro ordered, "between the air wings."

I managed, wincing at the sting of salt water on my left arm, where Maauro's grip had cut the skin, despite her best efforts.

"Now wrap your legs around my waist but keep them pulled up."

Maauro leaned forward as I did so and I found myself riding on her back. She began scissoring her legs back and forth and we started forward at a good speed. But a minute of two of climbing the Pacific waves revealed the futility of trying for quick progress. The waves knocked me off.

"Can we signal Jaelle, to come toward us?" I asked after the third time. "I'm nearing exhaustion."

"Unwise, the communication would be picked up. We make too good a sensor target on the surface. But unnecessary in any event, your air tank should be sufficiently recharged by now. We have to go underwater again. This time you hang on to me so I do not injure you further."

I nodded, too tired to argue against a return to the dark and the cold. Down we went. Relief from the waves was immediate, but the cold began eating through me. Fortunately Maauro's body was generating a lot of heat and I pressed against her, grateful for it.

Something flashed in the middle distance. Maauro swerved violently and whipped up her right arm. I heard the whoosh as she fired flechettes from her fingertips.

"What was that?" I shouted.

"A shark," she replied.

"Did you get it?" I said, trying to look in all directions.

"Yes. Hopefully it will give the others sufficient distraction as a food source to leave us alone."

"Others! No, don't tell me." I kept telling myself that so long as I was with Maauro I was safe, over and over.

We plowed on through the Pacific. *God, will this night never end,* I wondered. I felt like I'd been cold and wet forever. My eyes strained to pierce the blackness, but dreaded seeing anything. Gradually, I became aware that it was not all black, that lots of small pinpricks of light, some flashing, some pulsing, lay about me, like tiny bioluminescent stars.

Maauro pulled up and fired at something again. Then she sped up and we headed for the surface. I saw lights, the trawler, and was almost overcome by relief. But we were not out of the woods yet. The trawler rolled in the heavy seas as we broke the surface near it. Maauro shone lights from her big beautiful eyes at the trawler, shouts came immediately. I spotted Jaelle on the deck, grabbing men and pointing in our direction.

"Maauro," I managed. "I don't think I can climb out of the water."

"My energy is depleted too," she replied. "But I do not think we will need to. Look." The boom of the trawler reached out, a heavy fishing net dangling from it. As soon as it was close enough, Maauro reached up and grabbed it. I dimly heard Jaelle shout, then felt us lifted, Maauro had her left arm in the net and the right around me. My limbs had gone numb and I wasn't sure if I was holding onto her or not.

Jaelle and the men grabbed at us as they swung us onboard, but we still fell awkwardly to the deck, Maauro rolling under me to preserve me from the shock. But the last jolt was too much and I faded out.

CHAPTER 7

A feline face swam into view as my vision returned. Warm yellow light fell on my face. I realized I was in a bed, under a pile of blankets. I must have been out for a while.

"Wrik," Jaelle said. "Honey, are you all right?"

It was an effort to talk but I forced myself. "Yeah. Good to see you. Thought for a while there, we weren't going to make it."

"Here," she said. "Hot tea and soup."

She helped me up and I greedily slurped down the soup and the tea, the warmth spreading through me. "Is Maauro ok?"

Jaelle nodded. "She's down in engineering, plugged into the engine, sucking down as much power as she can without disrupting the ship's systems. I've never seen a haggard-looking android before, but even she looked like she'd been through the wringer."

I nodded, then caught myself. "Yeah, rough trip on the way out."

"Did you get what you needed?"

"Maauro has the samples in her body along with scans and records. She's probably already doing an analysis."

"Don't bet on that," Jaelle replied. "I think she's going to eat a small nuclear reactor before she does anything she doesn't need to."

"I know how she feels," I said.

Jaelle picked up the tray and locked it down on a nearby table. Then she came back and slipped under the blanket with me. "You still need some warming up."

"Sounds great to me." My arms slipped around her. I noticed the bandages on my torn left arm, remembered the sharks and shuddered.

"Very bad trip," Jaelle said. "Tomorrow, I want you to think about whether heading back to Star Central makes sense. How many more times will your luck hold?" Then her lips were on mine. "That's tomorrow. We have a few hours before the seajet takes us off this trawler. Forget about it for now. We'll be back at *Stardust* in 24 hours."

My head hit the pillow and I slid back into sleep.

CHAPTER 8

THE *SEAJET,* A STEALTHY MODEL, LANDED NEXT TO US in the darkness and we and Candace's crew transferred aboard. The trawler was fully automated, so there would be no one to question when the ISM investigated it later. The seajet took off, going supersonic and hypersonic shortly thereafter. It slid into the wake of a commercial transport bound for Gatwick. It made for a bouncy trip, but with the seajet's ECM and stealth mode, we'd be hard to spot even from satellites.

We landed in Spain and transferred to a legitimate short-haul airliner to London, with vacation clothes supplied for our cover. As promised, we were back at *Stardust* soon after. Maauro disappeared to the reactor room. Jaelle and I relieved Dusko so he could get away from the ship for a while. We were not to remain undisturbed long. Maauro appeared to tell me that Candace had sent her another message. This time the meet was at a private and exclusive restaurant, an easy place for Candace's security team, the Earthbound contingent of which she was evidently more confident in.

Jaelle remained with the ship. Maauro and I made our way to the Windsor after raiding our wardrobes for our best clothes. Well I raided mine. Maauro merely retexturized her exterior casing to a simple black dress and wore some of Jaelle's jewelry.

Seeing her so feminine, with her hair done in an elaborate style that had taken her mere seconds, given that she could literally tell it what to do, took me aback. I tried not to show my surprise.

We were picked up by a limousine and taken to a restaurant called the Criterion, then shown into a private room upstairs and in the back. We sat in the curtained alcove, under the antique lamps and ordered some appetizers. We weren't kept waiting long.

Candace Deveraux walked up to our table. The low-cut, orange gown she wore showed off winking Frosteer sunstones that glowed against her dark skin. "Good evening."

"Candace," I said. Maauro only nodded.

"ISM is up in arms. They're circulating artist sketches of both of you, seems that for some reason, no camera retained an image of either of you."

"How curious," Maauro said drolly.

"Don't get too confident," Candace said. "They're good likenesses of you anyway, Maauro."

"Well," I said to Maauro. "You are the pretty one."

"What progress have they made in regard to our intrusion?" Maauro asked.

"Very little; there were a lot of trawlers and small vessels in the area. There always are, that close to Japan. They could only do a cursory check and our trawler's memory banks retained no record of being boarded.

"They know where you were in the base and where you went, but not why. I doubt that their scans of the bodies and the lifeboat were detailed enough to determine what you did—"

"They should not be," Maauro said, "other than some small nondescript pieces of the shuttle, my work was on a molecular level. It would require their best machines and a perfect baseline to detect my sampling."

"So they have a mystery," Candace continued. "They think you escaped underwater to a submersible, or possibly drowned in the attempt. No one can understand how any being could have covered so much distance in so little time. They are still searching around the island, expecting you to wash up."

"It's too much to expect that they will write us off as dead," I added. "They know what we looked at. Whoever was involved in the Rainhell Op will put two and two together."

Candace shrugged. "People disappear at sea all the time. Even now. Still, big planet that it is, ISM has a lot of resources. I've blocked information on all of you out of every database I can. I still believe that no one outside of Confed Intelligence knows of Maauro's capabilities. To most you're just a big-eyed teenage girl from a lost colony. A junior member of Jaelle and Wrik's Lost Planet Company, but the sooner you get off Earth the better."

"Did you have some additional information for us?" I asked.

"What, I can't just drop in on two of my favorite operatives?" Candace said. The waiter came by with two bottles of wine and three glasses, Candace must have ordered them before coming over. We were quiet as the waiter poured.

I observe the Confederate spymaster closely while the waiter pours red fluid into our glasses. Deveraux would like to have me examined in detail by her scientists. Only the certain knowledge that I will destroy myself before permitting it forestalls her, that, and my avowed intention to take her with me. I do not trust this human and do not consider her part of my network.

"You did not come to enjoy our company or dine with us," I state.

Candace's friendly mien smoothes out into coolness. "You're right. I came with a mission specific reason. You have a problem, you're down an operative. Jaelle Tekala is not going. That leaves you and Maauro and one former Guilder. Not an ideal team."

CHAPTER 8

"How did you—" Wrik begins.

"How did I what?" Candace snaps. "Find shit out? I am a professional shit-finder-outer. Now back to the point. What do you plan to do about it?"

"No immediate solution occurs," I admit.

"One does for me," Candace says. "Take one of my people with you."

"No," Wrik and I chorus together.

"Hear me out," Candace says, raising a hand to ward off our protest.

"We are not taking on someone we don't know," Wrik states.

"You do know her and, in fact, it was your idea," Candace replies. Wrik looks confused, a feeling I share.

"What are you talking about?" Wrik says

"You did recommend Olivia Croyzer to me in the highest terms," Candace says.

"The police chief of Tir-a-mar," I add, giving Wrik a searching look, "formerly of the Confed Marine Military Police?"

A flush of anger crawls over Wrik's face. "I did recommend her, but not for this."

"Of course not," Candace says with feigned innocence. "This wasn't even in the cards when you did. But I took her on immediately after the Predictor mission, despite that little blot, well not so little blot, on her record."

I am in a dilemma. Croyzer was court-martialed for protecting the son of her former commanding officer in what had appeared to be justifiable self-defense, but was merely the overture for a serial-killer. The murderer had fooled her into believing his tale of being mugged until the other bodies showed up. Then it was too late. This information was told to Wrik in confidence and he does not know that I spied on the two of them, so I cannot use it.

"You were right, Wrik." Candace continues. "Human potential like hers isn't common and even that mistake didn't make her less valuable to me, or now to you. You know her—"

"Knowing her is not the same as trusting her," I say.

Candace picks up her glass and regards me over the rim of it. "Trust, Maauro? Do you trust Dusko or Jaelle? Do you even trust Wrik?"

She has passed my guard in a fashion I did not anticipate. Something in my demeanor warns her and she leans back, alarm in her face. Foolish, if I intended attack she would be dead before she could react. I am supersonic at need.

Wrik's hand has come to rest on mine. "That's enough," he says to Candace, his voice harsh.

"In any event," Candace says, putting the glass down with only a slight tremor in her hand. "She owes you, Wrik. She'll be easier to integrate into your team than anyone else and surely you can trust her more than anyone else you could find on your own."

I must admit the logic of what Candace says. Croyzer is tough and smart, so much so that I had wondered if she had abilities beyond normal humans. Despite her earlier misjudgment, she had proved incorruptible on Tir-a-Mar and instrumental in extracting Dusko and Jaelle from Guild trouble. While we could have succeeded without her help, we would not have, over her opposition.

"We wish to discuss the matter privately," *I advise Candace.*

"Sure, I'll go powder my nose. You two chat."

I wait until she is out of earshot before turning to him. "Wrik, I do trust you."

His expression toward me is neutral. "I know, Maauro. I return that trust. Even though I know you have occasionally lied to me, occasionally also withheld information. I know that even when you did that, you felt you were doing it for my own good."

I am disconcerted. This is not what I expected. I focus all my mental powers on an analysis of this issue for 1.233777 seconds, I go autistic to concentrate.

"Candace has made me angry," *I finally say,* "because as is often the case with her, she has told the truth. My trust with the others is rationed. Dusko has the smallest portion, gained only because he has seen that no enemy has survived engaging me. It is not in his Dua-Denlenn nature, with its totally self-centered moral code, for him to even resent this. I deal with him as his own would. Jaelle too, is closer to you than to me, while I have protected her with my life, she too has been subject to manipulation by me.

"Worse yet is the fact that what you have said is also true. I have on occasions lied, or withheld information from you. At those times I perceived this as for a greater good, or to cope with a flaw in you, such as when you were using Anodyne Dust back on Kandalor."

Wrik looks startled, even angry. "So that's why no one would sell to me."

"Yes. I eliminated several dealers and injured others to persuade them. It was effective."

He nods slowly. "I shouldn't have been doing it. I wish I could say that you should have talked to me first, but I was too broken to listen back then."

"Perhaps. The longer I operate networked to you, the more I have come to question myself. Maybe I should thank Candace for making me face this squarely. My believing that I know best is a failure of trust. Please forgive me. I will try to do better in the future."

"Dammit, Maauro, if you'd trusted me then, we'd be dead."

"That was then, this is now. I must change."

"I have no complaints of you," *he says, closing his hand on mine.*

"Perhaps you should. I may have been a bad friend."

"That's my call and I say no. Do you hear me? No."

"Thank you, Wrik. I am reassured and not so sad now."

"So what do we do about Croyzer?" he adds. "She's as good and as tough as anyone. We can certainly rely more on her than on anyone else outside of Lost Planet, so long as it doesn't cut against Candace's orders."

"As Jaelle is not going and I do not give Dusko a vote in such matters," I say, "it falls to you to choose."

"Maauro, I am not sure that I am completely objective when it comes to Olivia, she affected me in ways I didn't expect."

"You cannot defer this decision to me. I am not competent to judge human motivations to this degree and I have just been reminded of how very much I have to learn about such interactions."

Candace's walks up to our table. "Got a decision?"

I remain silent looking steadily at Wrik.

"How soon can Olivia join us?" he says

"She's en route to Earth and can be at your ship by 0400, two days from now. Girl travels light, well, except for guns. She'll be ready to go. But that brings up the question, where will you go?"

"We'll go to Eta Cassiopeia, the last place Bexlaw was seen," Wrik says. "We may find some clues there or in what Maauro sampled."

"Nothing now?" Candace asks, looking at me.

"No, but there are some unique signifiers in the material. Along the journey I may find traces on the subatomic level that correspond to the traces that the universe left on the molecules of the samples I have. It is a faint hope but better than none."

"I'll send couriers to both systems with instructions that any of my operatives out there are to help you. Once you leave Eta you'll be on your own."

"We are used to that," I say.

"Enjoy your evening," Candace said. "I have an opera to get to." She turned and sashayed away from us, perhaps glad to be putting distance between her and me.

Wrik raised his glass and indicated that I should do the same. I took the delicate crystal with my original right arm with its finer motor control. "It is perhaps a waste. I should leave the wine to you."

"We have two bottles of the finest kind. They're on Candace's tab. I know that you will enjoy it in your own way and that will be enough."

"Thank you," I say. I know that Wrik values time when it is just the two of us. This realization stirs something inchoate in me. I remember the possible futures that lay before us, some of which I saw when linked to the Ribisan Predictor. Some futures led to death or separation, others to success and at least one to something I could not presently comprehend, a joyful union of Wrik and me. Suddenly I am struck with fear over how fragile my friend is, how exposed to every danger. And now I propose to take him into more? I am made for war; he is made of flesh and easily shattered bone. Why am I doing this?

I must be malfunctioning

"*Maauro are you ok?*" *he says, concern on his face.*

I look at him, wanting to tell him, wanting to turn back. Yet another truth stops me. Both Wrik and I are on journeys to become. He will not allow me to preserve him at the cost of that journey. There are things that he needs to prove and reprove to himself. I do not want that to be true, but it is.

Also true, I cannot simply exist. I too must have purpose. Perhaps it is only balanced on the sword of that purpose that he and I can become what we must.

"*I am fine, Wrik. Merely glad that for tonight, at least, it will be just the two of us.*"

He smiles, "To us." We gently clink the glasses.

CHAPTER 9

THE NEXT TWO DAYS ARE SPENT IN PREPARATION FOR THE VOYAGE AND *we rarely leave the ship. Supplies of all sorts are purchased and secured aboard. Near the middle of the second day, Jaelle walks up to me on the bridge.*

"Good," she said. "I wanted a few moments alone with you."

"Yes, Jaelle," I reply cautiously, rising from my chair.

"I want to take my leave of you. Wrik and I are heading for the hotel for a last night together. I don't plan to come down to the ship tomorrow. You will all be busy with takeoff and it will only be awkward."

"Then this will be our goodbye," I say.

"Things are not always easy between us, Kit-sister."

"No," I reply. "I wish that they were."

"I know that it may seem illogical, but it does not mean that I do not care for you, or that I'm mad at you. It's important to me that you know that."

"I too want you to know how highly I value you. You are second only to Wrik in that. I suspect that I do not express this well—"

"It's all right, Maauro. Know that there is no one who I trust more with Wrik's life."

"I am honored. Know that I will not return if I fail to protect Wrik."

To my surprise, a look of anger crosses Jaelle's face. "You think I would want that? How would it help me to go from losing a lover to losing a lover and a friend? The universe is not so full of people dear to me that I can be so cavalier with them. You are not disposable to me. You do not exist only in relation to Wrik."

I walk forward and put my arms about Jaelle. She returns the embrace fiercely. I am troubled. Jaelle does not know, as I made Wrik promise to keep it secret, that the Ribisan Predictor has shown me possible futures, the most powerful of which showed a future that held only Wrik and me. Still there was no reason to believe the timeline we were in led to that future. Anything could lie in front of us.

Whatever comes, we were allied in our attachment to Wrik and our desire to preserve his existence. Beyond that, all I can do is try never to intentionally harm Jaelle.

"I will come back then, though it is unlikely that anything would get Wrik without having to destroy me first."

She rests her chin against the top of my head then strokes my hair. We stand that way for a few moments. She steps backward and kisses me on the cheek then walks out without looking back.

I wanted to spend my last night solely with Jaelle. Dusko and Maauro were down at the ship. Jaelle said she'd made her goodbyes with both already. We went to the nicest hotel near the ship, had the best dinner then went upstairs and made love with a single-minded intensity.

As we lay on the large, round bed trying to catch our breath, Jaelle turned to me. "It's not forever."

"I know," I said, but wondered if that was true.

"When you return, we will start again."

"We will," I said, "but Jaelle, we have to face it, we will be different people. Not only because of the time apart. You'll be a mother when I get back."

"I know that my getting pregnant by another male—"

"—Is not it. It hurts, as my journeying with Maauro hurts you. Something I'm sorry for. But it will be a different orbit for us around your children, around the things that you want to build for the future."

"So what are you saying?"

"God, Jaelle, I don't know. When I get back, we will make this work. Somehow. We're more different than we ever realized. Even the fact that whatever male gives you kits is so disposable to you is difficult for a human to understand. But somehow we will figure it out."

She smiled slowly. "That is a remarkably sophisticated thinking for someone so young."

I tugged her tail slightly. Jaelle sometimes teased me about being younger than her. "I'm told I was born old."

She swatted at my hand with her tail. But her serious mood reasserted itself. "Nekoans don't usually mate for life, or for long even. That scares you too, doesn't it?"

I wondered if this was the night to have this conversation, but found myself nodding. "I guess so."

"I am what I am, Wrik. Of a kind which has great passions, but which cool sooner than yours seem to. I cannot guarantee the future. Even your kind fails as much as it succeeds at long marriages. Can you guarantee your future feelings for me?"

"I would say, yes, Jaelle. But that may be because, as you say, I am young even for being young. Maybe having done without love before, I believe it can overcome anything."

"It's a good thing to believe. But all we can do is continue to care, continue to stay there for each other. God put us down here in two different species and we have to manage it as best we can."

"I promise you," I said, "that I will come back and whatever has changed, I'll do my best to understand and accept."

She rubbed the muscles of my back. "I guess I'll have to learn that you're a human and not a Nekoan without a tail."

"And I'll have to learn that you're female, but that your drives and desires aren't those of a human woman with big, beautiful ears."

"You've always loved my ears."

"I love everything about you.

"Do you? I fear that I have caused you as much pain as pleasure."

"You're wrong about that. Most of the happiness I have found in this life has come through you."

"I want you to know that I don't resent the one who brought the other part of your happiness. Not really anyway. If you're going, than she is my best hope for a protecting angel for you."

"I'm glad of that," I said, genuine relief flooding my soul.

"Did you want to sleep some?" Jaelle asked.

"No. Time enough for that aboard ship. We have two hours until I have to go. Maauro is down there doing most of the preflight work so we have this time together. I just want to spend it holding you."

"I could come down to the ship."

"No. I want to leave you here, safe in my memory. Not by shipside in the cold and the rush."

She nodded. "That was what I planned, which is why I made my farewells to the others earlier. I said my goodbyes to Maauro. Dusko got a wave."

I couldn't help but laugh, though there was a bitter edge in it. We lay together side by side, Jaelle's head on my chest, pretending we didn't see the clock. But soon it glowed 4AM. We stood and walked to the door.

Nekoans didn't cry and I didn't want her to see me doing so.

"I love you," I said. "I'll come back to you. What I don't understand, I'll learn to, or I'll learn to live with. In the end, so long as we put our heads down on the same pillow, we won't be doing too badly."

"Take no chances that you don't have to," Jaelle said. "Listen to Maauro. Remember that I love you and remember the way back to me."

Then it was time to go.

The cab took me to the spaceport. I'm not sure how I found my way to *Stardust* as I was so totally lost in my thoughts. I was surprised to find myself looking at my ship. I went up to my cabin, and dropped my flight bag on my bunk, reluctant now to face the others. I stopped in the galley. We had fine actual Earth-grown coffee aboard. I drank a cup, waiting for it to dispel the drowsiness of a late night and an early morning.

"Wrik," Maauro's voice sounded over the intercom.

I gave a guilty little start at her voice. "Yes."

"A vehicle bearing Olivia Croyzer is approaching."

"Ok, I'll get her."

"Thanks."

I drained my cup and secured it in the washer, then headed down the spiral staircase out onto the gantry. I wasn't alone. Launch crew were making checks on the gantry, disconnecting the power and sanitary lines to the ship. We were on our own now.

Olivia stepped out of a blue utility transport with a shoulder bag, and a rolling suitcase. She wore a long, black coat with which her bright-blond hair contrasted. A roboloader followed on her heels with an oblong case. I waited for her outside the amidships cargo hatch. She rode the gantry elevator up to my level. The lift stopped and left her two meters away from me. Her thick hair obscured her artificial right eye, but the other arctic-blue eye was fixed on me. Her face was expressionless.

"Hello, Olivia," I said.

"I understand your name is Wrik Trigardt this time," she replied.

It wasn't, but it was how I was known now. Only Maauro knew my original name, though I suspected Candace had traced me back to my old life. She'd never said and I was grateful for that.

"Yes," I relied. "You'll have to forget Jedaya Fels. That identity was left on Tir-a-mar."

"Nice to know who I am working with," she added dryly.

"Don't count too much on that Olivia. We all have our secrets." I only wanted to lie to her when I had to.

"Where's Maauro?"

"On the bridge, she wanted to give us a few minutes alone."

"What for?"

"Renew old acquaintances, I suppose."

The wind stirred her coat and hair, revealing her artificial eye, blue like the other, though without the icy sparkle. I knew the eye was functional and saw into the infra-red and other ranges. She didn't need the hair to be out of the way to see. "I'm grateful to you for recommending me to Confed Intelligence."

"Don't mention it," I replied. "We appreciated your help on Tir-a-mar. We might not have made it off that world except for your help, especially for Jaelle."

"I understand she's not coming on this trip."

"That's why you're here," I said. Determined to head off any discussion of Jaelle, I pointed to the squat roboloader and its crate.

"Weapons," she said. "I have my favorites."

"I'll show you to the armory." We walked into the ship, trailed by the robo. The armsroom was on this level, really just a walled off section of the main cargo hold. I noticed her looking at the three crab-robots secured to the walls. When we reached the armsroom, I opened the door. "Press your finger to the pad."

She did so.

"You're cleared for arms room access."

Olivia opened the crate, pulling out a variety of formidable looking weapons, including a sniper rifle. I scanned each one in and Olivia racked them. The roboloader made its way out on its own.

"You're in Cabin 5," I said as we finished. "I can show you—"

"I know Comet class ships," she interrupted. "One hundred fifty meters tall with main impellers on each of the three fins, 5,000 metric tons, class 13A hyperdrive, accommodations for 4-12 depending on duration, one pinnace and you've pulled out the bomb bay and converted it to cargo holds. I'll admit I've never seen one painted dark green and gold."

"Alright then," I said sealing the armsroom door. "Meet us in the mess at 0600 hours. Last check-in before launch."

"Aye, aye, sir."

"No need for any of that. This is a small ship and we run it civvy."

She gave me a long, measured look.

"Do you have something to say, Olivia?"

"Okay. This mission is a big one for me. I liked you when we first met on Tir-a-mar and I thought you were a simple line officer."

"You never believed that."

She shrugged. "My point is that you lead a complicated existence: a past no one seems to know, a Nekoan girlfriend, and some sort of relationship with an AI so powerful I can't imagine how anyone lets the thing run around loose—"

"Let me retract one thing I said about how I run this ship," I interrupted. "You don't refer to Maauro as it, or as a thing. You use her name, or the gender she's chosen for herself. You have a problem with that and you and your bag of fireworks can head back for the dock. Are we clear?"

"Yes, sir," she replied, again there was no trace of an expression on her face.

"Finish what you were saying."

"Whatever looked like it might be starting on Tir-a-Mar, stays on Tir-a-Mar. Your orbits are too complicated for this simple solider. I'm on my way to places again. There are things I want to do. Chances I have again. This is the last time I want to discuss it. After this, you and I are two pros on a mission. You can count on me completely, but it will be because it's my job."

"Sounds good to me," I replied. "As you say, it's a complicated orbit. I don't want it to get any more so either."

"Good, we understand each other."

"See you at 0600, Olivia," I forced myself to give a pleasant nod and walked out, trying hard not to show how pissed off I was, largely because I wasn't completely sure why I was angry. But I had a ship to lift and lot to do before we lifted. I put it out of my mind.

Two hours of frantic work later, I walked into the mess. Dusko was there already serving coffee and some pastry he'd whipped up. Maauro sat at the table nibbling the pastry with evident relish. I smiled at her, accepted the coffee from Dusko and dropped into a seat. At 0600 precisely, Olivia, in a dark-blue ship's jumpsuit, walked in, scanned the room and sat down at the table.

"Hello Dusko," she said, "that coffee smells good."

"Here you go," he said, sliding a cup before her. "Want to try the éclairs?"

"Sure."

Dusko fixed her up then joined us at the table. Olivia turned to study Maauro, who gazed back unperturbed.

"Welcome aboard," Maauro said.

"Who am I reporting to?" Olivia asked.

"Wrik and I share command," Maauro answered.

"Don't care much for a divided chain of command," Olivia said.

I shrugged. "Learn flexibility."

Dusko laughed. "Don't worry. You won't be getting any orders from me. I only outrank the dishwasher."

"Maauro is being sweet," I added. "She's the brains and does the planning. I fly the ship. Dusko makes sure all aboard runs smoothly. You back us up on the running and gunning and ship work."

She shrugged. "Those are my specialties. I'm an aerospace pilot too. I've got an atmospheric rating, I've flown nearspace too but I don't have a formal rating."

"Anybody who can fly in Cimer's atmosphere," Maauro said, "should have no problem with most conditions."

"I can stand a space watch," Olivia said. "But I've never flown anything bigger than a landing barge. I wouldn't want to handle anything this large in any but simple open-space maneuvers."

I nodded. "We'll work it out on the watches."

We reviewed all that had passed to date. Olivia brought nothing new from Candace beyond the fact that the ISM had not as yet figured out anything about us.

"Then I think we should get out of here before they do," I finished. "Maauro, please do an outside check, make sure no one has attached anything to us that shouldn't be there. I'll finish the launch checklist. Dusko you start yours. Olivia, you'll have nothing to do but ride up on this one."

She raised an eyebrow but said nothing. We scattered to our assignments.

I walk down and exit the ship to begin my exterior expectations. To my surprise Olivia Croyzer follows me. I gaze up at her, as she is three inches taller than I.

"I was hoping to catch you when it was just the two of us," she said, "if I won't distract you too much?"

"I am a quantum computer and can manage multiple tasks without a loss of efficiency." This is truer than she knows. *I am not only scanning the exterior of the starship, but over the days I have infiltrated more systems near our ship. It gives me a greater security picture than mere visual observation can supply.*

She follows me as I circle the towering starship and gantry.

"When I was chasing Jaelle Tekala though Tir-a-Mar, it was you hacking into the systems, frustrating everything I did," Olivia says. *"But for you, I would have gotten her. It was you I was battling all the while."*

"A battle of wits then," I reply, looking up at the ship, *"as I had no intention of harming you."*

"I read your file," she says, keeping pace with me. *"There's not much there and it's hard to credit what I did see. You're 50,000 years old?"*

"50,132 to be reasonably precise," I say.

"Well, by all means let's be precise. An AI, product of a species that vanished so long ago we know nothing about them. Wrik found you on an asteroid that you attacked during a war."

"Yes, my side was driven off after I and two other units subdued the base."

"I've never seen or even imagined a machine like you, an artificial intelligence so advanced as to mimic real life—"

"I mimic nothing. I live. I think. In my own fashion, I feel."

Olivia stared at me. *"I didn't intend to offend you. It just did not occur to me that it could be an issue."*

"Then perhaps, biological woman, you are not as aware of feelings as you should be."

Olivia laughs in evident surprise. *"Touché— a hit I do confess it. Sensitivity is not one of my strong suits and I'm only now learning how to interact with you."*

"It is perhaps less difficult than you anticipate."

"Certainly Wrik, interacts with you very well. He's even rather touchy about you."

"If by that you mean that he will not hear me insulted, then you are correct."

"You're very close."

"We are friends."

"More than that."

"You are correct in that ours is not a casual friendship. It is something defining to us both. If you imply something else, while I think of myself as female in an innate sense, my gender characteristics are both a matter of choice and mostly of appearance."

"So you say," she replied. *"Anyway, on to other matters. We may have to fight side by side and I don't know enough about what sort of abilities you have."*

I consider. Her request is a reasonable one. "I am a direct combat model though I am optimized for cyber-attack as a system infiltrator..." I go into some of my more obvious and known combat capabilities. Croyzer is after all part of Candace's operation and I no more trust her than I do Candace. Olivia's original eye widens at my descriptions.

"Quite the little death-dealer, aren't you?"

"Less than you think. For example I have already located and deactivated or reprogrammed the spying devices that Candace either gave or planted on you. She probably anticipated that I would, but nonetheless took the chance in the hope of getting more information on me. I won't bother asking you if you knew."

A spasm of anger flashes over Olivia's face. I suspect that she did not know.

"She knows I no longer destroy biological life casually, so there was little risk to you," I add. "My philosophy is to never kill unless I must. The corollary is I never fail to kill when I need to."

"A sensible sentiment I also subscribe to," Olivia says, her mouth a grim line.

"That would give us a basis for understanding each other," I reply.

She nods. We finish our circle and head back up in the gantry elevator.

For Olivia's benefit, I speak aloud as I broadcast to Wrik on the bridge. "All is secure outside. We are coming in."

"Ok, let me know when you're in. I'll have them roll back the gantry. T-minus twenty."

"We are at the hatch. You can have them roll it back now."

"Roger that," Wrik said, slipping back into ship-speak and sounding cheerful. He is always happiest at the controls of a ship.

We make our way up to the bridge. I strap into the seat next to Wrik. Dusko is already in his accustomed seat.

Olivia looks at hers. "Why is there a hole in the center? Oh right, Jaelle has a tail."

I am chagrinned. I have not thought about this. "We will modify it after we are under way."

The gantry reaches its lock down. I help Wrik finish his checklist. London Control gave us a very detailed exit plan. We input it into the ship's AI. Wrik would prefer to fly her himself, but Gatwick does not allow any but automatic launches.

The impellers build up power and Stardust *lifts, slowly at first but accelerating smoothly and quickly. We join the march of ships slipping Earth's gravity and into the freedom of space. The sky above brightens as we lift above the clouds of London and the early morning sunlight. The ports then show the dark-blue of high atmosphere and finally the blackness of star-studded space.*

As we reach orbit we head for the commercial accelerator. We pass through the rings of the accelerator with our AG field set on maximum as the accelerator flings us up to a high percentage of light speed. With money as no object, we will hit the Mars accelerator which is eighty five minutes away, it will greatly facilitate our flight to the outer edge of the system where the stardrive can operate free of the system's gravity well.

I excuse myself and retire to the engine compartment of Stardust *and plug into a special receptacle I had built into the reactor for this purpose. I top off, filling reserves and battery power.*

Now that we are in space and away from the interference of a planet's gravity well and EMG field, I can begin the detailed examination of the samples I have tucked into my body. This work requires precision and isolation. The shielded engine compartment blocks many emanations both from the outside and from the engines, which otherwise would kill the crew in short order. I add to that my personal EMG field and the fact I am designed to be radiation proof and I become an iso-lab. I sit on the deck, setting my motion dampers to keep me still on a nearly atomic level.

The level of detail of my exam will be well below the atomic level, down to elementary particles. I focus the full power of my quantum brain to begin an analysis that is far more detailed than any Confederate AI is capable of. Even still, it requires hours of real time to peel back the variables created by the handling of the artifacts and their relocation across space. Had I been present when they were found, I would have had much greater prospects of isolating the sector of space they were originally from.

What eludes me at the moment is how the lifeboat could have been so far from its launch point, even given that it might have been launched a hundred or more years ago. The lifeboat simply has no significant range, being designed for use within a few million miles of a planet. Confed ships discovered no habitable planet in the nearby system.

Either the lifeboat was launched from New *Hope, or some other starship after a hyperspace jump, or some new form of technology not resident in the boat was used. Yet the boat itself showed no sign of modification.*

Calculations that would have taken Confederate computers years, if they could have made them at all, unravel for me. The information in them is mostly negative but eliminates some areas of space from consideration. Elements and particles in the bodies indicate that they have not come from near the galactic core, nor from the outer edges, some combinations of particles suggest Hyades star cluster, which is congruent with what little we know of the technology and star-charting available to the original refugees. There are many other possibilities, but this is the highest probability, for all that it ranks little higher than random guesswork in an area parsecs wide.

CHAPTER 9

We are on our way to the last system where Maximillian's expeditions was seen, Eta Cassiopeiae. Perhaps I can find additional information there that will refine the variables further. I can do no more for now, but I have found the beginnings of a trail.

CHAPTER 10

WE CAME OUT OF HYPERDRIVE IN ETA CASSIOPEIAE almost twenty light years from Earth. I shook off the effects of the jump easily; the transit had been direct and quick. The others were getting up from their seats and, except for Maauro, sipping restorative drinks.

"Welcome to Eta Cassiopeiae," I said, "G5 star, four major planets, only one habitable and that one not very pleasant."

"Is that why humans didn't colonize it?" Dusko asked. "It's a bit odd to have a system so close to your home-system by hyperdrive, occupied by another species."

"Eta's hyperdrive shunt from Sol," Maauro began, "eluded detection due to an anomaly in Sol System. The hyperdrive entrance was masked by a gravitational effect caused by an immense chunk of space debris, possibly a dark planet, wandering through the outer part of the system. The dark object prevented the opening from being detected until it wandered out of Sol System.

"This direct route has only been known for forty-two years. Prior to that, it took 9.723 elapsed years of hyperdrive travel through many interchanges to reach Eta."

"Then why think *New Hope* would have used it?" Dusko demanded, stretching.

"Because the object was not close enough to obscure the jump point entrance during the time *New Hope* fled. They may have feared being caught by whatever power would triumph in Earth's wars and fled away from the nearer G-class stars."

I nodded. "Unfortunately there's always been a good hyperdrive path from Solari space to here. By the time humans bothered with the system, there was a small Frokossi colony there. It failed. Then the Solari moved in to squat in its ruins."

"Earth," Olivia added, "took a dim view of Solari this close to Homeworld and made sure the colony didn't prosper. The Solari only held on here to annoy us. After they became Confed members, we had to drop the embargoes, but nothing much in trade has developed. It seems to be the hiding hole for a fallen Solari dynasty, so they don't get much help from their own kind either."

Maauro nodded. "Bexlaw had no way of knowing how powerful *New Hope's* stardrive was, it had been an alien make, only possible for them to get their hands on in a world falling apart in war. Odds favored it not being as powerful as modern ones. It may have resulted in them being 'out' of the universe for far longer than we are in transit, decades, possibly centuries. There were seven G class stars within twenty lights of Sol. No sign of Lost Colony has been discovered on any of the other six, but Eta is special case. It's never been properly surveyed."

"So here we are," Dusko said, looking like someone who had lost interest in his own question. "I'll go check hydroponics."

"I'll check the drive units," Maauro said. "I want to hit my power tap."

Olivia grimaced. "My turn in the galley."

I sighed internally. We'd discovered on the transit out of Sol that Olivia was a worse cook than me, which was saying something. That meant soup and sandwiches if we were lucky.

Maauro perhaps read something in my face. "No need, Olivia. I will do it after I check the drives."

That drew a rare Olivia smile.

The others trooped off the bridge. I looked at the glowing star on the ship's screens. I tried not to dwell on the fact that I had now left Jaelle behind not only in distance, but in time. She would have left for Star Central not long after we did, a longer trip in reverse than outward time-wise due to the hyperspace currents. So for a while we had been out of the universe together and indeed she would still be out for a month or longer. But there was no way to tell how much time would elapse between our voyages and hers. No way to tell how long our actual time apart would be until we see each other.

I charted a course for Eta IV. Humans hadn't bothered to name it and if the Solari had, they hadn't told anyone. It was a world a little larger than Mars and also with two small, close moons. It was cold and arid, with more CO_2 then was healthful, conditions Solari tolerated better than humans.

After another check of instruments, I engaged the autopilot. *Stardust's* AI was a minor version of Maauro herself, truncated to fit into the ship's vastly more limited computers. To my surprise, she'd never invested it with a personality, any more than she had the crab-robots. The ship's voice remained neutral on the rare occasions we used the audio. Perhaps Maauro felt the need to make clear the separation between her and the lesser mechanisms.

I killed time with the others as we cruised inward. We had the momentum from the accelerators back in Sol System and I was saving fuel. We'd loop around Eta IV and gravity brake, though we didn't intend to land on the planet itself. We gathered on the bridge the next day, as I put us into a braking orbit around a world that was a larger duplicate of the now terraformed Mars, with its small seas and limited belts of green around the equator.

"Unlovely place," Olivia said. "Any contact from below?"

"No," I said. "And I don't like it. I sent the Confed mail transmission through. There wasn't a lot of it. They acknowledged receipt and made payment, but nothing came back. Otherwise they are studiously ignoring us."

Dusko shrugged. "Not that unusual. We haven't filed a flight plan for a landing. No trade opportunity."

Maauro turned from her contemplation of the screen. "Wrik, do you have any recommendations?"

I grinned mirthlessly at her. "Because I would have the best perspective on being a hunted human refugee, living in terror?"

She nodded slowly.

I gave it some thought. "These people didn't know the galaxy like we do. Everything would have been new and unknown. If they came this way, they were the first humans not only to be here, but to leave our solar system. They had no way of knowing how many habitable worlds are out here. Some of them would have been roused from cold sleep by automatics. They would have looked this place over well, but I doubt they would have risked a landing on Eta IV. The moons, on the other hand provided a place to scavenge some minerals and to study the planet from a safe and stable orbit. They would have landed on the planet-facing side of the inner moon."

"Agreed," Maauro said.

I oriented us for a landing on the inner moon. My charts said there were no Solari installations there. The Frokossi had put small bases on both the inner and outer moon, but as far as we knew, the Solari hadn't used either. The barren, airless moon grew in our view screens. It was as uninteresting a rock as I have ever seen, pitted and scarred with the usual meteorite damage. I placed *Stardust* in as low an orbit as was prudent.

"Your turn," I said to Maauro.

She nodded and headed for the airlock. Olivia's eyes widened as she simply walked in sans spacesuit. Next, we saw her walking outside to sit on the prow of the *Stardust*. She ran her hands through her silky black hair which splayed out. The hair began to wiggle, thinning and extending to form a huge nimbus around her head.

"A sensor array!" Olivia said.

"She's vastly more sensitive than any instrumentation we have," I said. "If there's something below, she'll find it. We can always check the outer moon later if I'm wrong."

We circled the moonlet for the hours until Maauro's voice sounded over the speakers. "Wrik, there's some disturbed ground below. Look on the screen. It may be a landing site."

Maauro transmitted to the screen, but the screen's resolution was insufficient for us to see what she did. I marked the coordinates on my board. "We'll land nearby on our next pass. I don't want to use the fuel for a hard brake on this pass. I'll allow enough distance so our set-down won't disturb the area you detected."

"Agreed," she said. "That will give me time to spin my hair back in."

"You don't hear that every day," Olivia observed.

"We say that a lot around Maauro," Dusko replied.

Maauro returned as I lined us up for a landing. We came in well short of the site.

"Shall we suit up?" Olivia asked.

"All of us?" Dusko asked with obvious reluctance.

"You need not go if you do not wish to," Maauro said.

"Then I pass. I'd rather be in my hydroponic garden with living things."

"Olivia?" she asked.

"Count me in. I like EVAs."

We headed for the lower airlock and an idea struck me. "Maauro, put a suit on. I don't know if anyone on the ground has instruments that could let them look up at us, but there's no need to advertise your presence and capability."

She nodded. "Excellent thinking."

Minutes later and all in suits, we walked toward the area Maauro indicated. Gravity was about a tenth of standard, so we moved carefully over the surface, each bound covered meters.

"You were right, Maauro," Olivia said pointing. "The area shows a clear set down from a ship, burn marks and a depression.

"Two ships," Maauro said. "Those are blast prints from two landings. Someone was not as cautious as we were in landing. The zones overlap."

We moved forward.

"There are indications of archeological style digging here as well," Maauro added

"Could this be it?" I asked, excitement bubbling up in me. "Could *New Hope* have landed here followed by Bexlaw's ship?"

"Difficult to say," Maauro began. "All we know is two ships landed. The fact that I see trenches is suggestive of an archeological dig. Unfortunately they would likely have removed any evidence."

"You mean other than that shiny object on the mound over there," Olivia said. We had just rounded a boulder and she was pointing at the back of it facing the landing site.

"What is it?" I said.

"A plaque," she said.

We loped over to the boulder. On it was a golden metal plaque sat. "Landing place of the *SS New Hope,* circa 2076CE," I read, "discovered by Bexlaw expedition 2880CE Galactic reckoning. From here they passed into the void."

"Good catch, Olivia," I said.

"Yes," Maauro added.

"You're not the only one with augmented vision," Olivia said, tapping the front of her faceplate. "Still I'm surprised that I spotted it before you."

"My attention was distracted by the aerospace bomber over us."

Olivia and I jerked as if touched with live wires.

"Do not move," Maauro cautioned.

We both disobeyed her enough to look up.

Hanging several hundred meters above us, a black and yellow fighter pointed its prow and weapons at us.

"A *Daitan*," Olivia said, "four-person, bomber. Old Confed model, they must have bought it surplus. It could scrag us and the *Stardust* in one salvo of those missiles on the hardpoints. Dammit, it must have been hiding on the other side of the moon and just popped over the horizon."

"Correct," Maauro said. "You were under its weapons from that instant. There was no opportunity to escape."

"Maauro," I asked. "Can you do anything?" We hadn't brought any weapons with us. Maauro was deadlier than anything we could carry.

"No, the bomber is too well shielded from cyber-hacks. I might confuse the missiles but not the chain gun in the nose. I have sent a message to Dusko to do nothing. If he warms up the laser or switches on the fire control, they will doubtless destroy our ship."

"Do not move," an artificial voice sounded in our ears, breaking in on our frequency. "Resist and we will kill you."

"What do you want?" I called.

"Male human, raise your arm."

I looked at Maauro and she nodded. I raised my hand, glaring at the black and yellow bomber.

"Female human, raise your arm."

"Maauro?" Olivia asked.

"Comply," Maauro said.

"Step away from the machine being," the voice ordered.

"Maauro," I yelled. "Run now. Run."

For once, she obeyed instantly. Maauro lunged, tumbled and changed directions with blinding speed. The *Daitan's* chain gun flared, silently spitting depleted uranium at Maauro. The slugs chewed up the moon's surface as Olivia and I threw ourselves flat, hoping that none of the rock chips hit our vulnerable suits. But the rounds trailed the racing android as she disappeared, zigzagging over the near horizon of the moonlet.

"Humans," the translated voice couldn't convey the fury its owner likely felt. "Move toward your ship or die." The fighter settled lower in the sky, with Eta IV glaring down behind it like the face of an angry god. Three Solari stepped out of its belly hatch and fell slowly, using jet belts to land near us. I'd entertained the hope that they'd try to pursue Maauro on foot, but unfortunately they showed no sign of it.

I could see inside the big bubble helmets of the Solari, who resembled a mix of Terran ant and beetle. They weren't insects, but their appearance suggested it. The faces in the helmets were devoid of any expression I could read, their black, beetle eyes stared at us, glinting in the reflected light. They held standard Confed carbines pointed at us.

I watched for Maauro, but with the bomber hovering over us there was no chance. It was one thing to dodge away, where they had no way of telling where she was heading. Coming to the attack, it would be too easy for the fighter lead her and destroy her.

"Dua-Denlenn," the voice came. "Open the ship or be destroyed."

Dusko opened the airlock and two Solari went in. The last one kept us covered. Olivia looked at me and I shook my head. Then it was our turn in the airlock. When we came through, it was to find Dusko staring sourly at two Solari who had shed their suits. They wore pants and vests over their dark and spindly-limbed bodies. The third one cycled in behind us and also shed his suit.

One Solari, wearing gold tabs on its vest collar turned to the others. It chittered something at them then headed for the bridge. The two with us gestured with their weapons.

"Cargo hold," one Solari said in Standard. We walked upward from the lower airlock. The Solari opened the hatch and ushered us in. The hold was crowded with supplies for the voyage, the crab-robots secured to the walls, crates and other gear. "On floor, sit."

The other Solari left, turning toward the hatch to the drive unit deck. The Solari with us sealed the hatch door.

"Good thing you made Maauro take that suit," Olivia said. "They couldn't tell which one of us was her. If she'd been out without one, they'd have sieved her on the first pass."

"Silence," the Solari said.

The vibration of the drive reached us through the deck plates and I realized what was happening. They were taking off, stranding Maauro on this moon.

"No," I said, standing, distantly surprised, as if I was watching myself from some safe place. "You're not stranding her on an airless rock. Not again."

The Solari stepped forward and made an abrupt gesture with the weapon. "Sit!"

"Wrik," Olivia said, alarmed. "Follow your own advice. Wait."

"No," I said, a frantic feeling welling in my chest. "She's not a machine. Not now. You can't leave her here, alone."

"Trigardt," Dusko snapped. "Don't be a fool."

"I won't let her be marooned."

The Solari struck me with a backhanded blow. I'd underestimated the distance between us— the long arm, with its horn-hard hand dazed me. I felt the hand with its pincer-like fingers cut it into my shoulder as it grabbed me and pitched me into Olivia, who'd gathered her feet under her. We tumbled to the deck.

Olivia grabbed my good arm and twisted it behind me. "Wrik, if I have to break your arm to keep you from getting killed, I will."

"I won't let her be left," I snarled.

"Trust Maauro," Dusko demanded. "Trust her and stop being a fool."

Dusko telling me to trust Maauro was like having a bucket of cold water thrown in my face. The insanity that drove me seconds ago, abated. I relaxed in Olivia's hold and she let go of my arm.

"You can't come back for her if you're dead," Olivia said. "Listen to Dusko."

I looked over at the Dua-Denlenn and nodded. "Thanks," I muttered, my breath slowing.

"Bah," he replied. "If we let you get killed she'd probably incinerate us, anyway."

"Let me look at that shoulder," Olivia said. "You're bleeding heavily."

I looked up at the Solari. *I'll kill you,* I thought. *I swear to God I'll kill all of you.*

CHAPTER 11

THE SOLARI TAKE OFF IN STARDUST, THEIR DAITAN BOMBER TRAILING. *I must make my move. I tear off the spacesuit I am wearing, which will not survive my actions and might impede me. I generate studs on the bottom of my feet as I start running. In seconds I am accelerating through 450kph, literally tearing up the ground as I bound over the surface of this moonlet. Quickly I achieve the maximum ground speed I can, then angle toward the largest rise in sight.*

At the apex of the rise, I fling myself spaceward then invert until the plasma torch in my right hand is pointed at the moon. I fire it at full power. My only chance is now. There is no point in holding back.

I turn my head through 180 degrees so I can optically focus on Stardust *and the bomber. I am relieved. The Solari are planning to land on Eta IV, as I suspected. They have not increased speed, having, like me, escaped the gravitational pull of the moonlet. With the close orbit of this moon, there is little reason for a power burn. It would just complicate the approach landing window for their home base.*

I calculate angles and trajectories. If the Stardust *does not alter course I can land on it in twenty minutes. I cease my plasma burn and reorient my body to face the fighter. I will use a small quick burn as I close in. I cannot interfere with the Daitan's instruments, but my own ECM is sufficient that the fighter's crude, passive search sensors do not detect me. Its active sensors would, but it has not occurred to them that I might be able to chase them this way.*

As I speed toward the fighter, I reach out through the ship's internal sensors and locate Wrik, Dusko and Olivia. All are present in the cargo hold, guarded by a Solari with a carbine. Wrik appears to be injured, bleeding from the shoulder. Anger lights within me.

The minutes crawl by. I find it difficult to be patient in these circumstances, but I prepare my counterattack. The Daitan grows larger and finally I fire my plasma torch, bringing me to a gentle stop between its two vertical tails. With a powerful pull, I launch myself to the back of the bubble canopy under which the pilot sits. The Solari looks up at me, too startled to react, as I slam my bunched fingers down through the canopy and into its brain. Circulatory fluids spray out and bubble. I pull the canopy open, grab the body and pitch it into space. I check the fighter's autopilot: a standard Confed model. It is undisturbed.

I look across to our ship only fifty meters away. It is time to retake my home and my network. I leap across and order the ship's AI to open the airlock for me.

CHAPTER 11

I launch a remote attack. In the hold, the Solari guard has but a second of surprise before the crab-robot, latched to the wall next to him, reaches over with two pincers and snips his head from his neck and his weapon hand from his arm. I lock all compartments that lead to the main hold. No additional Solari will reach my friends.

One is outside the airlock when I enter. The expression on his face is probably surprise as the inner airlock door opens and I plunge out, driving my stiffened hands through his body and slashing it into two pieces as I extract. Another Solari is on the bridge, he is squawking an alarm. I move quickly to the bridge area. Using the ship's cameras I see he is inside with a heavy powergun aimed at the door.

I return to the Solari I killed earlier. I remove its head and race back to the bridge. There is a view panel in the bridge door. I place the head against the panel and shriek in Solari. "Help! The android is onboard. Let me in."

The Solari inside unlatches the door, but leaps back, suspicious. The small opening is all I need. I spray in a biological agent based on one I used on the Infesters. There is an agonized screech as the agent freezes the Solari's body in one giant spasm. The nerve toxin causes instant paralysis, though apparently not of the vocal cords, as the screams continue for a few seconds. I would have preferred interrogation, but cannot risk heavy weapon fire inside the ship. I open the door and secure the enemy's weapon as the Solari expires on the deck.

I order the AI to suck the air in the room out, venting the poison into space. It should not affect my network, but I will not chance it. I toss the two bodies out the airlock as well.

I speed down to the hold and open the doors. Olivia is on the other side with the Solari power rifle leveled at the door. The dead Solari lies in a puddle of its circulatory fluids by the crab-robot. They shout with joy as I open the door, even Dusko. All race over to me.

"The ship is secure," I say.

"I told you to trust her," Dusko says, with what for him is an effusive smile. "I knew our Princess of Death wouldn't let us down." He pats me on the shoulder. He must have been very afraid. He has never touched me before.

Olivia slaps me on the back. "Hell of a job, Maauro." I am bemused by this and assume it is akin to Jaelle's mock attacks on me and a sign of being networked.

Wrik has hung back waiting for the others to move aside. He comes up to me and enfolds me in an embrace. This feels wonderful, though I am distracted by the crude bandaging done on his shoulder, I assume by Olivia, as the torn fabric is from the midriff of her shirt.

"Thank God, you are ok." he says his voice husky.

"Let us get to the dispensary and make sure we can say the same for you. I will clean up the Solari later. The ship is on autopilot. The fighter is secured as well. Come with me."

I look around at the bits of Solari scattered about. *"I should probably consider making a small maintenance robot for these sorts of tasks."*

Dusko nods, *"A good investment of time."*

I take Wrik to the dispensary. I have absorbed all the medical data on the Lost Planet members I might be called on to treat. Wrik's wounds are simple and I am able to close them with minimal scarring that I can eventually remove.

"How did you come by your wounds?" I ask. *"Was the enemy interrogating you?"*

He gives a rueful smile. *"I couldn't stand the thought of you being marooned on another miserable airless rock. I got a little stupid with the guard."*

I finish cleaning the wounds. *"I survived alone for 50,000 years."*

"You weren't Maauro then, you were M-7. You didn't need people."

I realize that his statement is more emotional than empirical and merely smile back. But the longer I consider it, the more I wonder if he might be correct. As M-7, a sentient weapon, I had little emotional life beyond a distant appreciation of the beauty of the stars. Now, having been exposed to wider universe— could I survive an extended period as I had before?

I touch his face with my right hand. *"Thank you for thinking of me in this way. You must promise to be more careful in the future."*

"I will," he said.

We stopped by his quarters for him to freshen up and get a new shirt. Then up to the bridge. Though in a real sense, I was never off the bridge, my AI in Stardust assures me that there are no vessels or weapons targeted on us. We are in deep space and there is no moon for an enemy to hide behind. The Daitan still trails us. I haven't decided what to do with it.

Olivia and Dusko await us. Both looked tired, but otherwise none-the-worse for wear.

"What now?" Olivia asks. *"Do we protest this attack to the authorities?"*

"I do not know," I respond. *"It is most likely that the local authorities are involved. This wasn't a pirate jacking. It's asking too much of coincidence that a raider showed up here just when we did."*

"Better to leave the area," Wrik says. *"They could tie us down with an investigation for months."*

"It was not practical to take prisoners and in an operation like this, it is unlikely the agents sent to confront us have any useful tactical knowledge. I will examine the fighter to see if there is any information in it." I add.

CHAPTER 11

"You know it might be a good idea to attach that fighter to us with the ship's external grapples," Wrik said. "It could be useful where we are going next."

"Very well," I say. "I will jump over to the fighter and bring it in while examining the records and contents."

CHAPTER 12

AS *STARDUST* DROVE AWAY FROM ETA IV AND OUR deadly encounter with the Solari, we spent many hours in the mess, debating what to do next. Maauro had found nothing of interest in the bomber that now rode in *Stardust's* grapples. She repaired the canopy. We could jump with the fighter attached, though we would have to detach it to land in any atmosphere. I spent a fair amount of time aboard it and Maauro rigged up a simulator program. It was not that different than my old ship, the *Sinner,* though shorter-ranged. We stripped out some changes that the Solari had made. It took longer to get the smell of them out of the ship. I made up my mind to take her on some test flights. Sims could only do so much and I needed to get to know the tubby bomber's idiosyncrasies. I was startled to find that, one morning watch, Maauro was outside, painting the black and yellow bomber to match the *Stardust's* green and gold, with a magnetic sprayer.

"It's ours now," she replied to my radioed question. "The color scheme indicated otherwise and most biologicals view that color combination as a warning. I wanted something that looked less menacing. Besides, it clashed badly."

I barked out a laugh. "Jaelle's been influencing you," I said. A stab of something troubled my heart at the mention of her, but I shrugged it off.

"Yes," Maauro said. "Ever since I came to work in that green and white jumpsuit, she worked rather intensively on my color-sense. She said she would not hang out with someone who dressed like a stick of holiday candy."

I laughed again and turned back to my morning coffee, then broke out starcharts and again pondered what direction to go. Space was mind-numbingly vast. Jumping without a clue wasn't like looking for a needle in a haystack; it was like looking for a needle in a continent. We were coming up on the trio of hyperspace entry points. One was the former roundabout way to Eta IV, abandoned after the direct route reopened. I thought it unlikely *New Hope* or Bexlaw's *Isadora* used that one, unless they simply came to grief in deep space and never planeted again. Otherwise some sign would have been found in the well-settled planets on that route. That left the second and third warp points. The one on the other side of the system led to multiple locations in Morok and Denlenn space. Again possible, but less likely they went that way. For lack of any real plan we headed for the third entry point.

CHAPTER 12

I walked into the rec room and stopped short. Olivia was there, her feet wedged under a bar doing pull-ups. She wore a black sports bra and black tights on her legs. As she pulled up the muscles of her belly and thighs tightened, which was quite a sight. I watched in admiration as she knocked off twenty-five reps without much strain.

The outfit didn't leave a lot to the imagination and Olivia was as hard-bodied as I'd ever seen. Physically perfect except for the artificial eye that replaced the one lost in...it occurred to me that I didn't know if it was an accident or combat.

She spotted me, put her hands down and came off the wall in a smooth move.

"Hello Wrik," she said reaching for towel. "Came for a workout?"

"Yes. Didn't mean to interrupt."

"No worries. I was just about done." Her skin glowed with health and sheen of fine perspiration. I found it hard to take my eyes off her body. The small smile on her face told me she knew it.

"Not much equipment here," she added.

"Yeah. The room is used for many different things. *Stardust* is too small for a real gym. Besides I'm the only one who uses it. Never saw Dusko here and other than wrestling the crab-robots there's nothing onboard that would serve as exercise for Maauro."

"What about Jaelle?" Olivia asked. "She looked pretty fit."

I was a little nonplussed by her mention of Jaelle. "Ah. Occasionally. She didn't seem to have to work at it as hard as a human. Nekoans are strong but not much on endurance. You'd have caught her on Tir-A-Mar but for Maauro."

"You keep in pretty good shape," she said.

"Not like you," I couldn't keep admiration from creeping into my voice.

"I could use some upper body work."

"Why? So you could kill a Conchirri with a single punch."

Her grin widened. "Wouldn't mind that but we'd have to find some that hadn't gone extinct. Then extinct 'em."

"God forbid those monsters still live."

"Space is wide. Who can say we got all of them?" She toweled her face. "What do you say to putting some mats down here and doing some sparring sometime?"

I nodded, but groaned inside seeing weeks of bruises ahead of me.

"Good," Olivia said. She walked past me and playfully snapped the towel at my butt.

I spent the next two hours breaking a sweat and trying to forget what she'd looked like walking away from me with the tights stretched over that taut body. I thought of Jaelle, the smell of her hair, the tigery way she walked across a room. How she liked being kissed on the neck. Then also how she'd told me that if I needed human women that I should indulge that need. Wasn't she somewhere getting pregnant by a Nekoan? Her need had been for family, for a future. Mine just seemed to be about sex. I worked out till I was too tired to think about it anymore.

The next morning I was sipping coffee and reading an old mystery novel on a tablet when Maauro called me to the bridge. The others joined me on the way. When we got there, Maauro pointed out what looked like a small silver ball with a few spiky antennas.

"It says *SS New Hope*," Maauro said without preamble.

"They left a marker?" Dusko said. "After all they did to avoid being trailed, why would they leave a marker buoy?"

I looked at the small silver globe sitting where it had for over eight hundred years. "They were going into the Great Dark," I said, slowly. "They didn't know what awaited them, if anything. Maybe they were afraid that no one would ever know what became of them."

"Or, it could be simpler," Olivia added. "If they jumped back this way they might have wanted a buoy to confirm this was the system they came out of while they were still near the warp point. You have to remember how primitive their equipment and techniques were. All this was being done for the first time. Parallax location confirmation would have taken them a long time."

"So we know they came to this warp point and jumped out. Where does it lead?" Dusko said.

I consulted my charts. "Depending on your angle of entry, this point can lead to three systems. Two are on the periphery of known space. RW Cephei, that's a hell of a jump, 11,000 lights. It's been made only once by an automated probe a century ago. It took seventy-three years out and twenty-three years elapsed galactic time back."

"Well we won't be doing that one," Olivia said, with a glance at Maauro, who nodded quickly.

"Nor is it likely Bexlaw, mad for the quest as he was, did so," Dusko added.

"The next is Wolf 363, but there is an old Enshari colony there. One of the few they ever had. It's abandoned now as they moved back to their homeworld to repopulate it after the disaster, but it was thriving eight hundred years ago." I said.

"Enshari are friendly," Olivia said.

"*New Hope* wouldn't have known that," Dusko said, "but it is likely that the Enshari would have detected the ship if it came close enough to the planet to scan it."

"True," Maauro said, "enough so to relegate it to the bottom of the probabilities."

"Great," I said, grimacing. "That leaves yellow-orange star about 695 lights from Earth on the other side of the Helix nebula."

"The old Voit-Veru border from before they joined the Confederacy," Olivia said.

CHAPTER 12

"Someone please tell me it isn't Mounus," Dusko groaned.

"No, that's some luck. Fenaday and Rainhell are too well remembered there," I said.

"That will happen when you atom bomb a port," Olivia said dryly.

"It's in the chart as 1363 Canum," Maauro said.

"Can we see it?" I asked.

A beam flickered from Maauro's right eye. She projected a blue world onto the table top. Charts and stats on the planet and its population accompanied it. "The Voit-Veru call it Velsust: one habitable planet, a world with a lot of water and not a lot of land. Some of that land is new, the Veru terraformed it by shading the poles so that some icecaps built up, draining some land. That colony was not there eight hundred years ago."

Olivia whistled at the hologram. "How do you do that? The image is perfect. Any better and I could see the fish."

I smiled. "Maauro has better holography then a high end theatre."

"The Voit-Veru won't be overly pleased to see us," Dusko said.

Olivia shrugged as she studied the screen. "All Voit-Veru aren't from the Aporek clan. Looks like there are Hersi clan there."

"Meaning?" Dusko snapped.

"The Hersi were the only Veru that Fenaday offered reparations to," I said. "The Aporek clan held Lisa Fenaday prisoner, and he never forgave that. But he hijacked a Hersi freighter, *The Queen of the Night,* to sneak onto Mounus. According to the few interviews he did on the subject, he regretted the necessity for that. With the fall of the Aporek clan, the Hersi led the Veru into the Confederacy. I agree a warm welcome is unlikely however."

"You talk like they're not part of the Confederacy anymore," Olivia said.

"By the time we get there," Dusko said. "Who knows? Maybe they won't be."

Maauro looked at me. "Wrik, I must leave this decision up to you. Do we proceed further or turn back?"

"What do you think?" I returned.

She shook her headful of glossy hair. "I will not influence you. I want you to make the choice. Of all of us, you have the most to lose by a long and mistaken voyage."

I stood and walked over to the portal, staring out at the stars and the small point of light that was *New Hope's* old beacon. I thought about Jaelle, about why I had come on this voyage. To turn back now, with so little to show, seemed to mock all the effort we'd made so far. Beyond that I found the thought of facing Shasti Rainhell and telling her we'd given up after two star jumps too grim to contemplate. To be found wanting in the jade-green eyes of a woman whose voyages I'd read about as a child? No, it was not to be contemplated.

CHAPTER 12

"I say we go to Velsust. It's the best bet. We've got plenty of trade goods on board to make a trade mission plausible, along with Confed starmail straight from Sol System. That in itself would make a voyage there worthwhile for a trader. We should arrive at Velsust before any word of us could catch up from our enemies."

"That should have been true here," Dusko said.

Again Maauro shook her head. "You must remember the ISM's assets. If an automated spacecraft were dispatched at max speed by parties who had greater knowledge of Bexlaw's route than we have, it may have preceded us."

"We'll have to risk it or turn back," I said. "My vote is we go on."

"I agree," Maauro said.

Olivia nodded. "Go on."

We looked at Dusko, who raised one of his pale eyebrows. "What? I get a vote this time?"

"You do," Maauro said.

"Then we'll make it unanimous. Jump."

"Okay— how soon?" Olivia demanded.

"Let's get some sack time," I said. "Eight hours, breakfast for those who jump on a full stomach, then we go. We'll be better prepared to face whatever happens if we are fresh.

Olivia, Dusko and I stood. Maauro merely smiled. "Go rest. I will keep watch here and start the jump calculations."

Nine hours later we had checked everything for the jump. Maauro inspected our new prize, and made sure of the grapples. I'd named the captured *Daitan* bomber after my old ship, the *Sinner II*.

Since we were going to an at least nominally friendly port, I let the engines go up to max cruise as we closed on the warp point.

I hooked into the jump rig, seeing the indicators for the warp point ahead of us. To an observer on our hull, it would have looked like any other empty patch of space. On the sensors it roiled and snarled with its warning of another reality waiting for those entering its grasp. I tweaked Maauro's approach vector some. The hyperdrive approach to a warp point was not strictly a mathematical endeavor; there was an element of "feel" to it. Humans with psi ability made the best pilots, having some ability to see into the point, almost to communicate with it. This ability eluded Maauro and a good approach could save weeks in elapsed transit.

"Everyone hold on to your underwear," I called.

"I'm not wearing any," Maauro said.

"I can never tell when she's trying to be funny," Dusko grumbled, staring at the screen.

"Five, four, three, two one, jump!"

We popped into a binary star system of a G-class star with a white dwarf only about a light year away. The sight would have been compelling but the proximity alarm demanded my attention. My board lit up as my hands seized the instruments. At our speed we could only turn so fast...

"Proximity alarm only," I called out as the board populated with data. "No collision. There's a vessel on scan about 180,000 kilometers ahead and five degrees below."

Olivia and Dusko exchanged worried looks. Maauro, standing next to me, directly accessed the ship's AI. "IFF is coming through now," she said. "Confederate light cruiser, *Hsien*. I am flashing ours across now. "

"From her course," I added, "she's headed for the warp point in about five minutes. Doesn't look like she was waiting on us."

"*Hsien* is hailing us," Maauro said. "Voice only."

"Open communications," I said, "voice only."

"This is Captain Charteis of the *CSS Hsien* to SS *Stardust*. Please advise your destination and intentions."

"Hello *Hsien,* this is *Stardust*, Wrik Trigardt, master. We are a general trade, break-bulk freighter. Our manifest and details are coming across in a data packet now along with Sol origin starmail. We are bound for trade on Velsust II."

"Acknowledged *Stardust*. Mail from Sol. Most welcome. We've credited your ship's account. I'll even do you a favor and take your download with me. You can resell it to the Veru."

"Thanks from one captain to another. I'm hoping to pick up a cargo here, then who knows? Didn't expect to see a Confed warship all the way out here."

"Well you won't again. Not a navy one anyway. We've been relieved and sent back to our homeport. ISM sent an auxiliary for system protection. It's not much, a 35,000 ton tender for corvettes and scouts. Still there's been no action in this area for decades."

"ISM?" I said. "Isn't that unusual?" I looked at Maauro and Olivia.

"It's strange days. Your manifest shows three humans and Due-Denlenn for crew."

"That's correct."

"A little bit of friendly advice. Don't linger on your business here. The Aporek run the planet for all that there are a considerable number of Hersi and lesser clans here. They haven't been overly hospitable to human, Moroks or Denlenns. Had a number of scrapes with my crew and the locals."

"Thank you, *Hsien,* that sounds like good advice to follow."

"*Stardust*, did you want us to tell anyone in particular that we saw you out here?"

I felt strongly that Hsien's captain was signaling to me. That there was more he wanted to say, but not on an open channel. The fact he had told me of a military deployment of an ISM tender was very odd, and in itself suggested he was warning me of more than surly locals.

"Check packet 53 Alpha in the data load we sent over to you," I said. "You might find that one particularly interesting."

"Got it, *Stardust*. We'll make sure it gets through. *Hsien* over and out."

"53 Alpha?" Dusko asked.

"It's to Candace, reporting where we are and what we have seen so far. God knows when she'll get it, but she will know we entered the system."

"Excellent," Dusko said. "When they lay a wreath for the repose of our souls at least it will be in the right system. Very comforting. I'll be in the galley."

I looked at his departing back. "Cheerful as always."

"A Confed frontier system with the Navy turning over security to the ISM?" Olivia said. "Sounds like things have worsened fast."

"Perhaps," Maauro said. "Or it might be related directly to us. Remember our enemies know at least some of the trail we must follow."

"Still, this is a civilized port," I said. "We can get refueled, reprovisioned and trade some. I don't think we have to fear pirates here."

"No. Worse," Olivia said. "Inspections, possible trumped up arrests, all manner of bureaucratic delays. If the ISM uses the color of law on us, we'll wish for pirates; we could kill those."

"Maybe we should have brought a lawyer with us," I said.

"An excellent idea, Wrik," Maauro said. "I shall see what is in the library computer on aerospace law."

"Well won't you be the proud poppa when your little girl gets her juris doctorate," Olivia said.

"Wrik's relationship to me is not parental," Maauro said.

"Oh," Olivia said, sweetly. "What is it?"

"I believe the human expression is, 'none of your goddamn business,'" Maauro returned, her expression pleasantly bland.

Red and unexpected alert, I thought, but before I found it necessary to intervene, Maauro stood, nodded and headed off the bridge.

"Hmmmm," Olivia said. "I wonder what that was about?"

"I don't know," I replied. "I didn't see that particular asteroid coming. However it might be as well for you to be a bit more careful about teasing Maauro. She has emotions, usually cooler than ours, but there. In some respects she's very young and you don't know her well enough to tease her. Don't forget that beneath the cute exterior—"

"Not likely to forget that," Olivia said, eyebrows raised. "A thin-skinned android, who'd have thought it?"

We came in to Velsust II Control Area two days later. The world of blue and white held so little land that at first it seemed to be all ocean.

"There's the ISM tender," Maauro said, pointing to the scanner for our benefit.

I looked over. The ship was only barely within visual range of our scanner and it showed a boxy vessel, not a sleek warship. Still the tender was armed and its force was in its small fleet of sloops and corvettes. There was no question but that we were seen and possibly known by this vessel.

Maauro parked the *Sinner II* in a geosynch orbit with a buoy, until we needed it again. Uncoupled, *Stardust* was now ready for landing. As we came into lower orbits we began to see scattered islands and archipelagos. Finally a large series of islands nearer the equator began to show up, through nothing that merited the word continent even as a joke.

Space control gave us an entry vector, took our starmail and uploaded payment to us. Everything was efficient and courteous and there was no sign of the hostility that *Hsien's* commander had warned of. We lined up for a powered landing with their automatic landing system. Maauro and I rode down on the bridge, ready to intervene immediately if anything suspicious happened with the ALS. Nothing did.

We came down slowly. I was able to look out at the spaceport both on the screens and through the ship's cockpit.

"Looks like the city is partially in the sea," I observed. It was true. The main spaceport and capitol lay spread over dozens of small islands that were linked by a spidery collection of bridges and causeways.

"It is similar in concept to Venice on Olivia's homeworld," Maauro said, "and Aria on Oceanus. All the land was built on and supplemented by artificial islands and recovered ground, as the freezing of the polar icecaps lowers the sea. They must live with the ocean in a way that few do. It is fortunate that the moon here is small and far away."

"Yeah, less in the way of tides and storms."

We came down on the Celbas, a large artificial island dotted with a dozen spaceships. Surface vessels and airships also used the island further to the deep ocean side. A huge causeway connected it with the city proper.

"Engines off," I called, "standby for customs and cargo."

"What shall I do?" Maauro asked.

"Stay with me," I said. "I doubt there will be any humans on the C&C crews, so they won't notice anything about you. If they know already, then hiding behind goggles won't help anyway."

We trooped down and opened the hatch, enjoying the smell of salt sea air. Mobile ramps and lifters rolled up to the ship, large vehicles all. Voit-Veru took up a lot of space. As they dismounted from the vehicles I looked them over. I'd never seen one in person before. They did bear some resemblance to Terran kangaroos, in the same sense that Jaelle did a cat, or I, a naked ape. They were as tall as men, but had legs made more for hopping then for walking. When they did hop, they held their tails out behind them. Around their middle were three thick ropy tentacles, the face held a muzzle and large mobile ears atop the heads. The eyes were curious, looking more like fuzzy patches of black then proper eyes. The effect was comical in some respects, but they were nuclear-armed and had developed stardrive on their own. Sixty years ago a military government under the Aporek had drawn them into a short war with the Confederacy after Fenaday and Rainhell discovered them backing a separatist movement on her homeworld of Olympia.

The vehicles positioned ramps around us and three Veru hopped up to meet us. They all spoke Confed Standard and the customs interview was brief and formal. They did not seem to notice anything about Maauro or the rest of us. The extensive weapons cache onboard was noticed and we were sternly admonished that this was a well-policed world and not even stunners were to be carried planetside.

Our cargo has been put up on the net long before we landed and those items that had sold were carried off by stevedores to the warehouses. As yet we made no pretense of looking for any further cargo for ourselves.

"Well we are down," Dusko said, looking at the rolling gentle seas beyond the breakwater outside the spaceport. "Now what do we do?"

"I will attempt to infiltrate any networks I can locate and seek for information," Maauro added. "This will take time as I wish to be undetected. Dusko should approach the local criminal classes as he would be most effective at that. If you run into any Guild, withdraw using my name. I do not believe you will be attacked.

"Wrik and Olivia should duplicate my efforts in the actual world. Seek for information about Bexlaw and the *Isadora*. It will likely be fruitless, but your making such efforts will be expected and it may then be easier for me to do so virtually. And you may, with your non-linear ways of doing things, discover things I cannot.

"Be wary, we cannot go armed here. Yet if we are to be effective, we must fan out and find what we can."

We left Maauro in what looked like a contemplative pose on the bridge. Since it risked suspicion if we stayed aboard the ship, we decided to head into town. We took coms and folding knives in our pockets, unable to bring any better weapons. We'd even ditch the knives before returning. Spaceport security would be far less concerned with what we carried into town then what we carried back into a secured area.

The port was a far cry from the usual primitive ones I'd put in at on the frontier. A slidewalk took the three of us to a monorail that whisked us over the causeway and the sparkling waters of the lagoon into the canaled city. At the end of the monorail, we stood outside, glad for our sunglasses and brimmed caps as we looked at the city. Everything looked new, sitting in and about the water, which was clear down to several feet. We could see small fish swim lazily. Light bounced back in eye-hurting ways from the glass and water.

Voit-Veru hopped or waddled around in bright-colored clothing. This near the spaceport, I did see some other Confed species; two Frokossi walked by, the sunlight shimmering off the lizard-like beings' skin. An

Okaran, with his fur close-clipped, panted as he stood on the deck of a nearby boat. In the distance I saw what were either humans or Denlenns walking away from us. Still more than ninety percent of the beings in sight were Veru.

Olivia smiled. "Venice, this isn't."

I looked a question at her.

She waved an arm. "This is all metal and steel, Venice is ancient stone. The water here is way clearer, also no brawny, handsome men poling gondolas along and singing in Italian."

Dusko and I looked at each other and shrugged.

"See that restaurant there," I pointed to a bistro with outside seating. The sign over it read, The Galactic, all species served. "Let's meet there at 2200 shiptime unless one of us gets a lead."

Dusko nodded and without a word walked off. Instinct would guide the longtime criminal to the Lowport and the sort of contacts he could effectively use.

I looked Olivia over, as she took off her light ship-jacket and tied it around her waist. Her pale arms were muscular in the bright sunlight and she produced a sunscreen spray and quickly applied it. I turned down the container. My shirt was long-sleeved but so light I barely felt it.

"Where to?" she asked.

"Maauro is checking all the port records that can be electronically tapped. Dusko will see what he can weasel out of dockers or anyone that worked on Bexlaw's ship. My thought is for us to hit the commercial end of things, where they bought supplies, any repairs, maybe the hotel they stayed at. Then we check the university here."

She snorted. "Might as well knock on the local ISM office door while we're at it."

I grimaced. "The further we can stay from them, the better."

We spent the rest of the day checking chandlers, suppliers and other repair outfits, occasionally calling Maauro for leads as to where payments had been made by Bexlaw. We found little that the official records didn't cover. Bexlaw hadn't been forthcoming with information. The only real excitement was when one of the chandlers mentioned that it had been Maximillian who'd come in to contract for foodstuffs. So he had been alive when the *Isadora* lifted off.

But that was the only information of interest that surfaced. As the sun drooped toward the horizon, we boarded a local waterbus and headed back to the Galactic. I felt a little winded and sunburned from a day on the water and more than a little tired. Olivia chided me about the sun and insisted on giving me a going over with a sprayer. I had to admit the sunscreen felt good as it repaired the cellular damage and blocked the setting sun's rays.

CHAPTER 12

We sat at the Galactic waiting for Dusko. The day had been long and toward the end of it I had begun thinking of Jaelle. Maybe it was partly brought on by spending the day with Olivia, who seemed more attractive by the day. Her manner toward me had become more open and friendly the longer we voyaged together. Today, at points had assumed some of the characteristics of a date, sightseeing, lunch out. Maybe if we had not planned to meet the others here we'd have found reasons for a more romantic ending to the evening.

Did I want to? That question kept jumping back into my face. At first the answer had been, no. It was too complicated, it was disloyal, but then came the doubts. First, my girlfriend was getting pregnant by one of her own. She'd given me her permission for me to be with a human woman. Olivia was here and seemed interested despite what she'd said when we first took off—"

"What are you thinking about?" Olivia asked.

And I wondered what she had seen in my face.

"Ah, wondering where Dusko is."

"Really?" she said. "I must be losing my touch."

I raised an eyebrow.

"First night off ship, you and me together all day and you're thinking about Dusko?"

"Other things may have crossed my mind."

"You know we don't have to stay on the ship tonight. There are certain things that we can leave planetside when we go back up. I know what I said when I came aboard and I still mean part of that. I want to keep it uncomplicated."

"Is it ever?" I wondered.

She shrugged. "It can be. I prefer it that way."

"I'm not sure what I prefer," I said with a sigh. "Things seem to turn out different for me than what I expect."

"You dated out of your species," she said. "Isn't that the basic recipe for the unexpected?"

"I guess I thought it would be easier than it is," I said, moodily clinking the ice in my glass. "To the extent I ever thought about it at all."

"It's not even that easy between two people in the same species. I found it hard making a go of it for four years with a husband from my planet, my species, hell, he was another Marine."

"You've been married?" I asked, struck by the thought.

"Yeah," she said. "Too early. It didn't last, and he wasn't a stand-by-his-girl type when I went down the tubes."

"I'm sorry."

"Thanks. Look, I don't doubt that Jaelle loves you in whatever fashion Nekoan's love, but you're missing a bigger picture."

"What would that be?"

"You sure you want to hear this?"

"Might as well, looks like there's nothing good on the Tri-dee tonight."

Olivia looked at me. "Ok spaceman, I warned you. Fasten your take-hold belt; this is going to leave a mark.

"Jaelle has life just the way she likes it. She's free of her father's domination. She'll have kits by a male of her choice that she can then be free of beyond some legal obligations, most of which don't come into play until the kits are near adult. Meanwhile she has a reasonably successful human male, who fulfills her emotional and sexual needs, yet will never interfere with her trade business, her future or her natural family. She couldn't have arranged her life better if she'd planned it from the start."

I stared at her.

"Your mouth is hanging open."

I closed it. "I believe she loves me."

"Consortship isn't marriage Wrik. Probably she sees it as a permanent part of her life. Probably. But you better realize that may be contingent on things staying the way she likes them."

"She's not selfish."

"Didn't say she was, but she's gonna have children soon, you're going to be number two to them anyway."

I shook my head. "I can navigate a starship. I can't seem to navigate women."

Olivia shrugged. "Bartender, same again." She turned back to me as he poured more vodka. "You've got some growing up to do."

"I want to make this work."

"Then you better realize that you have to make it work as a Nekoan and human. Stop seeing her as a human with fangs and a tail. She's going to have to stop seeing you as a Nekoan with ears in the wrong place."

I smiled as I knocked back the drink. "You know you are the most unlikely shrink I have ever met."

Olivia surprised me with a wicked grin. "I know men. Three brothers and Dad. Boys were after me from as soon as I strapped on a training bra. There isn't much about guys I don't understand."

She drained her glass and put it down. "I'm going back to the ship. I'll see you in the morning."

"What's your hurry?"

She looked me over. "You're not ready."

"Huh?"

"If you don't know, don't worry about it. Don't spend any more time here. Nothing good happens in bars."

"Maauro says the same thing."

"Then you're about to hear it again," she said, over her departing shoulder.

CHAPTER 12

I looked toward the entrance. Maauro was there and the expression on her face was not happy. By the time I looked back, Olivia had vanished.

Maauro walked up and sat down. The bartender looked at her as if he was about to ask for an ID.

"She'll just have a Virgin Mary," I said. "We're not going to stay long."

The bartender nodded. "What about you?"

"I'm switching to Ginger Ale."

"Good enough," he nodded.

Maauro's expression relented some. "I am pleased to see you discontinuing the alcohol."

"Wasn't doing much good anyway."

"Does it ever?" she asked.

"Only for short periods, if then."

The drinks slid in front of us.

The guy next to us looked at Maauro. "Hey babe, what are you doing with this guy?"

Maauro reached over and put her hand over his metal beer tankard and crushed it into a small ball. Fluid sloshed from between her fingertips. "I am not in a good mood. Go away."

The guy stood, eyes-wide and walked away quickly.

"Something wrong?" I said. Taking a sip of what passed for ginger ale.

"I have been infiltrating nets all day which can be frustrating and occasionally painful. Dusko called in, he has found some dubious company he prefers, but no useful information. He will not be returning to the ship tonight." She drank the Virgin Mary, gave it a curious look and sipped some more.

"Is that a problem?" I asked. While I had come a long way in forgiving Dusko for the things that lay between us in the past, the Dua-Denlenn was from a species that regarded trust as a character flaw. It didn't do to forget that.

"I do not believe so. He retains his healthy and sensible fear of me and we are not in a location or position where he could gain an advantage from selling us out. Not that outweighs the risks to his personal security. Without my protection, the Guild would likely find him and revenge themselves upon him for his actions with us."

"I find," she said, then hesitated, "that I am unsettled by Olivia's presence on the ship."

"And here I thought it was just me," I said, trying for lightness.

"I do not know her, or fully trust her, yet must rely on her. Beyond that her presence threatens additional vectors in the orbit that you, Jaelle and I have assumed about each other. Possibly deliberately and on instructions from Candace."

I hadn't considered that and stopped myself from the quick denial that I wanted to issue. How well did I really know Olivia? How much of the tension between us was being young and healthy and the only two of our kind on the ship and how much might be a manipulation at Candace's instigation to gain greater control over us?

"For what it is worth," I said mildly. "I don't think that is likely. I don't see Olivia doing something like that."

"Wrik, I sometime believe that you are naïve in matters involving females and that you invest them with virtues, merely because of their femininity, that they may not possess."

"Possibly, I seem to recall giving an almost endless supply of expensive yellow silk ribbons to a certain killer-android from the depths of time, just because she was so cute."

"My point exactly," she said, sipping her drink.

"None of which you are wearing tonight," I noted.

"They are precious to me," she said. "I try not to wear them in dangerous places where they might be destroyed."

"Couldn't you just retexturize some of your hair to simulate one?"

"Of course but then it wouldn't be the ones you gave me."

I laughed lightly. "Maauro, never tell me that you were not created female."

She sighed, then smiled back at me. "Shall we sit outside for a while? I have not seen these stars before."

"Sure," I said.

I turned to the bartender. "Same again to go."

"OK," he looked at the crushed tankard. "How'd that happen?"

"He must not have liked the beer," Maauro said.

The bartender grumbled, took the mashed tankard, and pitched it.

I paid the tab and grabbing a handful of pretzels, followed Maauro out. We walked onto a long pier, carrying our drinks. I found a bench and we sat, side by side. I passed her a pretzel. The sky was very dark and the stars seemed bright, the sea sloshed around in a comforting surration. I spent a few seconds thinking regretfully of Olivia's offer and the splendid body I'd seen in exercise clothes.

Somehow danger and complications seemed to recede with my small friend next to me. She drew her legs up to her chin on the fortunately sturdy bench and looked very young. It was hard to believe she'd first looked on stars when my ancestors were living in caves.

We didn't speak, just sat in the comfortable silence with our drinks and pretzels, watching boats and ships move across the sea and sky. Maauro kept most of her attention for her beloved stars. After a few minutes, I put an arm around her. She felt soft and warm, save for part of her left arm, which had been replaced with an Infestor robot arm after the original had been blown off. I left my hand on her left arm. I never

CHAPTER 12

wanted her to feel self-conscious about it. We sat that way for a long, peaceful time that I think we both needed.

CHAPTER 13

THE NEXT DAY MAAURO RETURNED TO HER HACKING AND scanning. Dusko appeared at the ship, asked Maauro for money and gems to spread around, and vanished again.

Olivia and I met at the ramp to the ship. By tacit agreement, we said nothing about last night's conversation and kept things light. Today we would get out of the port area and see more of the city proper. We boarded a public airboat at the main dock. The area was full of Veru in their colorful clothes. Though they were omnivores like us, there was an odd smell about them that reminded me of cattle.

Perhaps they didn't like the smell of us either. The Veru aboard shuffled away from us. I didn't know if this was a manifestation of hostility or not. I could read nothing in the patch-like eyes and muzzle faces that stared at us. The machine pulled smoothly from the dock and whisked its way up the canals. We stayed up on the open front deck. Many of the Veru went inside the glassed and air-conditioned cabin, the view probably of little interest to the frequent commuters among them.

For all the charm of buildings and water, I could see what Olivia meant about the city. It was mostly of recent manufacture, laid out in the orderly and rational way of new colonies. Homeworlds or older colonies had a more organic feel to them, with small, winding streets, odd buildings and other quaint features. This world was laid out with broad avenues and low, wide buildings. Veru were of human height but tailed, with hopping legs that were long and awkward compared to human legs, so the buildings were like stretched versions of what one would expect on most worlds. Doorways needed to be wider, rooms bigger. Even the airboat we stood on could have held four times as many bipeds as marsupial-like Veru.

"Don't get kicked by any of these guys," Olivia whispered, barely audible over the motor and the splashing of water shoved aside by the airfans. She showed no sign of worry however, smiling at the bright day and enjoying the sea air.

I nodded.

An older Veru standing in the front turned to me. "Greetings Humans. Welcome to our world. Do you know where you are going?"

"This is the airboat to the university?" I ventured.

"It is. Don't get off at the first dock though; the second one is closer to the admin museums and the colony museum."

We pulled up to a dock and some Veru shuffled on and off. One younger-looking Veru, turned as he stepped onto the dock. He made a noise in our direction that didn't need translation. Derision was also a universal language. Two Veru with him shook in what I took to be laughter.

"I apologize," the older Veru said. "Young people these days seem to have no manners."

"It's a common problem in the galaxy," I said.

"Maybe more so here for humans," the old Veru said. "Take some advice and do not wander about much after dark."

"That bad?" Olivia asked.

"Lately," the old Veru said.

A young female next to him piped in. "Not all of us feel that way, the Confederacy has friends here." The male Veru with her touched her with a tentacle and rumbled something in their native language. The female looked away.

"Ah," said the older Veru as the airboat surged up to the dock of a shopping district. "This is my stop. Good fortune and travels, Humans."

"Thank you," Olivia and I returned. The Veru moved off stiffly, along with most of the other beings aboard including the female and her reticent companion. The airboat pulled out quickly.

"University is the next stop," I said, observing the map.

"Let's take the old boy's advice," Olivia said.

"About the second stop?"

"Probably both pieces of advice were good," Olivia said.

We got off at a broad dock. Young Veru hopped about, getting on and off, some bouncing right over the airboats rails. We walked off and headed up a tree-lined street of broad but steep stairs, with Veru bouncing up and down them. I wondered what they did when they broke a leg or got old. We were both grateful for the shade of the tall, broad trees that resembled Terran willows, except for their great height.

The university occupied several hills and a broad valley with the usual wide buildings. Either a sporting event or a demonstration was creating noise and a crowd down at the admin end.

"Let's stay out of that," I said.

"Bexlaw would have come here," Olivia said. "But I bet he would have headed to the colony museum. Birds of a feather, you know."

I didn't, but I followed her as it made as much sense as anything else.

We found ourselves at a long, low building filled with photos, holos and scale models of the colony, from first landing to the building of the giant reflectors that had begun the cooling of the poles and the lowering of the sea levels.

I found a young, Veru female, chewing bubble-gum and reading a newsfolio. She looked up after we stood there for a few seconds. "Oh, sorry," she shook the folio in a sharp gesture and the paper instantly dissolved, the frame folded until next time she had it extrude something. "Can I help you?"

CHAPTER 13

"We were wondering if some colleagues of ours visited this university about a year ago," I said. I rattled off a list of the names of Bexlaw's expedition, including Maximillian.

The young Veru consulted her monitor. "Yes, they were here. The whole crew was using our research facility pretty extensively before they left."

"What were they looking at?" Olivia asked.

"Says here," the Veru replied, "they were doing work on an artifact recovered on the moon, some sort of encoded plaque. It was found about fifty years ago, not much was ever done with it until they showed up. Records say it was of human origin."

"And they didn't communicate with Earth about it?" I said.

She shrugged. "Doesn't say. But I'm guessing not. Fifty years ago, was pretty close to when the Confederacy forced us into it. Humans weren't that popular then."

"Little seems to have changed," I said.

"Hey," she said, "don't put any of that on me. I treat all species alike."

I nodded. "Yes, thanks. I didn't mean you, but it seems that there is some anti-Confederacy feeling around here."

She nodded reluctantly. "Yeah. Well, it's mainly the older generation. Live and let live I say. Too many people dwell in the past."

"Too true," I said. "Could we speak to the staff that Bexlaw's people were working with?"

"Not today," she said. "They are all at a seminar two islands over. If you want to come back tomorrow, I'll book you an appointment with Senior Professor Horst."

"Ok," I said.

After we made arrangements, Olivia and I went out, taking the path back to the boat dock. The noisy demonstration we had seen in the distance however, had rolled around the campus. The street between two large campus buildings ahead was full of shouting Veru bearing flags and signs. The crowd beat their hands in time to music and I could hear chanting. Some of the signs in Standard urged secession from the Confederacy.

"I don't like the look of this," I said to Olivia.

"Yeah," she said. "Let's backtrack and go around the white building to the left. We may skirt most of this and that side is closer to the docks if we have to run for it."

Olivia's suggestion took on some urgency as nearby Veru took notice of us. A few pointed. We faded back, ducked behind some shrubbery and made our way around the back of what appeared to be a dormitory. But ahead of us were more demonstrators.

"Crap," I said. "Backtrack again."

"No," Olivia said, glancing over her shoulder. "We're being followed, a number of Veru who were with the anti-Confed demonstrators. Wrik, they don't look like college kids to me."

I looked ahead again and noticed a difference. There were people waving the gold and blue Confed flag, these students were Veru and other races. "Hey, this is the counter demonstration."

Olivia glanced their way. "They're badly outnumbered."

"Not our problem. We should be able to get through them though."

We walked forward. "Smile," I said, "try to look friendly."

"Use your brain," she snapped. "Don't bare your teeth at anyone here. Veru don't smile."

We slipped into the crowd, which, smaller than the group overflowing the next street, was still noisy and sizeable. As we pushed forward the crowd got tighter. Some music blared and shouts came louder. People began to notice us.

"Hey," said one, well-meaning Veru. "Welcome Humans. Up the Confederacy."

I waved and shouted back. "Up the Confederacy."

My appearance spurred the crowd which, to my dismay, took up the cry and closed around Olivia and me. For a horrible second, I thought we would be lifted on their shoulders. We managed to elbow forward, being cheered and patted on the shoulder as we went.

The crowd's pressure pushed us to the front between the two groups, where we didn't want to be. Already I could see the anti-Confed line with their red and black secession signs. Only a few campus police separated the lines and I saw no riot gear on them.

Suddenly bottles flew through the air. Shouts turned to screams and a demonstrator near me went down, blood spurting from a head wound. Bodies crashed together as Verus made impossible leaps into each other. Flags became batons and staffs as demonstrators clashed. The police were shoved aside, and then began firing stunners into the crowd. In seconds a complete riot had broken out.

A wedge of secessionists crashed into the people near me. Olivia and I were engulfed in them. I easily blocked a strike by a Veru tentacle and gave back a straight right which dropped the Veru. I turned to Olivia who had wrestled a flagstaff out of a Veru's tentacles. Their ropy arms were no match for human muscle and bone. She slammed the Veru in the mid-section and head in a move almost too fast to see. Overhead, leaping Veru's exchanged kicks and bodies crashed down around us.

A flung bottle struck Olivia and she fell.

"Olivia," I shouted, shoved two Veru and a Morok aside as I headed to her. A stocky Veru in dark clothes stepped in my way. Dark Suit didn't look like a college kid. He knocked down the Morok. I took the advantage to throw a shoulder into him, knocking him over. Then I slammed

CHAPTER 13

a foot into the sternum of the Veru bending over Olivia, a bottle wrapped in his tentacle. He and the bottle flew in separate directions.

I turned, Dark Suit was back. I moved to face him and he leaned back, balanced on his tail and let fly with both feet. The wind left me in a way that made me doubt it would ever come back. I had the vague sense of flying through the air, crashing into bodies and then night fell on me.

I came to, bound to a chair, with a hood that smelled lousy over my head. I struggled for a second before realizing the futility of it and throttled down panic. There wasn't a lot of air in the hood. I heard Veru voices around me and got the sense of a crowded room.

A light shone through the hood, which was pulled off to leave me facing a bright lamp. I blinked, effectively blinded for a moment. I wasn't sure what to make of the hood being removed. Didn't they care I'd be able to see them?

A Veru sat opposite me on one of their peculiar chairs. I realized I was tied to something ad hoc, maybe nailed together just for me. They wouldn't have had a human chair handy. With the light facing me, I couldn't see a face, but the Veru was large; he might have been the one who'd decked me earlier.

"You are Wrik Trigardt off the *Stardust*," he said in excellent Gal-Standard.

"Yes, I'm a merchant. I was just visiting the university when I and my friend were swept up in the demonstration. Where's my friend? Is she ok?"

"I ask the questions. You are a Confed Intelligence agent on our world without authorization, in direct violation of the original Confederate charter."

"What?" I said. "Look, I'm not a legal scholar but the original Confed Charter was superseded by the Articles of Confederacy—"

The blow across my mouth was unexpected. Veru tentacles lacked the bone and muscle power of our limbs but they made very good thick whips. I tasted blood.

"We do not recognize the Articles," the Veru said. "They were forced on us by the Imperial Confederacy."

Great, I thought, *revolutionary rhetoric, always fun arguing with fanatics.* But on second thought, I wondered if my interrogator actually believed it, or if he was posing, either for the others in the room or some recording device.

"Assuming I was a Confed agent," I said, carefully and deliberately. "This is a Confed world and you don't get to pick which Confed laws you want to obey. Whatever I am, you have no right to detain or abuse me. Where is my friend?"

Again a blow rocked my head. *Ok,* I thought, blinking tears out of my eyes, *reconsider that strategy.*

"The Veru Alliance maintains," my interrogator growled, "that Confed agents must register with local authorities. You have not done so. You are here illegally."

Shouts came from outside the room. Suddenly the door opened and bodies pressed in. I tensed, to at least try and throw myself to the floor if shooting broke out, but instead the room became very quiet. Voices now spoke, low, urgent, with tones of respect. A VIP had arrived.

The light was turned from my face and a new Voit-Veru sat opposite me. His clothing was somber, but expensive, elegant on what was an awkward-looking creature. His muzzle and fur were grizzled and gray. I drew an impression of age from him. I could see almost a dozen Veru behind him.

The elderly Voit-Veru gazed impassively at me. I looked back steadily with a resolve that was a millimeter deep. Every part of my body ached.

"Greetings, Captain Trigardt," he said finally. "I wish to have a very careful conversation with you. I represent a party. My own name is of no significance. Call me Arzarafel."

"You're a little late on the careful," I said around swollen lips.

"Let us hope not for both our sakes. We are aware that...some force... protects you. Rumors of disastrous outcomes from conflicts with you and your team have reached our ears." As if to confirm that, the large vertical ears twitched.

"I'm listening."

"We are trapped, you and I here, and others elsewhere, in a situation that we did not make and would not have allowed to occur had we known of certain actions before they were taken. We can choose to remain trapped and allow the escalation to continue, with consequences that will multiply beyond our ken or control. Or," he leaned forward, "we can reverse course, stand down to the status quo ante. This would require demonstrations of good faith on both sides."

I licked my sore lips. "Would one of those demonstrations include getting these damn restraints off me?"

Arzarafel considered. He barked out a series of commands in his own tongue and the large Veru who had slugged me earlier, quickly undid my bonds with a wicked-looking knife. A smaller Veru, a female I thought, came in with a plate and a cup: water and bread.

Trying to preserve the dignity that I felt was some sort of protection; I sipped the water and slowly ate the bread, which was likely the best idea in my state anyway. I didn't know how long I had been out. I suspected from the groggy way I felt, that I might have been drugged to keep me unconscious longer. In any event I was starving. When I finished I turned back to the elderly Veru who'd waited patiently while I ate.

"Is my friend here?" I asked, "the human who was with me?"

CHAPTER 13

The old Veru turned to the younger interrogator and exchanged words with him, then faced me. "She was not taken. The circumstances did not permit it. Our information is she was detained by the campus police then returned to your ship."

I nodded, relieved. "Tell me more about your proposal. I'm not sure I understand what's going on."

Arzarafel nodded. "Let us discuss a hypothetical situation. Assume my master represents a power. Your master, whoever that may be, is another. Let us say that they are rivals. My master may have had a servant, who in the manner of those who seek advancement, does all he can to foster his master's aims."

I rubbed my wrists, impatient, but unwilling to risk provoking Arzarafel.

"As such," Arzarafel continued, "this servant knew of his master's enmity to your master. There is an old grudge against the other party. Let us refer to that one as the Death Angel."

My ears would have pricked up had they been as far up on my head as his. Death's Angel was an old nickname for Shasti Rainhell.

"The servant of my master set a trap for one of the relations of the Death Angel. This was not known, or sanctioned, by my master. Had he known, it would have been stopped. Such petty acts have no place on the stage of power and are only distractions from the greater game." Arzarafel looked at me with what I took for an expectant expression.

"So this overzealous servant," I began cautiously, "may have, let's say for now, leaked information to a certain party. That information would set that party in motion, a motion that would carry the relative of the Death Angel into danger."

"Just so," the old Veru said. "What seemed like a low cost way of dealing out some minor retribution has now taken on a life of its own. Assets were deployed by the Death Angel and then by the servant. This caused more assets to be deployed and the violence escalated.

"By the time my master learned of the plan, the relative had gone missing and a rescue was both in progress and being actively thwarted. I was commissioned by him to deal with the situation."

"And the manner of that dealing?" I asked.

"I disapprove of violence, most especially ineffective violence that merely incurs costs and no benefits. We could of course, with some effort, ensure that your small team and ship disappear, thus ending the matter."

"The power," I said slowly, "that protects me, would not appreciate that solution."

"One imagines you refer to the smallest member of your team, an apparent female in your crew we take to be the most recent model robot of the HCR series built for the Conchirri war. Something developed by Confed Intelligence."

"Then you take her for something vastly less dangerous then she is."

"Still, it is one mechanism. We can overwhelm it if needs be."

"You have either not fully believed what you learned from your sources about her, or you are misinformed. I take those sources to be Guild. They should have warned you better for whatever you paid them."

"It might," Arzarafel said, "have been in their interest to exaggerate, either in the hope of gaining more money for a more unusual tale, or covering up their own incompetence. As it is in your interest to exaggerate its abilities now."

"Her abilities," I stated, "and I do not overstate them. You can believe it, or learn and bitterly regret it later. I don't want a planet for my headstone. But that's what could happen. Maauro is her name and she doesn't place much stock in the concept of collateral damage. Once you are classed as enemy, she doesn't keep count. She just keeps at it until there is nothing left."

"We have a planetary militia and an ISM force—"

"She'll take those first," I said. Something in the conviction in my voice must have registered on the Veru. He sat back in his chair, placing his chin on one of his tentacles to study me.

"Say then," Arzarafel continued, "that we choose another option. De-escalation serves us all best in my view."

"Agreed," I said. "What's the deal on the table?"

"You will be returned to your ship. You will lift off immediately, proceed to the warp point and jump out. You forgo any retaliation and you will not be impeded or molested in any fashion."

I considered. "If we just jump out the way we came, this will not end. We'll report what happened to…the party that sent us. The next ships you see in your sky might be Confed Navy. Or, worse for you, the Death Angel has ships, not enough to penetrate a navy defense, but ISM auxiliaries won't stop them."

"You would be well-advised not to push your luck, young human. Your hand is not that strong."

I shook my head. "I'm offering solutions, not problems. Your people here know the course and speed Bexlaw's ship took when it hit the warp point. Maybe they know the coordinates or where that point leads as well."

"Say it was the former," Arzarafel said. "How does this profit my side?"

"Provide us with that information and we'll provide you with a digitally secure and confirmed message for Confed authorities that we left here on that course. If we don't come back, your hands are clean."

"And if you do come back? Perhaps bearing news of the Death Angel's kin having met a bad end?"

"Then you will have had time to prepare whatever idiot set this plan in motion for his eventual sacrifice to Rainhell," I said, tired of the pretense. "She believes you're behind it now and assumes her grandson is lost. Your situation will be no worse save, that I will have sold you a lot of time. Not something you can purchase elsewhere, your alternatives being rebellion, or civil war in the near future."

Arzarafel sat, pondering for what felt like an eternity, then spoke. "We do not know where Bexlaw went. He was given access to a time capsule found on our moon by a mining interest. It was clearly human made and from the *New Hope* but its contents were encoded. We did not break the code but, to be frank, there was little effort made. The artifact lay here in storage. The local authorities, out of mere spite, did not inform humans of the find, but the information made its way to the fool who put us all in this jeopardy. He then concocted this nightmare, intending to send Bexlaw and Rainhell's grandson into the void in the hope that disaster would, as it likely has, overcome them.

"He stupidly did not anticipate that Bexlaw would break the code, likely it was a simple book code for a common human book, something that we, culturally, would have trouble doing. Bexlaw took off before he could be stopped and refused to answer any requests for information by radio. We did not wish to involve the Confed Navy, so a small ISM cutter trailed them. It could not overtake Bexlaw, but did capture a course and speed to a hitherto unknown jump point.

"You're a star-pilot. You know that following a jump without true coordinates is rank guesswork."

"We'll take it," I said.

"And meet our other conditions?" Arzarafel pressed.

"Yes, step one of which is putting me in touch with Maauro, before she initiates action on her own."

Arzarafel touched a button on the table in front of him and a virtual screen popped up. He stabbed at it with his tentacle tips. "I am calling your ship now, asking for Maauro by name. Remain silent until I bid you to speak, you are off screen."

I nodded.

The screen lit and on it was Maauro's beautiful face, only her eyes were black from lid to lid and her mouth was full of serrated metal teeth. This was icy rage in Maauro and deliberate. She knew the effect it had on biologicals.

Arzarafel flinched visibly from the screen, then recovered. "Greetings, Maauro. I am Arzarafel. If any of what I have heard of you is true, then you're doubtless tearing through the network seeking my location. Do not exert yourself. What you seek is here, in my custody, in good health and will be returned to you shortly, if you agree to our terms."

"You would indeed be wise to return Wrik to me unharmed," she said, her voice flat and mechanical. "Others have experienced my vengeance before, though none now live who can testify to its completeness."

"So you say. For my part I find it troubling to deal with a machine. How do I know that you are self-aware enough for me to negotiate with? Your motivations are difficult for me to assess."

This time I winced.

"Your cavalier attitude toward me," Maauro grated, "tells me that you do not appreciate the threat that I pose to this colony and that you might lack motivation both to return what is mine and honor any agreement with me. I have been here days already and have not been idle. Let me give you a taste of what you should hope to avoid."

The room plunged into blackness. It could only have been thirty seconds but it seemed to drag on and on. Then the lights came back on and the connection reestablished itself.

Maauro glared at Arzarafel. "You will find that power failure was planet-wide on all but your most well-protected military systems. In the days that I have been here I have had abundant time to infiltrate your indifferently protected power grids, and through them, most other systems. In only a little more time I will defeat the defenses on your military systems as well. Your power plants, financial systems, even the terraforming equipment is infiltrated and permeated with virus by me.

"Shall I cause the space panels that shade the poles to fold and admit sunlight to the ice? Or explode a nuclear power plant?"

"No," Arzarafel gasped in horror.

"You will doubtless think to rescue yourselves with anti-virus protections and other network barriers. My intruder software is beyond your science to stop. Perhaps with a decade of non-stop work, your best programmers and computers might rid your systems of me. Your colony will be long-drowned by then."

"There is no need," Arzarafel said his tentacles waving in a placating gesture. "We have agreed with your Captain to stand down, to return him to your ship and to provide you with information critical to your mission!"

Arzarafel gestured frantically to me and I stepped into range of the pickup hoping my battered state would not provoke any further demonstrations.

Instantly her eyes turned their usual pacific green and the teeth were replaced with normal human ones a moment later. Her expression surveying my battered countenance was not happy. "Wrik, are you all right?"

"Yes. Is Olivia ok?"

"Minor injuries, but she is safe here at the ship."

"Arzarafel represents…a greater power. He's taken charge of the situation and is empowered to deal. He's made sure I am safe and treated well. I've promised that if we get all the information they have on Bexlaw, fuel and supplies and are allowed to go, that there will be no retaliation."

She looked at Arzarafel. "I will honor Wrik's agreement. I am a logical being and do not pursue quarrels where there is no need, any more than I shrink from such pursuit when necessary. But do not take me lightly again."

"No, no," Arzarafel said, "of course not. We will return your friend immediately."

"You personally will do so," Maauro directed, "as you now know what will follow either failure or treachery."

"And our systems?" Arzarafel demanded.

"The viruses are dormant and can only be triggered by me. They will expire within a local solar year if I do not."

"What guarantee are we offered?"

"I have no desire to be regarded as a criminal by the Confederacy, who would likely regard my destruction of a colony that is nominally theirs as excessive. I do not fear Confed law. I need only wait for a hundred years or so for these governments to fail and pass if I need to, but while my network is alive and intact I have a reason to regard the law. However, I will not tolerate further damage to my network."

"We are leaving now," Arzarafel assured her. Only now was the true nature of the force he had provoked becoming clear to him. He clearly wanted me back in its hands as soon as possible.

"I will await you at the base of the ship," Maauro said. She then turned to me and with a gentle smile added. "See you soon, Wrik."

Arzarafel broke the connections and shouted orders to his staff. Veru were running everywhere in seconds. Two of the large males moved forward as if to take hold of me.

"Do not touch him, you fools!" Arzarafel demanded in Standard. "See to his comfort. Protect him with your lives until we get him back to his ship."

The guards, well-trained, turned from suspicious to solicitous in the same instant.

"Hurry, hurry," Arzarafel called to the hopping Veru. "Bring the aircar. Now!"

We were ushered out front of the massive warehouse we had been in, to a large, comfortable aircar with two escorting utility vehicles. In seconds we took off into a lowering, cloudy sky. The car accelerated to a cruising speed I estimated at just subsonic.

Now that we were moving, Arzarafel seemed to relax. He reached into the limousine's bar and poured us both large drinks. I accepted my much improved beverage with gratitude.

"There is food here that is safe for a human, though I cannot answer for the flavor," he said.

"I'll wait until I am home," I said.

"Doubtless wise," he said. Then with a surprisingly human-like sigh. "Do not become old and stupid, young Trigardt. I was curious about your

Maauro, seeing in her a mere mechanism such as we create. I decided to probe her and nearly brought on disaster. Who knows what damage was wrought or lives lost by the power loss? She spoke the truth and disrupted every power source on the planet. She spared only aircraft in flight or the casualties would number into the thousands.

"I allowed my personal curiosity to provoke me into pushing a negotiation when I had already succeeded in my objective. Very stupid."

I enjoyed my drink and the softness of the cushions, but couldn't control a grunt of pain as I sat back.

"It might be as well if you did not emphasize your pains from the recent unpleasantness that transpired before I took charge," the Veru said.

"I think I can be induced to minimize my pains," I said.

"Perhaps we can supply some additional inducements," he reached into a compartment on his side and produced a small pouch. He dropped it in my hand, seeming no more interested in touching my hand, than I was the ropy and repulsive tentacle.

I opened the package to find a fortune in sunstones, moondrops and other exotic gems winking up at me from a bed of black velvet. I hadn't intended to ask for a bribe but saw no reason to turn one down. "My aches are already receding on account of your generosity."

"Oh there is no generosity, my young friend. All that has been tendered to you will be extracted from the hide of the fool that set this in motion, with interest added. I promise you that much."

Ahead I could see the spaceport coming into view and the seaport behind it. Lights glowed despite the hour on account of the weather.

"It's good," I said suddenly, "to have a contact on the other side. One empowered to make sensible bargains to keep open lines of communication."

"Yes," Arzarafel replied. "It is an effective ward against disaster. Try not to die on this adventure, young man. You may be a useful acquaintance in times to come."

"Hard times to come," I said.

"Yes, I fear it is so. What we have treated here is a symptom, not the disease itself. Whatever one's allegiances are in these matters, we will all be sorely tested before much longer. I hope, by my own efforts, to put if off far enough in the future so I may die in a time of peace. And to leave what follows to the younger, hotter souls who are always so willing to pay for change with lives, especially if those lives are not their own."

"It would be good to know that if I got a message from you," I said as *Stardust* grew in our window, "that I could trust the source."

"Yes," the old Veru said quickly. "Yes, authentications. Quickly. We do not have much time."

"A message from me will have the name Emma Ferlan with it," I said. Few people knew the vanished Guildmaster's name or would associate it with me.

"And a message from me will come under the name, Adan. She was, if you recall, the captain of The Queen of the Night, the ship Fenaday used to destroy one of our ports."

The limo settled on the permacrete of the field, with only a slight jar, well short of *Stardust's* gantry and rolled forward on its wheels. The utility vehicles continued to circle above us. *Stardust* stood, embraced by the usual utility lines, but I could still see the communications laser poking out of its aperture. Halfway up one of the hatches was open and unless I missed my bet, Olivia was in there with her sniper rifle.

Maauro stood in the open near one of the fins. The wind was kicking up and her long hair trailed out behind her. A fine sheet of rain began to fall but she ignored it as we rolled up.

The driver got out and opened the doors. Both I and Arzarafel stepped out into the chilly rain. I was glad for my ship jacket. The old Veru looked a bit shrunken and clutched his coat closer to him with two of his tentacle arms, waving the other at Maauro in greeting. "Here is your companion, returned to you safe and sound."

"Safe, yes," she said, coming forward to lay a hand on my arm. "His soundness I will judge for myself."

I knew she was scanning me finding bruising that went to the bone. "All's well. Arzarafel put a stop to the interrogation as soon as he arrived."

"Wise Arzarafel," Maauro said, but the look was not friendly.

For his part the old Veru stood looking at Maauro in dawning wonder. The incongruities of her appearance, fairly obvious to a human, were doubtless lost on him, but her animation and self-awareness were not.

"I misjudged you very badly," he said. "Our intelligence on you was ludicrously off the mark. The Confederacy never made such a machine as you. Not in a thousand years could it be done."

"I will not disagree with the obvious, that I am not of Confederation make. For the present I and my network serve the Confederacy, to some degree, and those patrons who seek to find the lost. Whether those lost are loved ones, friends, or something else, so long as we find merit in their quest. This does not make us enemies, save that you impede us, or attack my network."

"Those attempts will not be repeated," Arzarafel said. "We have offered our amends to Trigardt and he has accepted them. The subordinate who brought this about will be disciplined severely for bringing us into a conflict we did not want."

"I would know the identity of this person," Maauro said. "His account with me remains open."

"I cannot share that," Arzarafel said, shading his face from a gust of wet wind.

Maauro seemed to contemplate that for a few seconds. I gave a tiny shake of my head and she nodded.

"May I ask how far you are from launching?" Arzarafel asked.

"We are fully supplied and prepared. With Wrik aboard and clearance from Space Control we can launch in twenty-nine minutes."

"Then please do so. You have already been given unconditional exit priority. Once you are in orbit, we will send you the Bexlaw data in return for the digital confirmation Trigardt agreed to, absolving us from whatever happens if you follow it."

"Agreed," Maauro returned. "No ship is to approach us or trail us to the warp point. You could not destroy *Stardust* quickly enough to prevent me from sending the trigger code."

"There will be no vessel near you after you leave orbit," Arzarafel assured. He turned to me. "Go now, Trigardt. I will remember the name you gave and you remember the one I gave you. It may serve our principals well that this pipeline continue to exist."

I nodded.

Arzarafel again looked at Maauro. "As for you, unique and unprecedented being. You are enough to make an old Veru believe in miracles. I have seen much and traveled far in a long life. Now I have met a living machine. It is clear to me that the universe is a vast unknown and my own understanding of it shallow and incomplete.

"I regret that we met in conflict. Perhaps other future meetings will be more gentle."

Maauro raised an eyebrow. "From what I can see of that future it seems unlikely. Still there are many possibilities. For your intercession on Wrik's behalf, you have my thanks."

Arzarafel backed away and retreated to his car as the rain came down harder. The limo pulled away. From the corner of my eye I saw the hatch above, where I believed Olivia laired, close.

Maauro, still holding my arm gently, led me to the gantry way to the lower hatch. I felt the chill in my aches and bruises. The water simply sluiced off her; she didn't bother to even wipe it off her face. "You need food and rest."

"After we lift off."

"They will not annoy us further."

"Trust me, Maauro, my appetite will be much better when we kick free of this miserable, water-soaked rock."

"Do you wish to take her up?" she asked.

"No. I am too tired and shaky. You do it. I'll ride shotgun."

Maauro sealed the hatch. I looked at the spiral staircase that lead upward while the *Stardust* was in vertical mode. She shook her head and belted me into a personnel lift that went up the wall that was our floor when the AG field was on. I let her secure the straps then we went up, Maauro keeping pace on the staircase, only pausing when the stairs snapped out of the way to let my lift through. When we got to the control level, Dusko and Olivia were there. Olivia was grinning. She looked almost as banged up as I was.

CHAPTER 13

"Back alive, Trigardt?" Dusko said. "You certainly have the luck."

I grimaced. "Yeah. Luck enough to not get killed in the trouble I wasn't lucky enough to avoid.

"You okay?" I asked of Olivia.

"Hah," she said. "I got worse than this my first week in basic. Looks like you still have all your parts in working order."

"Yeah. We're getting out of here."

"Great news," Dusko said. "What friendly port are we bound to next?"

"The Voit-Veru don't know where Bexlaw jumped to exactly. He went into an unknown warp point, but we have his course and speed. Not enough for an exact coordinate match, but it should be one, or at the most two, exits to deal with."

"Not so great news," Dusko answered, "and this place is beginning to look better to me."

"You want to take up fishing, be my guest," I replied.

"That was very obliging of the Veru," Olivia said, raising an eyebrow.

"We proposed a deal where they gave us what we wanted and Maauro didn't drown the whole colony world by reversing their terraforming."

"Oh," she said, then looked at Maauro. "Would she really have...never mind. I might be happier not knowing for certain."

"Please make final launch prep and strap in," Maauro said. "I will be taking us up in twenty minutes.

They both nodded and moved off. I settled into the second seat with a sigh. Maauro took the pilot's chair. "The ship's AI and I have been working the checklist in preparation. We are in countdown mode now."

Olivia and Dusko returned at T minus five minutes and strapped in, as usual, we would ride up together. Maauro communicated with Launch and Space Control which tersely told us we could do anything we wanted so long as we left.

We lifted with the smooth power of our impellers. I felt a knot of tension loosen in my chest even as I was pressed back in my seat. True relief waited for me where the blue of the sky turned to the starry black of space. Launch was our most vulnerable point and while the old Veru has seemed a sensible person, not everyone involved had behaved so nicely. I checked scan, for all that I knew Maauro was watching. I noted with approval that only one object was near us, *Sinner II* right where we had parked it in orbit.

A thought struck me. "What if they—"

"Sabotaged the *Sinner?*" Maauro finished. "I programmed it to avoid any vessel approaching it and to signal me if anything did."

"You sneaked up on it."

"My programming is superior to what it had and I doubt anyone else will leap on it from deep space as I did. Nonetheless, I will check it out before I replace it on the grapples."

Maauro did that while I set up a course out of system. As usual, I scrounged speed from rotational orbits of the planet and moon, gaining velocity for the trip to the outer system. We'd grab more speed from the medium-sized gas giant en route. I observed the ISM auxiliary hanging in orbit with its cutters and small patrol vessels, but it studiously ignored us.

The ship's AI chimed for my attention. "Message received and secured in security buffer."

"I have it," Maauro said, from outside where she was finishing securing the green and gold fighter. "It is clear of viruses. I am routing it to your nav board and sending back the digital message relieving them of any responsibility for what happens to us. It appears Arzarafel is as good as his word. We have all the flight data on Bexlaw's escape from the system."

Maauro entered the airlock and since she wore no suit was almost immediately in the bridge with me. I still found it disconcerting that she could walk in from deep space with no more transition than a moment or two to warm up to a reasonable temperature. She nodded at Olivia and Dusko who had come in with some drinks.

"You seem to have formed a network with this Arzarafel," Maauro said.

"One only of mutual convenience," I said. "I have no doubt that he is one of Aporek's senior advisors. From him I get the impression that, much as Aporek wants to increase Voit-Veru power at the cost of humans and their allies, he is not interested in an out and out rebellion or civil war, at least not now."

"It would not be in his interest," she agreed. "Humans are the most effective mass-fighters the Confederacy has. Aporek's plan should be to avoid armed conflict while he builds alliances and saps the power of his enemies."

"Spoken like a chess player," Olivia said, as she handed me a drink and fell into a chair, draping one leg over it. "Politics is much more a game of poker, with an occasional demented player who doesn't know how to bet and ends up trying to throw the table over. Sometimes you don't even know who is sitting at the table."

"That's what happened here," Dusko added.

I smiled at Maauro as she sat next to me, taking one of her sweet concoctions off the tray. "Yes, the cat got out of the bag and Arzarafel wanted our help getting it back in before things got totally out of control."

"What cat?" Maauro said. "Ah, a metaphor. What a silly way of trading clarity of expression for colorful confusion."

"Thought you were talking about Jaelle for a second," Olivia said with a sly smile.

I snorted. "They haven't made the bag that can hold that kitty."

Maauro opened her mouth then shut it quickly. Whatever comment has occurred to her, she thought better of it,

"Well at least we won't be interfered with this side of jump," Dusko said. "God knows what waits us on the other side, though."

"For now," Maauro said, "what awaits Wrik is rest and a proper meal. We have two days until we reach jumpspace."

CHAPTER 14

TWO DAYS LATER, HAVING BOOSTED UP TO THE SAME speed as Bexlaw had, we closed in on the warp point. Unlike most, this one had no buoy or other markings. The Voit-Veru had not explored it, nor wanted to call attention to it. Again we four were on the bridge as Maauro and I set up the jump. Our instruments showed the roiling in space of the entry point. We were tight to the course we'd been given, but the cutter had trailed Bexlaw's *Isadora* by a long distance and the last fine tuning of a jump, done when the pilot used his "feel" for the point, could not be recorded from outside the warp point.

Olivia and Dusko were silent as Maauro and I examined the readings. "Damn it," I said.

"Yes," Maauro replied, "two warp point entries almost side by side and within the margin for error of this course."

I placed my hand on the gravimetric sensor, through this device a starpilot "felt" space. Anyone could use it and the other scanners to control a jump, but most true pilots "felt" something through the instruments. It was a form of psi power not understood by science. In my mind's eye, I could see a pair of "holes" in space, one at a shallower level to our course than the other. There was something in the roiling pattern of the lower one that told me this was a faster current or shorter jump.

"My thought is to go for EP2," I said. "The pattern says short fast jump to me."

"I defer to you," Maauro said. "This is something I cannot sense."

"Stand by for transition," I said, tweaking the angle. I watched the jump clock, and continued the tiny adjustments well within the math of the jump and now working by feel. Minutes rolled away. "Jump in ten seconds."

We came out of hyperspace and every sense I had screamed in revolt. I'd never felt the sensations, seen the colors, or the burnt smells that came with this space.

"Jesus Christ," Olivia said, gagging.

"What's burning?" Dusko said, his head twisting around as if he expected smoke to be billowing.

For me it was the most intense as I still had my hand on the gravimetric control and I was fighting physical sickness. It felt as if space around us was screaming from being tortured. Conviction filled me instantly. "We have to get out of here." I spun *Stardust* on her axis to bring her fusion torch to bear against our course. Before we could regain the warp point I had to kill our forward momentum. It would take minutes at this speed even with the engines on full.

"Wrik, what is wrong?" Maauro demanded, anxiety in her face.

"There's something wrong with this space," I said, "something deadly. I don't know how I know, but I know."

"He's right," Olivia said. "I feel it too."

Dusko looked at her. "I don't know. The jump was bad, unpleasant, something does feel wrong. But I don't know what. I thought it was an electrical fire."

Maauro stared at my face, but made no move to stop me as I slammed the torch on full standard power. The AG field instantly adjusted, but I pressed its limits so that we began to feel the pressure as we braked.

"I detect nothing in the immediate area. Space is empty," Maauro said.

I struggled for words to make sure I could convince her before she acted to stop me. "Maauro, you know a human pilot has a 'feel' for space, that we interpret the data through our senses on entry and exit in jump. This space, it feels like death."

"I feel nothing and detect nothing," she stated.

"There is something wrong," Olivia insisted.

I wasn't sure where I drew that certainty from, but I knew if we didn't get back to the jump point, we'd die here. I watched as our forward momentum slowed until we could finally overcome our inertia and start back to the jump point.

I cast a sidewise look at Maauro. All she said was. "I am expanding my search but again all I can see is that this area of space is extraordinarily clean and—" She froze for a second. "Wrik, put the engine into emergency power, disregard the coolant alarms."

I pushed the controls through the safety stops as we stopped and finally began to start back. The AG field again struggled and *Stardust* began to complain of the mistreatment with yellow and some red warning lights appearing on our boards.

"What is it?" Olivia demanded.

"You were correct about the feel of space being wrong. We have emerged near a dark-matter-fed Preon star."

"Gods," Dusko said, turning ashen, "what's its interval? How long do we have?"

"What's a Preon star?" Olivia said.

"I do not yet have enough data to judge the interval between radiation blasts, but we will be indeed fortunate to regain the warp point before one swings our way." Maauro turned to Olivia. "You know what a pulsar is?"

"Of course," Olivia snapped.

"A Preon star is similar, denser than a neutron star, yet smaller than a white dwarf. They are the densest objects that exist outside of black holes. Even my Creators knew little about them, save that they are in part made of dark matter. They rotate. Not so quickly as a pulsar, or we'd be destroyed already. The rotation condenses gamma radiation into something like a pinwheel. We must have emerged between the arms of the pinwheel. The radiation is so intense it has destroyed or swept away everything in this system down to hydrogen atoms."

"We're far out in the system," Olivia began.

Maauro shook her head. "Irrelevant with this level of power. I will see if I can detect the wave front approaching. As it is not as condensed as a pulsar, there should be some level of gradation."

"What good will that do us?" Olivia said.

"None," Maauro said, as if discussing the lunch menu. "We will not suffer if we cannot make it back. Even the leading edge of the radiation wave will vaporize the ship instantly."

"Well," Olivia said, leaning back in her seat. "It's been nice knowing you all."

"Not really," Dusko said, crossing his arms.

"Two minutes and five seconds to warp point entry," I announced, my eyes locked on my gauges more of which glowed red.

"Can you get any more speed out of her?" Dusko asked.

I shook my head. "No. I may even have to cut back, there's a stress alert on one of the fusion tubes."

The indicator flared and I vented some plasma, adding five seconds that I didn't know we had, to the escape.

"This is going to be rough even if we make it," I said.

"Understatement," Dusko said, "a double-jump, no rest, no time for restoratives and I know who gets to clean the puke off everything."

"Radiation levels are increasing," Maauro said, her voice soft and quiet.

I looked at her. "Do we have time?"

"I cannot tell, but lose no more time. It will be fatal."

Inspiration hit. "Maauro, fire the engines on the *Daitan*."

She didn't debate, or point out that it would likely shear off from the grapples, possibly killing us. The bomber's engine lit furiously. I countered the roll it induced by seat of the pants flying. "Maauro, can you compensate for the thrust vector it's giving us?"

"I am angling its engines now."

It wasn't a lot but I had those five seconds back and more.

"Warp point acquired," I shouted. There would be no time for finesse. This was going to be brutal. "Jump in 10, 9, 8—"

"Radiation spiking," Maauro said.

"5,4,3,2,1, Jump!"

CHAPTER 15

MY EYES OPENED SLOWLY AND I WONDERED IF I WAS dead. After a few seconds I thought I might prefer being dead, as it could not feel this bad. My eyes focused and I realized I was in my cabin. I stirred and groaned.

"Wrik! You're awake," Maauro's voice came. A second later her face swam into view above me. I didn't dare turn my head. I heard her administer some shots and the room began to stabilize. She lifted me carefully into a sitting position and handed me a tall glass of restorative fluid. I was grateful for its lack of taste, as anything more would have made me vomit. We sat together for about twenty seconds while I gathered the energy to ask about our status.

"I think I'd rather have been hit by the Preon star," I managed.

"I marvel that we were not," she replied. "As best I can tell we were 1.783 seconds ahead of the front of the wave."

"Ah, plenty of time," I said.

"We emerged back in the Voit-Veru System. I shut down the *Daitan's* drive before it broke free and shut ours off so it could cool."

"If Bexlaw jumped in there, then he and everyone with him are dead," I said. "Isadora was an old freighter. It could never have turned around fast enough. *Stardust* was built as a courier and we barely made it."

"True for *New Hope* as well," Maauro said. "We know that they landed somewhere and met an alien species that we have not encountered. They clearly did not do so near the Preon star. So we must try the other warp point. Same approach .345187 up the z-axis."

I looked at her. "We've got to be low on fuel and we have damage. I pushed the engines past the stops. There was a spike in the fusion tube."

"The spike was a faulty sensor," she said.

"Crap, and I slowed down for it!"

"There was nothing else to be done. I have inspected our tubes and all are sound, though it will move up the date of our next refit. The other repairs have been minor and I have been engaged with those in between nursing you three."

"How long were we out?"

"You and Olivia, three days. Dusko is still out."

"Three days!"

"It was not so bad," she assured. "You have been intermittently aware and able to follow instructions for bathing and food, but none of you seemed to remember awakening each time. Only now are you oriented properly."

"In the meanwhile, I ordered spares and a full refuel sent out by tanker. It will put a noticeable crimp in Candace's budget, but there is no help for that. We will leave as well provisioned as when we set out a few days ago.

"Feel free to sleep on," she said. "The situation is in hand and beyond the minor repairs there is nothing to do until the tanker arrives tomorrow."

I nodded as she rose off my bed.

"Oh and of course, Dusko was wrong about who ended up cleaning up all the puke on the bridge," Maauro added.

Which, of course, was the wrong thing to say.

The tanker appeared as promised, with some additional supplies strapped to its dull-orange carcass. It was as crude a device as could be imagined: a drive, a framework for hanging tanks and containers and a simple AI to get it there and back again. I didn't trust the AI and did all the work of maneuvering alongside it. Maauro then saved us hours by handling all the EVA work, refueling both *Stardust* and the *Sinner II* with enriched deuterium. I think she had some for herself as well.

"Okay to detach," I sent over the com.

Maauro stepped back as the shielded lines withdrew from us back into the tanker. It started the long slow fall back toward the inner system where it would be picked up.

"Ready for Take Two?" I said after Maauro returned to the bridge. Dusko and Olivia both nodded. I took a deep breath. Despite Maauro's assurances, there was still a funny smell to the bridge, or maybe it was just in my nose.

"This won't get any easier hanging around here," Dusko said. "Try not to discover anything else lethal and exotic on this jump."

"It it makes you feel any better," I said, "we'll name the Preon star after you. It's the first one anyone has found."

"In the Confederacy," Maauro said. "My makers knew of two, though this was not one of those."

"Thanks, I'll pass," Dusko replied, "couldn't sell any real estate there anyway."

I set our course and repeated the steps that had nearly brought us disaster days before. This time the approach was shallower. The roiling mass, color-contrasted on my instruments for better visibility, now said mid-level jump to me. I slightly goosed the drive for a further shallowing. The colors and smells of hyperspace fell on me again and I ceased to exist…for a few seconds.

The downshift wasn't bad for a mid-jump. Nothing screamed strangeness at our emergence, but we quickly grabbed our restoratives and meds. No one wanted to chance another jump back out without them.

"Scan is clear and normal in near space," Maauro said. "Pushing scan out as far as I can, as fast as I can, but all remains nominal. An F5 Sol class star is ahead. I'll have our location and time in transit shortly, but I am estimating four weeks out of space-time. That was a moderate current out. I doubt it will be any longer back."

"Planets?" Olivia asked.

"Will take several hours study. May I recommend reducing speed to one-third?"

I hesitated. "Maauro, I'd rather not. We're still pretty nimble even at this velocity. Anything scan pulls up we should be able to react to it and maneuver around. If we slow, we'll use fuel and we're far from home."

She considered. "Sensible, I concur—though if we come up on a sizeable asteroid we can use it for braking."

We headed inward. Despite Maauro's watchfulness and that of her AI, I stayed on the bridge. Exploring an unknown system was a hazardous business and the disappearance and disaster rate among first-in scouts was still high, despite the safeguards. Maauro remained unusually silent, using a great deal of her processing power. Even for a quantum computer, charting a system using only occlusion and gravity distortion was clearly tasking.

Olivia and Dusko tended to the ship and their own special concerns. Dusko worked his hydroponics garden and whipped up the meals. Olivia prepared her weapons and exercised even harder. Something I hadn't thought possible.

On the third day insystem, Olivia walked into the bridge in her usual set of black leotards and a halter top. "Thought I'd drop in and see how things were going." She'd brought a tray and some drinks with her and put them down on the arm of my flight chair.

"One of your energy drinks," she passed Maauro one of the sweet concoctions. It smelled syrupy enough to induce insulin shock. "No actual deuterium. Sorry."

"Well that should have enough calories in it to recharge you," I said.

"Thank you," Maauro said, but otherwise did not move. Her air of abstraction remained.

"Any luck on planets?" Olivia said.

"Not so far," I replied, when Maauro didn't.

I picked up an iced tea. Olivia picked up the other glass. Her body shone with a fine perspiration.

"You need to get back to the gym before you get soft," she said. "Maybe another bout of MA."

"Please," I said. "I need these arms to steer the ship with. You almost pulled the left one out of the socket last time."

"Yeah, sorry about that," she said, putting a hand on my shoulder. "You'd fallen better than that before. Guess you got tired."

Her hand was very warm through my shirt.

"Well I'm for a shower. See you for dinner in an hour?"

"You need not remain on the bridge, Wrik," Maauro said. "I will call you in the event of a change."

"OK," I said. "I'll see you down there, Olivia."

Olivia gave me a wink and left. I couldn't help trailing her with my eyes.

"Why," Maauro said in a low voice after Olivia disappeared down the companionway, "do you pretend not to look? If she didn't want you to, she would not dress in such an eye-catching fashion."

"Well maybe that's the only gym set she brought."

Maauro gave me a small smile. "Since I have done the ship's laundry, I know that not to be the case. She is not wearing that outfit for my benefit, or Dusko's, so clearly she is trying to attract your attention." She picked up her sweet drink and sipped it delicately.

I shifted, uncomfortable as always with such discussions. "I think Olivia prefers to be admired, rather than touched. She also indicated when she first came aboard that she had little interest in joining what she referred to as 'the confusion.'" I didn't mention the more recent conversation on Velsust.

"That may have changed. You are both young and healthy members of species. Her sexual attractiveness is far above average."

"Hey, what about mine?"

She sipped her drink again.

"Great, thanks a lot. Anyway hasn't life been complicated enough with Jaelle and the two of us? Weren't you just telling me about how you didn't like having Olivia onboard one planet ago?"

"The complications with Jaelle are largely of your own making," Maauro said tartly. "She is a practical being, too practical to live without access to her own kind for all of her life or to believe that you can do so."

"But not so practical that she doesn't resent my friendship with you."

Maauro hesitated for a few seconds and I began to repent of having said it. "Jaelle believes in the physical and psychological necessity that, if for nothing else than children, she must share you, as you must share her. She does not see that as optional, so she accepts it. It's made easier by her culture, a permanent pair bond is rare among Nekoans.

"She does not consider your relationship with me to be a necessity and thus resents the division of your 'heart' between us. I am a part without a place in her view. I am not a Nekoan, which she would not tolerate, nor a human, which she feels she must tolerate. So there is a rivalry between us. It has not overwhelmed our own relationship, but it may someday."

"It will be a long while," I said slowly, "before she forgives the fact that I felt I had to come with you on this trip. I told her it was a much about me as about you—"

"Did she believe that?"

CHAPTER 15

"I don't know."

"Do you believe it, Wrik?"

"I don't have an answer for that just now. But you haven't answered my question either. You're encouraging my interest in Olivia. Why?"

"Perhaps," she said, and now I knew I heard sadness in her voice, "perhaps I fear that my love for you is selfish. That I am keeping you from something that could be very important to you."

"What?" I said. Forget the new star system, now I was really entering uncharted space.

"I want to be with you," she said, looking away. "Yet I cannot give you the physical love that Jaelle or Olivia can. Even if I altered my body to permit it, it would merely be a simulation. I have no such drives, nor the body that would give rise to such needs and desires.

"My love may even be dangerous to you. You follow me into these adventures, these mission and battles, yet you are a frail being. How many more times can you do so without death claiming you? You were missing for two days on the Veru world. I had many long hours to wonder about the morality of what happens between us. Would you not live a longer life if I left you with your own kind?"

"Longer, maybe?" I replied. "I wasn't long for the world when you met me. I don't know that Olivia's company is much safer in any event. But Maauro, life with you in it, long or short, that's what I want."

"I feel that if I really loved you, I would have left you on Star Central."

"I couldn't have stayed behind. God, I'd have lost my mind wondering what was happening."

"Jaelle is right," Maauro said, looking away. "I do divide your heart." She sighed, a very deliberate act. Maauro rarely showed any great degree of emotion. Once before had I seen such, when she pulled free of the Predictor on Cimer, near hysterical with grief and pain, with actual tears running down her synthetic face. In at least one of the futures that combination of being and machine had showed her, she had seen my death and, I sensed, something more.

"You're thinking of the triple-ringed world, aren't you?" I added.

Maauro had seen a ringed world, unlike any in known space, through the Predictor. While she would not say what else she had seen in this one of the many possible futures the Predictor showed her, she'd voiced the one warning. "We must avoid such a place should it ever be found."

"Yes," she whispered. "How do I know that this isn't the system of that world?"

"If it is," I said, standing. "We will face it together."

She looked at me and her face was troubled and though I felt the same in my heart, I smiled. "See you later."

The next day Maauro called all of us to the bridge. When we gathered she turned to us. "I have finished my scan of the system. I find five planets. Two are in habitable zones. Indeed their orbits are unusually close."

"A shared orbit?" Olivia asked.

"No," Maauro said, "though about as close as it could be without gravitational effects guaranteeing an eventual collision.

"There is a Mercury-like planet inward and two gas giants." She looked at me. "Only the gas giants are ringed and the rings are standard equatorial ones."

I nodded and breathed a sigh of relief. Olivia looked at me curiously, but asked nothing.

"I may have missed asteroid bodies, but certainly no other world, or major moons," Maauro concluded.

"Are any of the moons in habitable zones or large enough for an O^2 atmosphere?" I asked.

Maauro shook her head. "If the New Hope came here then they headed for those two worlds in the habitable zone. They'd have shaped course for the one with the closest orbit to Earth's. That's where we will go first."

"Agreed," everyone said.

Two days later, we closed in on the outer world's orbit. All of us were again on the bridge, staring at the monitor at the bright world ahead. It was further out than Earth's orbit around Sol and two mid-size moons circled it, one so far that it might have been an accidental capture.

It was immediately clear something was very wrong.

"No radio traffic on any band," Maauro said. "No microwave or other transmissions that I can detect either.""

"We're coming up on dayside and just now in visual range. If it were nightside we could at least see if there were lights," I added.

"Anything visual?" Olivia added, shifting impatiently.

"No, lots of clouds."

"I do not think we will find power or much of anything else operating," Maauro said. "I am detecting high levels of radiation for an Earth-type world: Strontium 90 and other elements that indicate a large scale use of nuclear weapons in airburst."

"Crap," Olivia said. "Sounds like it's been fried."

"Let's see if we can get some better visuals now," I leaned forward and programmed the scanners. On the main screen, the planet snapped into focus, but all that could be seen were vast gray clouds and immense featureless sheets of shining ice. The world below reflected sunlight like a mirror.

"Nuclear winter," Olivia said, from behind my seat. "That was a heavy, heavy strike then. Not just a few tactical, or even theatre weapons. Somebody wanted to put the whole planet down."

"Reminds me of what Rainhell's logs said about Vania after the Conchirri had their way with it," I said. "If this is like Vania, then the only place anything might survive is about the equator where the ice sheets haven't reached. I'll recalculate our orbit so we pass over all of it."

Maauro nodded her approval. *Stardust*'s approach slowed as she caught up to the frozen world. As we settled into orbit, I scanned a major continent at the equator. Its northern and southern edges were glaciated, but the center remained free of ice. The land mass showed the signs of a great burn off. How long ago we couldn't tell, but nothing green had come to reclaim the scarred wastes.

"Damn," Dusko said, "excessive by anyone's standards." The Dua leaned against the bulkhead, his cold blue eyes seemed to mirror the world ahead.

Olivia nodded. "It's like they were trying to swamp some defenses that either didn't respond, or weren't effective and 100% of the attack got through. This is overkill."

"Means that whoever did it didn't plan to land and occupy the real estate," I added. "Maauro, any idea how long ago this happened?"

She considered. "A crude estimate would be five hundred years or so. But that has quite a margin for error that embraces the period during which *New Hope* might have arrived here. If the stardrive they had was only as efficient as the early models humans produced, they could have been out of the galaxy for decades or even a century on some of jumps that took us only weeks."

"*New Hope* carried no significant weapons," Olivia said.

"No, whatever happened here was local," I said. "It would take fleets to do this or massive, long distance bombardments from the inner world."

We slid over to the nightside. Night's reign was undisturbed by any glimmer of light.

"Can we scan for Bexlaw's ship?" Dusko asked.

"Only visually," Maauro said. "The planet has cities buried under the ice and blasted into fragments around the equator. There will be false positives in abundance. The radiation levels are too high for us to pick up the Isadora's engines even if they were hot."

"That is a lot of planet to scan," Dusko said, "even figuring that they would have put down at the equator if they came in anywhere." He looked at the grim world with distaste. Even the insular Dua-Denlenn seemed depressed by the world-sized headstone.

"Unless we pick up something very interesting on our first complete orbit, I see no reason to consider a landing." I drew an immediate and hearty agreement from Olivia and Dusko.

"I concur," Maauro said. "There may be surviving animal life down there, particularly in the seas. We could be overlooking some land animals, or areas of vegetation, but I see no evidence of even small bands of humanoids like the one we found in the lifeboat. There are no towns, no villages, no power generation. If any natives survived down there, it will be in the most primitive of conditions."

"We'll alert Confed when we get back," I said. "They can send a proper planetary assessment team."

"So we head for the inner planet?" Olivia asked, standing.

"At the completion of the next orbit," Maauro said. "We will have overflown all of the areas free from ice by then."

Nothing showed up at the conclusion of the last orbit and I used the planet's mass and a judicious burn of our engine to slingshot us toward the inner world. It took a ship day for us to close on this world.

"This is our last real hope," I said as we again gathered on the bridge.

"Yes," Maauro agreed. "We could risk another starjump outward with our supplies, but it would cut too far into our safety margin. And in any event, we have no clues as to where to go. The *Isadora* would have been marginal coming even this far. Bexlaw was an obsessive to take such risks."

I checked my instruments. "We have plenty of time for dinner before we can get anywhere near visual range. It'll be at least six more hours."

"Sounds good," Olivia said, stretching as she rose. "If I log anymore chair time on this bridge my butt will fall off."

"I would hate that," I said. I couldn't help the goofy grin that slipped over my face.

"Bet you would," Olivia said. "You know you still haven't taken me up on that sparring session."

"We need everyone operational," Maauro said. "Your training methods are somewhat rough."

"Whoops," Olivia said. "I better be careful. Wouldn't want to get beaten up by your girlfriend."

"No," Maauro agreed. "You really wouldn't."

"Now, now," I said, "Let's all play nice."

"I'm always nice," Olivia said.

Dusko snorted and rose and left. Olivia followed.

"You still think she's a good choice for me?" I said in a teasing tone.

"Yes. I do confess to finding it somewhat wearying that every female that takes an interest in you, seems to feel the need to needle me. Doubtless they would feel ill-used if I returned the favor."

"Possibly because you would use real needles."

"Probably would," she said.

"It wouldn't be any different if the genders were reversed. Probably worse, guys would have come to blows quickly. It's how we resolve things."

"Oh? Dumbly?"

"Yes, dumbly."

"Dinner?"

"Sounds good," I said, rising. I didn't even have to flick on the AI, Maauro did it automatically. "At least we'll face whatever is coming on a full stomach."

We came up on viewing distance of the inner world in the middle of the night watch. Most of us had catnapped in our cabins, waking when Maauro called us back to the bridge. We came in to find the main screen already focused on the inner planet and at full magnification.

"Lights," Olivia said, with a grin, relief plain on her face.

"Don't get too hopeful," I said. "It's not a lot of lights and they are well separated. Earth or Star Central practically glow on their night sides. Still, we are far out. There may be more to be seen as we close."

"I am again picking up indications," Maauro said, "of nuclear attack, but at a vastly lesser level. No nuclear winter here."

"So some chance of life and civilization," Dusko said. "Maybe even a decent bar or two. Is a casino too much to ask?" He leaned against the bulkhead with a mug of whatever nasty-smelling brew Dua-Denlenn used in place of coffee.

"There are radio transmissions as well: low power and no visual, Maauro continued. "I can make no sense of it, of course, without mathematical constants, it's just random noise. With visuals I could pick up enough clues to eventually construct a translation program from gestures and obvious nouns. No chance here.

"IR and other scans show some anomalies. There are large, dead cities down there. Still intact, but empty of life, heat or power, some show blast damage."

"Kinetic energy weapons then," Olivia said. "Rocks or spheres of dense metals sent down out of orbit, nuclear level damage with way less radiation. Standard if you plan to land troops."

"Remember the note that was found with the alien corpse in the lifeboat 'Help Seddon' this may be Seddon."

Maauro nodded. "It will do for an identifier for now, though Seddon could be a person or something else."

The images sharpened as we closed the distance.

Dusko whistled. "Look at those cities. Whoever built them had no fear of heights."

I nudged the sensor and it added building heights to the imagery. I too whistled. "Some of those towers go up one thousand five hundred meters. They're connected at multiple levels by skybridges and elevated roadways."

"Intriguing," Maauro said, "and it causes me to reassess my thoughts on the technological level of this society."

"Yeah," Dusko said. "A nuclear conflict maybe five hundred years ago and the cities are that intact? Okara Prime was blasted by the Conchirri only ninety years ago and it looks worse than this already. What did these people build with?"

"This implies this society was at least equal and probably more advanced than the Confederacy," Maauro said.

"Except for stardrive," I added. "If these people had been out among the stars we'd have run into them, or found some evidence before this."

"Remember the Voit-Veru," Olivia cautioned. "No one knew they were there."

"True," I conceded, "but they were on the other side of a nebula. Also a star-faring race would have had buoys, accelerators, deep space stations and navigation aids in the outer system. We've seen nothing."

"Could have crashed or been deactivated," Dusko said. "It's been centuries."

"Possible," I said. "But you'd think something would still be up, even if not operational. They were master builders. No, I think they just didn't go out to the outer system. There's no reason to head for deep space unless you're going to a warp entry point. Everything I see tells me these folks were confined to this system, unable to get away from each other and at each other's throats. Whether they were two species or it was a civil war I don't know."

"My preliminary analysis," Maauro said, "is that this world was attacked with NCBO."

"The unholy trinity," Olivia said, "Nuclear, chemical, and biological. God, they had it all. It must have felt like the apocalypse."

"We're talking about casualties into the billions," I said. "Two planets close by each other, genocidal warfare between two species?"

"Possible, but unlikely," Maauro said. "That two species would develop with sufficient similar levels of technology to battle on such nearly equal terms, each able to hit the other's homeworld, the odds are astronomical. More probably this was a conflict between a mother world and a colony."

"Civil war, fratricide," I responded, "a particular level of evil to extinguish your own kind."

"You humans seem prone to it," Dusko said. "Get ten humans in a room and you have ten religions, four different skin tones and eleven opinions on any subject. You're a fractious bunch."

"It is rather true," Maauro said with an apologetic air. "Humans vary more in appearance and socio-religious organization than any other species."

"We organize pretty well when it comes to kicking the asses of annoying aliens," Olivia nettled.

"True enough," Maauro said. "Let us hope that the next need to do so is far in the future."

"But you doubt it," Dusko said.

"There was a large scale die off of life," Maauro said, returning to the topic at hand, "though with no nuclear winter. There is evidence of later beam and kinetic weapon fire on many buildings in cities. This implies a massive ground invasion."

"Bodies lying about?" I asked.

CHAPTER 15

"Not after so long," she responded. "They would have long since completely decomposed or been buried naturally. Even most soft-skinned vehicles would have decayed by now. I am detecting some large AFV's—"

"What?" Dusko said.

"Tanks, APC, missile and artillery launchers," Olivia supplied.

"Most of these too are badly deteriorated, but because of the material they were made from they are still recognizable."

"Life?" Dusko asked.

"Scattered life signs, either herd animals, or small groups of sentients in the area below us. This section of the world was roughly treated, population does not seem to have recovered much," Maauro replied.

We continued to close, passing over the dead night side of the world. Our orbit had not taken us within range of the lit section of the northern continent. We would catch that on the next orbit.

"Coming over the terminator into daylight," I said. "I am kicking our velocity down, entering the highest orbit I can and still get a good ground view."

"You are cautious?" Maauro said.

"I've seen some very old weapon systems that were still dangerous," I replied, giving her a grin.

She nodded. "Sound thinking, though I am doubtful we will find anything capable of firing on us in orbit."

"Look," Olivia said.

The screen showed a devastated city at the edge of an ocean, its center cored out either by a nuke, or chunk of rock hitting at high velocity. But toward the coast in the broad bay, a surface ship was moving. No, multiple surface ships.

"A fishing village or a small port," Maauro said with a trace of excitement in her voice. "Indications of significant electrical power in the area of the city near the coast."

"Is that ship on fire?" Olivia asked, pointing at the plume of smoke as the scanner zoomed in slightly.

A memory clicked into place for me. "More likely a fossil fuel, coal or something else that burns and operates a reciprocating engine. The smaller vessels look to be sail-powered."

Maauro panned the scanner over the city. "Wrik can you lower our orbit? The resolution is not enough for me to see the beings who operate the ships."

I worked the controls dropping and slowing *Stardust* further. Meanwhile Maauro had taken control of the scanner and was zooming in on various points below us.

"Interesting," she said. "There are signs of habitation and recovery, spreading out from this landing point. However there are no roads, or rather they are completely overgrown and broken up, outside of this port. Nor did we see signs of other than perhaps small bands of beings further into this continent."

"Meaning that it's being resettled from a site that was less damaged, or more recovered, on the other side of this ocean." I finished. "This is a colony. That explains why we didn't see anything further inland. All these small ships are coming out to greet the big one, well it's like when one of our starships puts in at a new colony. It's a big holiday, a huge event for the colony. Probably it's bringing in more colonists too."

"Only now are they resettling this area?" Dusko said.

"Remember the die off," Maauro said. "The only reason that Confed worlds hit during the war recovered so fast, is that there were outside forces to come to their relief. On Vania the population was annihilated."

The image on screen froze and zoomed on a building in bright sunlight. We saw a cart being pulled by a being. As we watched, it stopped to rest and looked up. The image stabilized and Maauro froze it.

The porter had taken off his hat and wiped his brow in a very human gesture, but the face of the humanoid alien below was a rough duplicate of the alien body from the lifeboat.

"Bingo," I said, " a Seddonese."

"We found them," Olivia breathed, her eyes wide.

"Yes," Maauro agreed. "He is of the same species as the corpse. Now that we are lower, let's look at those ships. The screen flashed back to the vessels in a dizzying flash and we were looking at images of the natives that became clearer every moment. As they wore clothes and hats, from above they looked like humans until one could see the dark green skin with its varying shades of fine feathery hair.

"I see no signs of humans in the area," Maauro said, "but it will be difficult to pick them out save visually. Body temperature and mass of these natives are similar to humans. Our sensors are not made for such delicate work."

"Maauro," I asked. "What do you estimate for a population in that city?"

"Somewhere between 20,000 and 40,000 beings. It would depend how many are occupying the old structures where we cannot see them. Clearly the city was made for over a million. Many of its buildings must, however well-built they were originally, be uninhabitable, at least without extensive restoration."

We were overtaking the colony below and passing beyond them.

"What do you want to do?" I asked. "Slow to a geosynch orbit or keep moving?"

"Continue moving, I think," Maauro replied. "Alter orbit to take us over the most brightly lit area, in daylight. That should be the seat of whatever government and power there is on this world."

I nodded and began to set up the course change. "We should get landing prep under way."

"I'll check the planetary supplies, bio-filters and the like," Dusko said. "We shouldn't need much, if anything, since humans must have lived with these people."

"I'll check weapons," Olivia said. They both left quickly.

"Maauro," I said, turning to her. "We'll have to detach the *Sinner II* but it gives us options we can either leave *Stardust* in orbit and fly down in the bomber."

"Yes..." she paused. "That is odd."

The image on screen blurred again. Now we were looking down at an island off the coast. I could see devastated ships rotting by the piers of a base or small city. But Maauro focused on something largely buried in the sand.

"Is that a body?" I wondered. In the sand was a shape, with what looked like four limbs, one of those seemed to be in fragments.

"No," she said. "Look at the scale. It is over thirty meters tall."

"A statue then," I hazarded, "the local Colossus of Rhodes, perhaps?"

Maauro stared at the screen as if willing it to provide greater clarity and pierce the covering shroud of sand. "Perhaps," she said.

CHAPTER 16

WE CRUISED OVER THE NORTHERN LATITUDES, SEEING cities that were occupied by only small percentages of their former populations, and some newer and lower-built towns. There were trains of a sort and road traffic, though the highway system was crude at best.

Once we hit a radiation spike in a destroyed city. Maauro and I examined the scans.

"This is incongruous," she said. "This small city was struck with a nuclear weapon once, but it seems to have relatively high and fresh radiation."

"An old site uncovered?" I hazarded. "Some old weapon or power source that detonated lately?"

"Possible, though unlikely. Another explanation would be a recently destroyed modern ship."

"Can you see any sign of *Isadora?*" I demanded.

"No, but the center of the city is a mass of fallen metal and building material from the fall of some giant towers. Anything could be under it."

We drifted further north on the next pass. This time we could see evidence of a local war from our height with recently burned cities and towns Corpses appeared occasionally in the streets.

"I also see evidence of evacuations," Maauro said. "There are trails of abandoned goods, sometimes of vehicles and transports that were overtaken by what was pursuing them.

"In terms of your Earthly history," Maauro continued. "This area resembles Europe or North America in the period between 1850 and 1900, complicated by the fact that there are huge disparities in population and technological levels."

"That would be similar to Earth's overall history at that point as well," Olivia said. "Most of the planet was a thousand or more years behind the technological leaders."

"Even more so," Maauro said. "These people know of many things that were possible from before. Even if they do not know how to do them, they know of flight, both in atmosphere and space. If not from legends, or surviving old records of their own, but from the presence of humans among them and the recent visit of Bexlaw."

"Assuming there are still humans," Dusko said.

"Even if there weren't, there would be bones, artifacts and legends," I said.

"We haven't seen a live human," Olivia added.

"It it is difficult at this height to tell," Maauro added. "In clothes and unless we catch one looking up, they are too similar to tell apart. If there are humans, they would be a very small percentage of the population, records indicate that there were only about 250 humans aboard New Hope. Not all of them would have been of breeding age, some likely would have died without issue. Five hundred years is not a long time for population increase, even assuming there were no local hostile factors."

"If it is like Earth at that period of time," Olivia said, "then warfare is likely constant and we have seen some evidence of that. They almost certainly do not have a central government, so lots of small regional wars."

I stood up. "I think our best move it to take the *Sinner* down and leave *Stardust* up here with Olivia and Dusko aboard, at least until we have some idea what is waiting us. We'll check out the city I designated as Alpha, it's the furthest north one that we have seen that looks to have been recently attacked. Maybe we can find out what is going on."

Olivia immediately looked like she might protest, but I held my hand up. "Bexlaw's ship didn't come back and we haven't seen it. Nor have we picked up the radiation from its engines. Either it was destroyed, or it's hidden and either way that means trouble. Having you up here means options."

Olivia subsided but looked unhappy, mostly at the chance for missing some excitement.

"We'll mind the store," Dusko said.

Sinner II kicked free of *Stardust's* green and gold hull. I spun the bomber on her axis and lined up on the planet below. I looked over the dark green nose of the ship as we angled downward at the scarred and mysterious world below. Maauro sat in the second seat alongside me. Her small frame barely filled the standard ejection seat. The cockpit of the bomber was surprisingly tight for all the capacious weapons bay. The Solari must have been cramped when they used it.

"No reaction to our orbital approach on any system," Maauro said, her hands poised over the weapons and ECM panel.

"Good," I said. "I like quiet trips. Wouldn't want this ship to go the way of the original *Sinner.*"

"Me neither," Maauro said, waving her left arm, replacement for the one severed in the loss of my original ship. "I'm well out of warranty."

I fingered a virtual switch. "Com check, *Stardust.*"

"5 by 5," Dusko responded with his usual economy of speech.

"Good luck," Olivia added.

"Thanks. We're entering the thermal zone. Communications blackout in 145 seconds."

CHAPTER 16

As if to confirm me, the heat shield slid up over the canopy, blocking our view of the cherry glow spreading on Sinner II's nose. We wouldn't be able to effectively maneuver in reentry, but Maauro could still use our ECM and weapons. We bumped and slewed as the fighter struggled through the planet's cloak of atmosphere. I had plotted our course so we would enter over ocean, less chance of anyone attacking us from the sea. As the bumping subsided, the canopy shield slid open. I could see perfectly well through my screen and other instruments, but, like most pilots, I preferred to have my eyes on the sky.

I tilted the nose down and could see white clouds scudding below us across a vast dark-blue sea. The planet, we opted to call it Seddon after the mention made in the lifeboat's records, was not as sea-covered as the Voit-Veru world but it had oceans in abundance.

"No vessels or other contacts," Maauro said, "nothing but a wide and deep ocean."

"*Sinner* to *Stardust*," I called, "reestablishing communication."

"We read you." Dusko said, sounding bored.

"We'll keep you posted, as we go," I said. "Automatics will relay all our scan and vid."

"S.O.P" he replied.

Yeah, I thought, *easy for you to be blasé, you're still in orbit.*

"We're stable at mach 2.5," I replied. "I'll go subsonic well before the coast. I don't want a sonic boom— could scare the locals."

Seventeen minutes later I slowed to about three hundred knots and dropped below the cloud deck. It had been sunny at sea, but we'd crossed a cold front and the clouds were heavy with rain and only about five hundred meters up. I slowed further so we could see objects on the ground better. This area however was devoid of any significant habitation beyond blasted and abandoned cities from centuries ago.

"We're crossing onto the continent down below where we saw lights," I reported. "We can check out that dead city, then work out way up toward the occupied areas."

"Okay, Wrik." This time it was Olivia. "Stay nimble."

I goosed the speed and decided to climb back over the cloud deck just as the clouds let loose their burden of rain. After an hour's travel we were approaching the city that had caught our eye from orbit. I nosed down as Maauro activated the weapon suite. We dropped through the cloud deck and saw a medium size city below us. It was less filled with sky-climbing towers than most.

"Hey," I said. "Some of those buildings past the towers, they're made of stone or wood—"

"Yes," Maauro said. "Likely that means more recent manufacture. This town was reoccupied until recently." Her voice ended on a grim note. "Wrik there are decomposed bodies in the streets. Skeletons. I also see blast and fire damage in the sections of recent construction."

"That's a stockade there," I said, pointing. "It looks like it was hit by a tornado, that's not blast damage."

"No," Maauro said. "It looks more like it was trampled."

I stared at her, but before I could ask more, Maauro said. "Let us land and examine the area."

I looked down at the dead city and the more recently destroyed village that had sat snug alongside it. Reluctance filled me.

"What happened here," she added, "was not very recent. Months, I judge."

Maauro's instincts were usually sound. I sighed. "Ok."

"*Stardust,* we're landing in City Alpha," I relayed. "It looks like it was attacked in the last year. Standby."

"We've got you covered from up here," Olivia's voice called. "Main laser warmed up and ready."

"Roger that," I said, privately doubting that even our improved laser would do much at this range and through this much cloud. Still it was comforting to think someone was watching.

I circled, bled off some more airspeed, then went into hover over what had been a parking lot some long time ago. The pavement was cracked and trees poked through much of it. But here was a large enough area where only tall grasses projected through. I slowly dropped us down, realizing that it was even more broken than I'd thought. Fortunately none of the landing gear went into any of the abundance of holes.

"Any landing you can walk away from," I quoted. Maauro just shook her head. She went to a locker and drew her armspac, and I pulled out a triple-auto carbine. I added raingear to my haul. Maauro was indifferent to weather.

I opened the bomber's weapons bay, which doubled as airlock. I had to squat as the clearance under the bomber was only a meter and half. Still, it kept the rain off. Maauro walked out into the rain and, grumbling, I followed. It was a cold drizzle, my helmet kept it off my head but I had to raise the visor to see better. My hands projecting through the poncho sleeves were immediately wet, though I had shooting gloves on.

We stood, looking in a circle. The towers of the original city actually disappeared into the clouds above. No light showed there and many of the towers were mere skeletons of their former glory, with all their windows out and their interiors long ravaged by the elements. Still, they stood, even after centuries of abandonment, and they looked none the less strong for that broad march of time. None had collapsed or tilted. Some further to the center of the city and perhaps better shielded from the elements, still boasted glass, or whatever strong clear material it was.

But we turned ourselves toward the smaller, more recent habitations that been built by the last inhabitants. These were shattered to the point where it was hard to say what they had originally looked like. Walls of tumbled stone, burnt wood, mixed with some of the ancient buildings that had been put back into use but with more crude materials.

"Maauro?"

"Beam gun fire, some evidence of high explosives and then something large rammed or otherwise attacked these structures. It is as if they were pulled down by cranes or wrecking balls."

We walked forward side by side. Maauro with her armspac aimed to the left while I covered the right. We marched down the destroyed roads until we came to the first skeletons. White bone lay scattered about a field, whether by scavengers or the original attacker we could not tell. Seddonese were a humanoid species, the skulls looked depressingly similar.

"A lot of these," I said, quietly, "were children, from the size of the skulls. Oh God, this must have been a schoolyard!"

"Yes," Maauro said, her face and voice distant.

"Son of a bitch," I muttered.

We walked on. There were more bodies. I saw no weapons, no sign of a battle, only a slaughter.

Maauro and I inspected artifacts from the destroyed town. The objects were of cunning make, but the metals were of simple steels or basic alloys.

"Interesting," Maauro said. "This confirms a society that has at least recovered into the early industrial age."

I looked around, the rain was coming down in sheets and it was hard to see any distance. "Is there anything more to be gained by remaining here?"

She placed a hand on my arm. "No, we should go. It is time to look for the living. But we have learned something valuable. The Seddonese have a living enemy and it is hunting them. Its technology is equal to ours. The beam fire I have seen here could have come from any land fortress of your people. Even one of my creators land vehicles could have used it as secondary armament. What form this enemy has taken is yet to be determined."

"Let's get the hell out of here," I said.

We returned to the *Sinner II* and stowed our weapons and gear. I reported developments to *Stardust* and we lifted off, heading northward to the area where we knew there were people and power generation.

The land below was shrouded in clouds and rain. Our instruments probed through but found only empty lands. We passed what might have been a battlefield, with signs of chemical explosions cratering the ground as if from artillery.

We broke into clear sky. The land ahead lay flat, crisscrossed by small rivers and the broken remnants of highways running through forests of dark-green trees that had a silvery and reflective tone to their foliage.

Somehow the site of the open ground cheered me and I increased our speed.

"No sign of combat below," Maauro said. "Nothing has tracked us."

"We are coming up on the southernmost point of power generation," I said. "ETA five minutes at present speed."

"Let's not head directly at it," Maauro said. "Lower and slower. Unless we see some evidence of danger, we should land and reconnoiter, then make contact."

I rubbed my hand over my face. "Well it's what we came for. If we are going to find Maximillian and the others we'll need some local help. It's a big planet."

We scanned and dropped altitude until we were flying nape of the earth. I popped up over one hill to see a town. Again it was new construction huddling near a series of the sky towers. These however went only a few hundred feet above. The new construction was lower, but it still showed the longing of a people to move back into the sky. Even the more recent construction had an ethereal quality to it. In the distance I could see the skyline of a major city in the distance.

I switched into hover as Maauro studied the town through eyes that were superior to the *Sinner II's* instruments. "There are lines of fortifications in front of this town, Wrik. I believe I see entrenched artillery of a primitive sort."

"Sounds like we are in front of a main line of resistance," I said. "They're expecting whatever danger it is, from the same vector we are approaching from. Not good."

"Agreed. Let us circle around this town and head for the city beyond. We can land behind that city. We will present a less threatening aspect on foot."

I flew *Sinner II* around the foothills, well away from the town, then headed north until we could see a city split by a large river. We circled behind it, avoiding the occasional buildings and villages around it which seemed abandoned.

Once we were well past the city, we turned back to approach it, following a road back toward the city, until we saw what looked like a column of refugees. Then I cut over the woods until we could continue south, parallel to the road but out of sight if not earshot. Finally I could see, on the horizon, the great city with the river running through it.

"The fortified town was about ten miles past this city," I said. "I think we should land well short of it. They might not be looking for something hostile coming from this direction but I wouldn't want to bank on it."

Maauro nodded. "We should land here. It is as close as we can get without being seen in the air.

I called up to *Stardust*. Dusko located a nearby clearing. He had to do so quickly as *Stardust's* orbit was taking them away from us. I ordered Dusko to bring *Stardust* into geosynch orbit on the next pass, then I dropped the bomber into the clearing. The grass was wet from recent rains and fortunately did not catch fire.

"The question becomes do we travel armed or not?" I asked of Maauro.

"My thought is that you carry a sidearm," she said. "Our greatest advantage should it come to any combat, is that no one will likely realize what I am, or have any remote idea of my capabilities, even if they do. The armspac and carbine could cause some frightened trooper to take a shot at us. Our best hope is to meet a patrol with a sensible officer who takes us up the chain of command rapidly."

"I agree. Our safety here is going to be based on being underestimated, in your case, or being taken for friendly humans."

"Carry a homing tracker set for the *Sinner*," Maauro said, "should we become separated."

I nodded, then drew a holstered laser pistol from the locker, leaving the larger carbine behind. I tossed Maauro a jacket and pulled out one for myself. It would be cool outside. She wouldn't need the jacket, but it might seem odd for a small, slender female to be walking around in a form-fitting bodysuit in the cold. Canteens and small packs with food and toiletries had been readied before we left the starship. I opened the bomb-bay hatch and we dropped into the wet grass, and edged out from under the bomber. Then I resealed and code-locked the hatches.

We stood next to *Sinner II* for a few seconds, taking in the smell of the forest, the wet ground and grass, some of which smoldered from our landing. Maauro stomped out any patches that looked like they had the potential to burn on. A breeze tugged at us, but it wasn't strong and came in irregular surges. Trees rustled. They looked like a mix of pines, though the branches seemed dusted with silver. Red fruit hung from something that looked like a smooth-boled oak. The sight reminded me of the Christmas trees of my childhood.

We walked on, heading for the road. I had no need of my compass with Maauro leading. We walked through thigh high blue-green grass, which my moisture-proof pants shed easily, though it did strike a chill through me. Water beaded on Maauro's legs. Her chassis was textured to look like fabric but water didn't quite react to it the same way. I made a mental note to mention it to her.

As we passed under the trees, I put on a soft cap to keep dripping water off my head. I'd left the helmet behind, not wanting to look too much like a soldier.

Something rustled in the undergrowth. I put a hand on my pistol.

"Small animal, fleeing," Maauro said, not breaking stride.

The ground was soft and spongy, which gave Maauro more trouble than it did me. She kept sinking into the soil, looking annoyed at each step. Finally, we reached the open area near the road to her evident relief. Nothing was in sight as we came out of the forest. As we stepped out to examine the asphalt road, Maauro shook first one leg and then the other at such speed that they blurred, dirt and moisture were flung off. Fortunately I was far enough away that none hit me. The sight was so peculiar, and so reminiscent of a dog drying itself that I simply could not stop myself from bursting into laughter.

Maauro gave me a hurt look and I walked over to her, putting an arm around her and struggling to bury my mirth. "I'm sorry," I fought down a grin. "Really, honestly, I shouldn't have laughed. Sorry."

She gave me a dubious look. "I suppose it did look funny."

I wiped the grin away. "Just unexpected. Forget about it. Remember I'm descended from monkeys. It's amazing we ever got out of the trees."

"Well, not literally monkeys," she said.

"You don't know that much about my family," I joked, surprised at myself for doing so. I never mentioned my family, even to Maauro, who knew who I really was. I realized there was some relief in that.

Her serious look told me that she realized the significance of this. This was one of those secret places, the unique bridges between only the two of us. It was the place where my love for her lived.

She placed her right hand over the one I rested on her arm and smiled gently at me.

"Let's go find some Seddonese," I said.

She nodded. We both turned to the south and began walking down the sun-warmed asphalt road. "Isn't it ironic," I said, after we'd gone a kilometer. "We came here at many times the speed of light, flew around the atmosphere at supersonic speed. Here we are hoofing it down the road at foot speed."

"You could hop on my back," she offered. "Even carrying you I can run at highway speed."

"Thanks, I'll pass on the windburn. Besides if someone saw us..."

"I would guard against that, but perhaps as you say it is safer to proceed thus. When we bring *Stardust* down I can assemble the cargo mule, or we could ride on one of the crab-robots."

"If wishes were horses beggars would ride," I quoted.

We walked on in companionable silence. I took off my jacket and tied it around my waist. The sun was climbing in the sky and the heat reflected back off the road. Maauro noticed and unzipped her jacket.

Ten minutes later, Maauro raised an arm. "It looks like another refugee column, coming this way. There's a small military escort of an armored car preceding it."

"Well might as well wait for them here."

"Wrik, I think you should handle the contact. I will speak as little as I must and avoid attention as I can."

I nodded. Now I could see the column as they came on. We waited in the center of the road. The armored car leading the marching civilians was camouflaged in gray and dark green. It had a long engine compartment and a small turret atop it. I could see some helmeted men in back standing and staring at us. The car accelerated on its six wheels and advanced on us, pulling up only twenty meters away. A Seddonese stood in the turret and shouted something at us. We walked forward. I held my hands well away from my pistol.

"Hello," I called back, wondering if there was any chance I would be understood. "We're humans from the Confederacy."

The Seddonese stared at me with its large purple eyes. Four more dismounted from the back of the vehicle. They held their weapons level, but their demeanor was more curious then hostile.

"They have seen humans before," Maauro said, softly. "No panic, they almost seem unsurprised to see us."

I nodded, keeping my hands open and level. The office said something. It sounded almost familiar.

We looked at each other. I took a deep breath and said. "Bexlaw."

The officer started and the men looked at each other in excitement, babbling to each other. The officer recovered himself first and snapped orders to the men who fell silent immediately. The officer in the turret gave me a long searching look. "Bexlaw," he repeated.

"Bexlaw," I agreed, at least we had one word in common.

He turned to the soldiers and told them something. One, a sergeant, I guessed waved us forward with one hand. We came around past the foul-smelling machine and climbed onto the back of the open metal compartment in back of it.

One of the soldiers looked surprised when Maauro got on and the machine sank under her weight. I didn't like the look the officer gave both of us at that moment. He said something to the sergeant-type and two of the soldiers got off, evidently demoted to infantry and told to wait for the column. We drove off with the two guards sitting opposite us on the hard bench seats. The officer was on a set of headphones of what looked like a crude radio, speaking urgently.

We drove back and edged around the refugee column. The road was full of Seddonese, some carrying parcels. Many of the Seddonese were accompanied by carts pulled by four-legged animals of varying sizes, small wheeled vehicles and some by Seddonese themselves. They glanced at us with curiosity and many pointed, especially among the subdued-looking children. I longed to be able to ask questions but there was no present way.

The column wended its way for hundred of meters, brought up at the rear by another armored car and a squad of troopers. Once clear of the column our vehicle sped up. The road ahead was empty and we made good time. Soon, I could see tents and smoke arising from campfires. We drove into a good size military encampment on the edge of the city. Looking around, it was obvious that, while this was one of the ancient cities and still largely abandoned, it had been resettled for a long while and boasted a sizeable population. Here there had been less new construction. It seemed more effort had been expended in moving back into the ancient buildings. Some had been refurbished and reoccupied. Vehicles, both self-propelled and animal-drawn bustled, about. Seddonese were on foot all over the place. Most were soldiers. I did not see any humans, but again the people's lack of reaction told me that we were not the first they had seen.

The car rolled up to a prestigious building surrounded by soldiers and military vehicles. We pulled up and the guards jumped out. Maauro and I followed. I winced as the vehicle's shocks showed her weight, though she tried to minimize it by getting off slowly. The officer climbed out of the vehicle jumping down next to me.

We looked each other over. He wore a dark-green uniform with braid on it but it was suppressed in color, unlike many of the more colorful soldiers bustling about. It made sense. The inside of the armored car must have been a greasy and dirty place as the uniform was well-soiled. A revolver rode on his hip. The helmet he wore was of what looked like a soft, thick leather. He was shorter than I was, with dark-green skin that looked like it had the texture of velvet, only a few shades lighter than his uniform. The face was nearly triangular and hairless and with the large purple eyes lent him a somewhat feminine look. Seeing a live Seddonese this close was very different from examining a desiccated and autopsied corpse.

The officer pointed at my sidearm, holstered on my hip and held out his hand. I slowly unbelted the weapon and handed it to him. He made a curious hand gesture and something like a bow, perhaps a gesture of conciliation and respect.

He nodded and pointed to the stairs, waving invitingly with his other hand. The two guards he brought fell in behind us and he commandeered another soldier who was passing by with a rifle slung on his back. The new soldier stared at us, said something to me. I raised my hands in non-comprehension; he seemed to understand the gesture.

The officer said one word, "Bexlaw."

The new soldier sucked in his breath and fell in with the others. At the officer's urging we quickly headed up the stairs. The Seddonese guards closed up, watching us warily over weapons that they kept handy, but did not point at us. They'd clearly not realized anything about Maauro's nature. While there were two guards on me, only the new guard trailed her, his triangular bayonet pointed skyward. It wouldn't even have scratched the pigment of her outer casing.

We reached the foot of a sky-soaring tower. From what I could see only the lower stories were occupied. "The technology for pumping water and waste around something so tall hasn't been reacquired as yet." I said.

Maauro nodded. "They are only now reacquiring electrical power and their mechanical skills are very uneven, as you would expect. Some rediscoveries are more fortunate or easy then others." Military preparations were going on all around us. Wheeled guns were being towed by on an elevated highway by a local herbivore. Small armored vehicles similar to the one we came in were lined up in the plaza next to the tower. Some trailed what Maauro confirmed where hydrocarbons, indicating fossil fuels of some kind. Everywhere brightly-colored infantry moved. Evidently guerillas wars weren't an issue, or these were dress uniforms. Given the practical look of the weapons everyone had, I didn't think so.

Another vehicle moved smoothly onto the plaza and this one caused me a double-take. It looked of modern design like a Confed air transport, but a second look told me it as an ancient machine restored to some use with a combustion engine. Once it had clearly been meant to fly. Now it rolled on its ground wheels, but it looked quicker and more efficient than any of the recent make. Given the high tech metals and ceramics of its body, it might have been the most effective fighting machine present, for all that the gun in its turret looked more like the wheeled ones being pulled by animals.

Our young officer made a gesture and gave a sharp command. We followed him into the sky tower, past groups of other soldiers and what might have been Seddonese civilians, who stared at us. We were ushered into what was clearly officer country and passed from company to battalion and to regiment in a tedious process. We retained the original quartet of Seddonese we came with.

"Have you mastered their language?" I asked Maauro when we were given food and water and a place on a couch, by a window, overlooking the plaza and elevated roadway. Maauro checked the food and opined it safe. The officer and guards took some themselves and sat a distance away, watching us.

"Only basics," she said, drinking some water for appearances sake. "If someone points at or references an object in a clear way, I acquire a noun. However the word for food could be specific to this bread-like substance, or might mean food generally. It will take me only a little while longer to be able to do simple sentences. Minutes after that I would be fluent, but I am not sure I want them to realize that I know their language just yet."

"What have you picked up?"

"The guards are very reticent, they have just been told to take us to various officers of increasing rank and have reported the circumstances of our meeting. The senior officer we last saw directed them to take us to what I believe is a scientific or political leader.

"They aren't acting like people who have never seen an alien before," I said, "They were surprised, but unless I am not reading them at all correctly, they didn't seem shocked or overly frightened."

"Your observation is sound. They are handling us as if they knew the capabilities of a human male and a small female. Yes, I believe they know of other races. They either know of the *New Hope,* the *Isadora* or perhaps humans survive here still."

"Yes. First contact is usually a civilization-shaking event."

"As it was the first time our kinds first met," a voice said in badly accented Standard.

We both turned to see one of the purple-eyed, green-skinned Seddonese standing near us. He wore loose robes and cut a professorial figure.

"You speak our language," I said, rising. Maauro stood as well and in the background the guards also climbed to their feet.

"Poorly," he said. "I am Dr. Parisha, a language master and I welcome you to Seddon. I speak the languages of my kind, the corrupted language of our extinct enemies and the main tongue of the humans who first came here so long ago in the *New Hope.*"

"And you learned Gal-Standard," Maauro said, "from Professor Bexlaw's expedition from the *Isadora.*"

Parisha looked at her in what seemed mild surprise that she addressed him. "Yes, it would seem that disaster, unintended, but disaster nonetheless, is always heralded by the arrival of your people."

"Trouble?" I thought. "What do you mean?" I asked, speaking slowly as he concentrated on my words.

"First," Parisha said, "tell me why you are here. Then if I deem it safe I will bring you to someone who can speak to you in greater ease and answer your questions." Parisha was looking at me, I assumed because I was older and male he thought I was in charge. That was fine. It was always useful to divert attention off of Maauro, though nonhumans rarely detected that she was an android.

"We were hired by the family of one of the Professor's students to find and recover them," I said. "The expedition was overdue and was not supposed to have left charted space in the first place. It was feared they were all lost."

Parisha was visibly surprised, if I interpreted his body language correctly. "You are the most diligent of rescuers to have come so far across the stars. Is the one you seek a prince that such an expedition was commissioned?"

"Let's just say his grandmother is no one to be trifled with," I said.

Parisha gave us a long and searching look. "It may be that you can rescue more than just the survivors of Bexlaw's group. Please follow me."

Before I could follow-up on "survivors" Parisha turned and walked off. We rose to follow him and the three guards and their officer trailed us. We went down a hallway, then up a broad flight of stairs.

"Look," Maauro said, as we reached the top of the staircase to face a large open room before towering glass walls. I spotted what she was gesturing at immediately. A human male, gray-haired, middle-aged and wearing a Seddonese military uniform, stood with several of the green-skinned people deep in discussion. Other than the unusual feathery-appearing haircut, he would not have attracted a second glance on Earth. I noted the braid and decorations on his uniform that suggested he was a senior officer. He spotted us at that moment and stared at us.

"Come, come," Parisha said.

"This is good news," I said to Maauro as we walked on in a widening pool of silence and stares. "A human, and he appeared to have both rank and respect among the natives."

Parisha did not comment on our observation, but we marched steadily down a series of halls until we came to one with bright, electric lights. Here an escalator took us further.

"Welcome to our government center," Parisha said with evident pride. "We have restored many levels and functions of it. This was once a hospital and functions as such again."

We emerged onto a guarded floor to see more humans, a man and woman. It concerned me a little, the local humans might spot that Maauro was not one. Still, they had been out of the galaxy for eight hundred or more years. They'd have little idea of what to expect of a human mutation.

The humans called out questions to Parisha in a language I didn't know, but he waved them off. We entered what was clearly a medical area with the usual and recognizable equipment of hospitals. It seemed that scrubs, gurneys and white coats were a staple of healers everywhere. Seddonese walked about, intent on their tasks, or giving us curious looks.

We came to a door that Parisha knocked on, then opened. The guards deployed behind us and we followed Parisha in.

Inside, a Morok lay in a bed. I thought it was a younger female. The blue-skinned goblin-like being was propped up on pillows, connected to an IV, and looked at us with bright-red eyes.

"Please God," she said in Gal-Standard. "Tell me you're from the Confederacy."

"We are," I assured her, "Captain Wrik Trigardt, SS Stardust, and Maauro.

She coughed. "Ezlen Elgee from the Bexlaw Expedition."

"You're sick, Miss Elgee?" I asked.

She nodded her head. "It's a rare form of genetic disorder among Moroks. I need general spectrum genix drugs, but ours were destroyed with the ship."

"Destroyed?" Maauro said.

"Do you have any with you?" she asked. The desperate hope on the young face was almost painful to see.

"Yes," I said, "aboard ship."

She struggled with her emotions for a few seconds. Moroks cry like humans do and tears trickled down the slate-blue cheeks. "Could you send for some? I'm in a bad way—"

"Not necessary," Maauro said. "I too have a condition that requires genix general spectrums. I always carry a supply with me."

Maauro, of course, knew the formula and must have been working on creating them inside her body from the second the girl revealed her problem. She'd have created the container and slid it into the pocket of her jumpsuit. Likely the container was still warm.

Elgee gave a cry of joy. Parisha demanded something in his native tongue. Elgee rattled something back to him as Maauro handed the girl both the container and a glass of water.

"This is a standard ten day supply," Maauro said. "If you tell me more of your condition, I will come up with a course of therapy for you after I conduct some research. My memory is eidetic and I can supply the formulation to your doctors here."

Elgee, between tears, relayed this to Parisha, who demanded to know if the new wonder medicine would work for his kind.

Maauro demurred. "Likely but it will require study. The drugs work on almost any creature that uses DNA or something similar. But as yet I know little of your biology. It will work on the local humans."

"Maauro is our ship's medic," I added as Parisha stared at her.

"Impressive in one so young."

"She's older than she looks," I added, reluctant to out and out lie. "The work can be done. If not now by us, then by properly trained scientists who will follow us here, if there is a desire for trade and normal interstellar relations with our Confederacy."

"It seems," Parisha struggled some, his grip on Gal-Standard slipping due to excitement, "that an age of wonders is upon us again. But, as always, it is on the doorway of such that the ax falls on us. It seems the doom of my people."

I turned to Elgee, who had finished the water and pills and lay back against her pillows, looking exhausted. "What's happened here? Where's Bexlaw and the rest of the expedition. What happened to the *Isadora?*"

For a second I was afraid the young Morok might not be up to answering. She was after all, a young being who'd just received a reprieve from a death sentence.

She drew a deep breath. "Professor Bexlaw and most of the expedition are dead." She was dry-eyed now, but grief still showed on her face. "Our ship, *Isadora,* was destroyed by a reactivated ancient war machine of Kolzi, that's the next planet out in the system.

"Ancient war machine?" Maauro asked. I wanted to know who had survived from the expedition but bided my time.

"I know," Elgee said. "It sounds mad to think a war machine from five hundred years ago could still be dangerous."

"Less than you think," I said dryly.

"We found it underground. The Seddonese military had uncovered one of their old subterranean forts shortly before we arrived and in a great state of preservation. They couldn't do anything with the technology, then we came. We were greeted like rescuers out of a myth. Evidently after the war, they'd sent *New Hope* back toward Earth with a mixed Seddonese and human crew, hoping for help. The ship jumped out but nothing was heard of until—"

"We know about the lifeboat," I said.

Elgee looked startled but continued. "What do you know about the war here?"

"Assume we know nothing," Maauro replied. I shifted in impatience, but allowed her to lead the conversation.

Elgee nodded. "Kolzi, the next planet out, was a colony of Seddon. Bitter irony, Kolzi means Beautiful House of the Winter Sun. The Kolzi colony fell into a dictatorship generations before *New Hope* arrived. A dictatorship so thorough, that it rewrote their history. The Kolizens were like inmates in an asylum. All they knew of the Seddonese was the twisted fictional history the ruling family fed them. They produced a huge military, while the democracies on Seddon bickered about how to deal with it.

"The situation was heading for a war, with one side armed and prepared for it and with the other, even though they had vaster resources, in a desperate scramble to catch up. Then *New Hope* came into the system. Her stardrive wasn't like one of ours and she'd wandered in hyperspace with far more time out of the universe than we spend in a transit. Best guess is her various transits took her over three hundred years.

"She encountered a Seddonese ship and was escorted here. That was too much for the Kolzi and their mad rulers. They attacked, fearing that with stardrive technology the Seddonese would dominate the future.

"The Kolzi came down in waves, mobile land forts like ours, small tanks and armored vehicles and then something uniquely theirs. Giant machines in humanoid-shape, weapons of terror, thirty-meters tall. These were targeted at the civilian centers, spreading plague, chemical and radiological warfare. They weren't robots. Each contained a Kolzi soldier mated to it as part of its CPU. Rumor was that they were suicide warriors. Once they became joined to the giant fighting machines, they seldom, if ever, came out.

"We found one of those machines in the fort. It was undamaged. The pilot must have died when it landed. The Seddonese asked if we could get it going. They wanted to use it for construction and to excavate the rest of the underground fort, looking for more treasure." The last came out dripping bitterness.

"Bexlaw wanted to help. We'd been giving them information, technology and medicine from when we arrived but we had no heavy machinery with us. We did have a portable nuclear APU on the *Isadora*.

"Bexlaw and Maximillian from our expedition worked with the Seddonese and hooked the, well they now call it the Destroyer, up to the APU. The auxiliary power unit had plenty of juice and the machine started up in just a few minutes."

"Maximillian Vaughn?" I interjected. "Is he alive?"

"I don't know," she whispered. "For his sake I hope not. You see he was in the machine when it reactivated. I heard him scream, saw wires and cables wrapping themselves around him as if they were alive. Then the chest cavity of it closed up and he was gone.

"It started moving...we didn't know... we didn't know. It began firing almost immediately, attacking everything in sight. Seddonese started dying all around us. It must have released some bacteriological agent, or a poison gas specific for them. We fled, alerted the military but it was hopeless. When the machine emerged, it simply destroyed them. It must have either drained the reactor or incorporated it in its huge body.

"We called for the *Isadora,* for help. But *Isadora* tried to flee. They were too close. The machine fired some form of beam weapon, blew off part of the stern and *Isadora* came down in a fireball, wiped out a town. Only I, Tomas Schim, and a Frokossi named Fitaz from the expedition made it out of the underground fort alive."

"Bexlaw," I said, "was a reckless idiot."

"We cannot evade our own responsibility," Parisha said. I'd almost forgotten he was in room. "It was we who pressed Bexlaw. He'd opened a box of wonders for us and like greedy children we kept pressing for more. Some feared a future where we would be wholly at the mercy of aliens, not even humans who we at least knew, but true aliens, who would dole out such technology as they chose to for us and at what prices and conditions we could not tell. We had been a great people and we sought to regain as much of that as we could before we came face to face with your Confederacy. Remember that the humans who came here were refugees from the cruelty of your own species. We did not know what to expect. Some feared the worst.

"Bexlaw may have been a brilliant professor, but he was a child in politics. It was easy to trade him our past for his help in securing what we thought would be our future. In doing so, we may have killed both our kinds."

"The Destroyer," Eljee said, "with Maximillian aboard as its new brain, has rampaged through their country for over a year, a festering vector of disease, poison and radiation. Their military has only slowed it, never turned it aside and they've have had to abandon city after city to its advance with untold casualties."

"Good God," I said.

"The only good news is that it seems to have exhausted it supplies of chemical and biological weapons," Parisha added. "Still, with its size and other weapons, it remains a deadly foe. Our end is only delayed not averted. We have been driven north here to the capitol on this peninsula. Some have escaped past it into wilderness areas, but they have no future beyond mere survival there."

"Do you have weapons?" Elgee asked.

"We're not a warship," I said slowly. "But we have weapons and a few tricks up our sleeve that may come in useful."

"If you can help," she said fiercely, "then you must. We brought this on them, just when they were beginning to recover: tens of thousands, maybe hundreds of thousands, dead. The only reason it hasn't been worse if they've been able to outrun it until now."

I reached for the water and another glass and poured some for myself, my head buzzing with all I had learned. "We were sent, hired in fact, to find the expedition, but specifically Maximillian, by his grandmother, Shasti Rainhell. Our first job would be to determine if he is still alive inside that thing."

She made a Morok gesture I guessed was a shrug. "We don't know. If he is, then he has no control over it. Max was…is… a nice young man. He wouldn't hurt anything if he could avoid it. He fled Olympia to get away from his father and that whole way of life. We tried reaching him by radio, no response. No one who's gotten near the machine has survived trying to communicate with it."

"So you see," she lay back against her pillows. "The Great War here was inevitable but the *New Hope* humans coming triggered it, the match to the tinder. Then we came along. We didn't make the Destroyer, but we resurrected it and set it killing again. Will you help?"

"Yes," Parisha echoed, "will you help?"

I looked at Maauro but she gave no sign. I realized that once again, she was deferring entirely to me. "We will, if we can."

Eljee collapsed back onto her pillows and her eyes closed. Maauro moved instantly, placing a hand on the young Morok. "Natural sleep and exhaustion. Wrik, we must leave this young woman to recuperate."

She turned to Dr. Parisha and spoke quickly in Seddonese, then turned to me. "I have given medical instructions."

Parisha gaped at her. "Your mastery of our language is astonishing."

"I will also require a complete tactical briefing with your senior military staff, all that is known of the Destroyer and previous engagements."

"You interests extend beyond the medical sciences?" Parisha said. I could see total confusion on his face.

"Dr. Parisha," I said. "Please sit down."

The older being reached for a chair and sat, staring at me.

"I don't want you to be frightened," I began. "But for us to work effectively together there are some things that you must know. Maauro is a living being, but she is artificial in origin. She is made of ceramics and metals and her brain is a computer such as Bexlaw must have told you about, only vastly more complicated."

The Seddonese gripped his chair with hands that showed white through the green skin.

"Please do not be afraid of me unnecessarily," Maauro said. "I am in the same service as Wrik and follow his orders—"

Sometimes, I thought.

"—I do not harm anyone who does not threaten myself or my companions."

"But," I added, "she is not the little girl she appears and she is vastly stronger and more dangerous than you could ever believe. Elgee will be no less surprised when she learns of it. Maauro was made by an unknown species long ago. She's far beyond even Confederate science."

"You can think?" Parisha asked her tentatively.

"Yes, I do," she said. "I also feel, joy, sorrow, even love, in my own way."

"Gods," he whispered, "a living machine. With a mind...dare I ask, a soul?"

"You may ask, but for your last inquiry I have as yet no ready answer. Once I would have said, no. Now, I do not know."

"May I," he hesitated, "may I touch you?"

Maauro walked slowly over to him. "Anywhere but my left arm, which will only feel metallic and cold to you, it is not original."

Parisha slowly extended a hand to stroke Maauro's cheek. She stood motionless as he did so. It occurred to me that no one touched Maauro regularly other than myself and Jaelle.

"You do feel alive," he said. "You face is as soft and smooth as my granddaughter's."

"And yet would survive a direct hit by any weapon a being might lift," I said.

Maauro picked up a metal stool and with no fuss and only minimal noise folded it into smaller shapes until it was crushed to a ball that glowed in her hand from the heat.

"Like the Destroyer," Maauro said. "I too, was created for war, only in my case eons ago. I fight now to save lives, to find the lost and to help biological life. Wrik has said we will help you. We will do so. I will caution you, that like the Destroyer itself, I am an implacable enemy if those I value are threatened and harmed. You mentioned your manipulations of Bexlaw. Be careful not to make such moves with me and mine. In return, I will do battle for you."

"No enemy," I said, looking at the sleeping Morok girl, "has survived Maauro."

"I will...I will brief my superiors," Parisha said, eyeing the crushed ball and clearly struggling to keep his grip. "Please go with the guards. They will not harm you. I will be sure of that. You will be given quarters, but it must take some time for me to convey this, for the shock to be overcome..."

Maauro put the ball in the sink and ran water over it which hissed and crackled, then placed it in a trash can. "We will await you as requested. If I could be given a grammatical dictionary it will facilitate communication. More so, if any of the expedition's computer equipment is available. They must have digitized some of this it will speed the process from tedious minutes to seconds."

"Really?" Parisha said, dazed, as he stood and went to the door. He spoke to the officer outside in very, slow and deliberate speech, apparently to make sure there could be no error in his orders. I noted a human soldier had joined them, a young man. He nodded to me and spoke, haltingly in something that almost sounded familiar.

"He is using an old variant of a human language called English," Maauro said. "There's a lot of it in Gal-Standard. He assures us we will be treated well." Maauro answered the young man, who smiled in relief. We followed them up the hall to another floor and a well-appointed room.

The Seddonese guards were more alert now, more careful. I noted that when we reached the new room that were a lot more guards, but they stayed well away from us. Only the human came into the room with us. There he brought us food and water and carefully explained each item to Maauro. I ate slowly anything that she suggested would be safe, though one local dish smelled so bad, I asked them to remove it so I could enjoy the other food.

"What's his name?" I asked Maauro. She translated.

"Enso Pape," the young man said. He was of a medium complexion, shorter than I with a wiry build and dark hair and eyes.

"I believe he is of some form of special forces or intelligence," Maauro added. "His rank, which appears to be the equivalent of a major, seems very high for his youth. I suspect this is a very intelligent young man who has been placed here to handle us."

"Well," I yawned picking up a drink and leaning back on a comfortable couch, facing away from the sun setting through the golden drapes. "I am sure you can defend your virtue if he seeks to handle you."

"That is not what I meant."

"Kidding," I said with a smile.

Pape watched our interactions closely and I suspect with an understanding of Gal-Standard that equaled Parisha's.

I looked at him. "Do you want to continue having Maauro translate? Or would you rather fill us in on the local history while we are waiting for Dr. Parisha? I am sure you speak our language, or they wouldn't have put you here."

He looked at me for a second, his face void of expression then said. "I speak Gal-Standard about as well as anyone. I've spent a lot of time in the field with Tomas and Fitaz, trying to find ways to slow up the Destroyer. I have a better grasp then Parisha on colloquialisms."

I nodded. "Can't blame you for pretending. We were doing some of the same."

Pape looked at Maauro. "Did you really crush the stool into a small ball?"

"Yes,"

"And you are really a machine?"

"Yes."

"And you think? He does not control you?" Pape pointed at me.

"I think and Wrik is my friend. I consult with him on my actions but he does not control me."

"I don't even have that luxury with my girlfriend," I joked.

Maauro smiled.

Pape merely shook his head in wonder.

"Tell me about the humans here," I said. "You seem on good terms with the Seddonese."

"Now," he said. "It hasn't always been the case. There aren't a lot of records from before the fall but most Seddonese knew about the Kolzins and didn't blame us for the war that broke out. So we weathered the worst of it with the Alish, the local Seddonian democracy we landed in. Human fortunes have waxed and waned over the centuries. Our numbers grew slowly but we have a lot of immunities to native germs and diseases.

"When Bexlaw came and the Seddonese found out about how much humans figured in the Confederacy, our stock went through the roof. Then, of course, came the Destroyer, now you. Not sure where the credit balance stands today.

"I will get you the grammar books that you asked for," he said.

"Unnecessary," Maauro said. "I detected an active computer from the Bexlaw group on a floor below. Your military is using it, I imagine with the help of one of the survivors you mentioned, but it contains the grammar that I needed I have downloaded all information in it."

He froze looking at her.

"It will facilitate our military briefing when we get it," she said, smiling sweetly.

"Don't worry about it," I said, knowing it was pointless. "She is on my side."

"Always," Maauro nodded.

CHAPTER 17

STARDUST ENTERED GEOSYNCHRONOUS ORBIT OVER THE capitol city of Revived Tur-Sharaa. As soon as they were within range, Maauro updated Dusko and Olivia on what had transpired. She was able to use the *Sinner II* to relay the signals up to the orbiting starship. All this occurred while we were in the room with Pape, talking to the young operative. Parisha checked back in with us to advise we were invited to a meeting with the Seddonese president of Alish. There was no world government, but Alish was the leading force in the world recovery, with its mix of human and Seddonese and their contacts with Bexlaw.

"Are you too fatigued for this meeting?" Pape asked. Parisha hovered anxiously behind him.

Truth was I was tired, but I wanted to see the powers as soon as possible. "I'm good. I'd like to bring our ship down and recover our smaller ship."

"Do not worry about the vessel you came in," Pape said. "It has been secured by our special forces."

I smiled. "No doubt. I hope they didn't try the locks."

Pape's face was carefully neutral. "The vessel is undamaged and we will see to it that it remains unmolested."

"Good."

He turned to Maauro, "And you?"

She gave him a pleasant smile. "I do not fatigue in biological terms."

I nodded. So long as she wasn't using vast amounts of power in battle-mode, she didn't need to recharge, drawing power from everything from sunlight and ordinary food, to hydrocarbons or fuel cells.

"The counsel is assembling," Parisha said. "If you will follow me."

We followed Parisha out the door, trailed by Pape. I noticed that the guards had changed. The Seddonese and two humans around us now wore much more subdued uniforms. None of them spoke and they seemed to watch both us and the area around us. I suspected we were now in the hands of Pape's Special Forces. Probably good, less chance for someone to make a mistake, I thought. However, most of them had some form of grenade on their belt, worthless against Maauro, but more than enough to take care of me.

We went down the escalator, and across the building into what was apparently the political wing. This part of the building was opulent, with chandeliers, thick rugs and curtains on all the massive windows. Even at this late hour, the halls were full of Seddonese and the occasional human rushing about on tasks. Parisha was known and expected as we

CHAPTER 17

were passed through layers of security and bureaucrats. Finally we came to a set of ornate white and gold doors under bright flags. The attendants opened the doors. Our security detail split. Only a few of the most formidable-looking followed Pape into the round chamber room before us.

The room was filled with rings of concentric desks, all unoccupied. However there was a central dais and six Seddonese stood there, awaiting us.

As we walked up to the area in front of the dais, I studied the Seddonese before us, noting no humans were present. Of the six, one I guessed might be female. The two at either end wore military uniforms. I suspected they were service commanders, likely a general and an admiral.

Parisha paused before them and gave a small bow. He turned back to us. "Given your friend's mastery of our language, I will propose that she translate for you. And I will translate for the Emergency Committee."

"As you wish," I said.

Parisha turned to the six on the dais and began speaking.

Maauro immediately translated. "He is addressing and identifying the committee. Center right, in the black suit and white shirt is President Landertan. The Prime Minister is the female with the longer hair/feathering and dark red clothes. Next to her is Barocorpin, Minister of Defense. Beside the President is the Minister of Species Relations Naracorpin. At the far end, in the red and gold uniform, is General Telmas. At the other end is Admiral Bernarin."

President Landertan began speaking. He was a small being but somehow seemed to convey a great authority, his voice deep for a Seddonese.

"The President welcomes us in this dire time," Maauro translated. "He invites us to sit. He confesses both relief at our appearance and some amazement and trepidation at meeting a living machine like me."

We sat in the indicated seats before the dais, looking up at those in power.

"They ask for a briefing on why we have come," Maauro said.

"Fill them in completely," I said, "including about finding Maximillian."

Maauro did so, taking a few minutes. Since she did so in their language, Parisha did not have to translate.

"I am commended on my Seddonese," Maauro said. "They say I speak like a native, if formally."

"Tell them that I would like to bring down the *Stardust* as near to the capitol as is practical and to bring the *Sinner* here tomorrow. I want to concentrate our assets as we explore a way to stop the machine and save Maximillian. Ask if they have a suitable site nearby and tell them what we need for a landing."

"The President says a suitable site is nearby. He will direct that it be prepared. The General asks if we have the capacity to attack the Destroyer from our ships."

"Unlikely," I replied, as Parisha translated. "My vessel was originally a military courier, optimized for speed, not armor or firepower. We have a smaller vessel with us that has armament, but from what I heard of how Bexlaw's ship was brought down, I think a direct attack in line of sight from the air would be very risky. We have three small but efficient fighting machines aboard *Stardust* we can employ, but truth be told be told our best chance lies with Maauro."

There was a long and pregnant silence.

"I believe a demonstration is in order," Maauro said. She walked over to a heavy white stone bench and causally lifted it into the air with her left hand.

"Impressive," the Prime Minister said through Parisha, "but hardly—"

Maauro's right hand lit in the plasma torch and she sheared the bench in two in an instant.

The guards around me all twitched, then subsided.

"Maauro is far stronger, faster and more deadly than you can imagine," I said into the astonished silence. "But her greatest strength is in her ability to intrude into and control almost all machines she meets."

"Including ours?" demanded the Admiral.

Maauro shook her head and answered for herself. "No. For me to control a machine it must be computerized, like our machinery. Your machines have no artificial brains to control."

"And you think you can do this to the Destroyer?"

"Only time and combat will tell. My biggest problem is, that in order to take over something, I must, if you will pardon an analogy, first be able to speak its language."

"I speak Kolzin," Parisha said.

"You speak the language of the biological entities, while that will serve as a starting place for my attack, it is not the language of a battle-computer. I must somehow acquire an ability to translate my attacks into its language before I can even begin to batter my way through the programs defenses."

"Are there any other examples of Kolzin machinery that we could examine?" I asked.

"No," Parisha said. "General Telmas says that few of the Kolzin machines survived their battles with our ancestor's forces. We have broken parts in museums and we will make those available to you, but for hundreds of years, the Kolzin machines were avoided as they leaked poisons and radiation. They were not preserved."

"An examination of what you have may still be useful," Maauro said.

The politicians and soldiers questioned us for an hour further before the President brought the meeting to a close. "You have come far and we have kept you late. Rooms are prepared for your rest. In the morning, you will be taken to your small ship and may summon your large one. After that I will leave you in the hands of our military commanders to plan a strategy.

"We have not seen the Destroyer for some days. It has been most effective at eliminating our scouts, or losing them. We do not know where our enemy is or where it will strike next."

"We can't risk our starship to hunt for it," I said. "Perhaps we can do something with our bomber. We will need a briefing on all that is known of the Destroyer's ability before we take that chance."

"Until the morning," the President said.

Our escorts took us to another area, where well-appointed rooms awaited us. Maauro demurred at being given a separate room. The major domo who showed us the rooms didn't seem quite sure what to make of the propriety of that until Pape assured him that she was a machine and his sensibilities need not be ruffled over it.

I shut the door, assuming Maauro would deal with any surveillance devices focused on us. To be frank there was nothing really to be concerned about, we had in fact come to help these people, though they may not have appreciated our emphasis on saving Maximillian. *Hard to blame them,* I thought. If someone handed me a weapon that could stop a monster is such circumstances, the life of one young man wouldn't weigh heavily in that calculus, but we were agents of Shasti Rainhell and if we could recover him, we were bound to do so.

Maauro examined an electric socket in the wall, sighed, then extruded some device that she plugged into it. "Never turn down free power after a plasma burn," she said. "However I must be careful or I risk blowing their fuses."

"I think you blew a lot of the fuses in the Emergency Committee's brains," I replied, as I dropped onto a large plush bed with a groan. "They will still have a hard time seeing someone who looks like a young girl as a threat to a huge monstrosity."

She shrugged. "I may not be. It depends on how the Destroyer functions. Remember, every other system I have ever encountered: Confed, Ribisan, Voit-Veru, Infestor, I already spoke the basic programming language of. This machine is something new. I may have to defeat it in close physical combat. It would surely find it difficult to cope with me at close range. But enough for tonight."

"Agreed," I said, "a shower for me and some sleep."

"As for me," she said, "mere low quality AC current and a spot on the floor."

"You're welcome to half of the bed."

"The bed is old and wooden and might not take my weight, not to mention the scandal to the major domo should I be discovered there in the morning."

I laughed and headed for the shower.

CHAPTER 18

N THE MORNING MAAURO RELAYED THE UPDATE TO STAR-
dust about where to land. They started lining up for a landing in the
late morning, giving us time for breakfast and for Pape to arrange
transportation to take us back to *Sinner*. We were to meet with General
Staff on our return in the afternoon. I sighed internally, foreseeing an
interminable series of technical meetings and other time-wasters. In this
regard the Seddonese seemed very human.

Breakfast was excellent, with Pape supervising what was likely to
appeal to a human. The fact that Maauro participated with gusto seemed
to bemuse the native human.

Afterward, Maauro and I were taken out to the area we'd parked
Sinner II and an escort brought us to the bomber. We rode out in the
armored car, similar to the one we'd ridden in a day before. The day was
only partly cloudy, we'd landed in late winter, almost to spring. Clouds
and rain were the mark of the season. I caught a glimpse of the glow of
Stardust's entry through scudding clouds, but could not hear her engines
over the dull rumble of the armored car's engine and the wind blowing
over us.

Maauro leaned close on the hard bench. "Dusko says entry normal.
He is estimating set down at the field in ten minutes. He wants to know
what is for lunch as he does not plan on cooking."

I laughed. "Tell him the local food is well worth the visit and to save
his appetite."

Pape looked over from the bench opposite. "Everything all right?"

"Yes, our starship is landing," I replied, raising my voice. "It'll be
there when we return. "

The armored car pulled over. I saw four Seddonese soldiers waiting
by the roadside.

Pape nodded to them and spoke in the local language, trivialities
Maauro did not bother to translate. Accompanied by Pape and the escort
of four Seddonese soldiers, we started off into the forest. Pape told me
of growing up in woods like these as a child and some of the animal life
that lived in them.

I'd developed a liking for the *New Hope* descendant and offered him
a ride back in the *Sinner II*. His men would have to head back in the
armored car. He told me his sergeant was glad to be making the trip
back on ground-based wheels. Pape sent them back after we opened up
the bomber's hatch.

Pape was amazed at the bomber.

"It's actually an older vessel, a *Daitan,* means 'Daring' in some old language," I told him as I did my walk around. "We took it off some pirates, or rather Maauro did."

Maauro had preceded us to the bomber. A few days dryness had made the ground much firmer and she wasn't sinking in as she had before. She'd completed the walk-around and some of the safety checks by the time we caught up to her.

"It's hard to believe," Pape said, looking at Maauro disappearing into the green and gold bomber. "Her capabilities,...they seem like magic. She could be a demon from the outer hells, well other than the fact that she's as cute as a new puppy."

I wondered briefly what the local form of puppy looked like. "Yes, she is that."

He hesitated. "Do you mind a personal question?"

"No." I said, as I checked a flap. Maauro may have pre-flighted it but I was too much of a pilot to leave that duty entirely to someone else.

"You seem more like, well more like a couple than..." Words seemed to fail him as he searched for what we might be.

"My girlfriend sometimes makes the same point," I said. "Maauro is... unique and we are very close. In many ways I am closer to her than to anyone else."

Pape whistled. "That's a recipe for trouble."

"Sometimes."

"What's her name?" Pape asked. "Your girlfriend, I mean."

"Jaelle Tekala," I thought about it a second. "She's not a human, she's a Nekoan." I pulled my com from my pocket. A picture of Jaelle glowed on its screen. She wore a bathing suit from one of our trips to the sea. The two piece suit showed off her fine, taut body, her tail projecting from a slit in the back. Her face was lit by a wicked grin and her golden eyes were filled with her usual joy at being alive.

"She is beautiful," Pape said, "very exotic. I'm married, myself. Here, take a look." He reached into his blue and gold jacket and pulled out a leather wallet. When he opened it, there was a picture inside. To my surprise, a golden-eyed Seddonese looked out of it at me. She wore a swirling gown and her face was lit in a smile.

"Beautiful," I said, and meant it. "I didn't know Seddonese had golden eyes."

"It's rare except in this part of the country. Purple is the most common but you'll occasionally see orange or black even."

"Looks like we have something in common," I said

"Is it...is it unusual," Pape asked, with a sudden shyness, "for humans to marry or date out of our species in the galaxy?"

"It's not common, but it's not frowned on. We have a legal union called a consortship, for people of different species, since you can't reproduce. Some simply use their local customs to marry. I'm in a consortship with Jaelle."

"Nice," he said. "That's nice."

"How is it here?" I asked.

"Pretty rare. Some regard it as scandalous, some as an abomination. We are one of the few to do so in our generation. Fortunately she's from a powerful family, or we'd likely have been stopped. It must be nice to be from the stars where love is so much less questioned."

"It's not always easy," I said.

"Still you have laws."

"They'll be your laws if you join the Confederacy," I said.

"Something to live for," Pape said, his face solemn.

"Come on," I said, as I edged under the bomber. Pape followed me up through the hatch and stared around the interior. Maauro had turned up the lights.

We strapped into our seats after I finished preflighting Sinner. Maauro gave Pape her usual seat. "The view is better," she said, while strapping him in. "It will mean more to you than me."

He smiled and thanked her.

I nudged the throttle into hover and *Sinner* lurched into the air. As soon as we reached five hundred meters I moved her into forward flight. We headed toward the field where *Stardust* had landed an hour before.

"We have nothing like this," Pape said, as he pressed his face against the canopy. "There were some balloons and dirigibles, some gliders but nothing to compare with this. We'd started on regaining flight when the Destroyer awakened. Nothing we had could survive in the air within line of sight of the monster."

"You have been unable to keep patrols in contact with the enemy," Maauro said.

"We tried. Again anything in line of sight drew beam fire. The Seddonese couldn't get even that close until recently. It was using chemical or biological agents deadly to them. It seems to have used up most of those but may retain a small amount for dealing with patrols. We've used human scouts, but casualties are heavy and it can break contact pretty easily, especially in open country."

"Undesirable," she mused. "I must consider means by which we can keep tabs on our adversary."

As we neared *Stardust's* landing site a vibration started in the right engine.

"Dammit," I said.

"What's wrong?" Pape demanded, suddenly losing his enthusiasm for air travel.

"Picking up a vibration in the number two," I said as I shut the engine down and ran up power on number one. "Don't worry. We can fly on the one engine."

"Do not blame yourself," Maauro said. "I checked the engine out as well. Whatever defect it is, was well hidden. One suspects the pirates we took it from did not maintain factory specifications."

"You'll have to tell them off if you see them again," Pape said with a sickly grin, his hands white-knuckled on his seat arm.

"She told them off pretty thoroughly the first time," I said. "Fact is she'd have to visit them in Hell to follow-up."

"Which would seem pretty redundant," Maauro added.

Pape turned from his tense scan of the outside to look at her. She noted his regard and smiled sweetly. He turned back to me. "I have a feeling it's a good thing she's on our side."

"You have no idea, my friend," I said, eyes glued to my instruments. "None at all."

"*Stardust* to *Sinner*," came Dusko's voice. "We see you. You look wobbly."

"*Stardust,* we're having some engine trouble. Tell everyone to keep off the field. It isn't serious, but I want to get down as soon as we can. I don't like running on one engine."

"Very sensible. Try not to prang into us while you are doing it."

A few tense minutes later I brought *Sinner* in. Since I didn't wish to use hover on one engine, I took a brief landing run on the wheels for safety and was relieved when the bomber rolled to a stop.

"We'll have to do a tear down on that engine," I said to Maauro.

She nodded. "There's Dusko and Olivia coming down the cargo ramp. I see they have unpacked the mule and the crab-robots. Good."

When we climbed out it was immediately clear something was up with the Seddonese. People were running, vehicles and riding animals raced in every direction. We paused as Olivia trotted over, Dusko trailing her.

"What's going on?" I asked.

"I don't know," Olivia said, she had her hand on her sidearm and watched the scurry with a suspicious gaze.

"It all happened just as you came in," Dusko added.

"I'll find out," Pape said and ran off to flag down an approaching staff car. The dark green and gray vehicle screeched to a halt and the braided and decorated occupant inside exchanged words with Pape. The news was clearly bad, the young human staggered back, his face stricken. The Seddonese officer got out of the vehicle and gestured at us. Pape nodded and they both ran over.

"It's a disaster," Pape said, as he came up to us. "The Destroyer is on the move. It came through the Mellifan swamp near the town of Chlor. We don't know how. That should have been impassible but it did it. The population is fleeing now."

"Why weren't they evacuated before this?" Maauro asked.

CHAPTER 18

Pape's face was tight. "We have only so many resources. We evacuated the towns on the plains south of here. We never thought it would sweep around the flank and head for Chlor though a swamp. None of the cities and towns in that sector have been evacuated."

The general rapped something out to Pape.

Maauro translated for us. "They are sending forces south to help the refugee column: vehicles to help the civilians outrun the Destroyer, and military forces to delay it."

"It's hopeless," Pape interjected. "We don't have enough transport to do it. The only thing our military can do is delay the Destroyer by forcing it to battle. No unit of ours has survived that unless it broke and fled."

He grabbed my arm. "Wrik, Chlor is where my wife Corra and her family live. Is there anything you can do? The bomber—"

"Not with the *Sinner* on one engine," I said. "She'd be a sitting duck. *Stardust* is even less maneuverable and has less armament." I looked at Maauro. "If we are going to do anything it will have to be on the ground." Behind her a troop of mounted Seddonese, carbines in their scabbards thundered past. A steam cart pulled a piece of artillery slowly in their wake. They looked pathetically antiquated.

"Wrik," Maauro said, quietly. "Again, it falls to you to make this decision."

"Is there any chance?" I ask.

"We have not taken the measure of our enemy," she replied. "I cannot tell."

Pape watched us in an agony of suspense.

"We're all they've got," I said, despite the dryness in my mouth and the thudding of my heart. "Dusko get to work on the *Sinner's* right engine. Olivia—"

"I'm going with you." Olivia said. "I'll get my sniper rifle and some LAWs."

I opened my mouth to argue but she was already racing off.

"I will get my armspac from the *Stardust*," Maauro said. Then she moved, speeding past Olivia at a rate that made the human woman look like she was standing still.

"Your vehicle is fast?" Pape demanded, looking dubiously at the mule.

"Faster than anything else around here over smooth ground," I replied.

"Then I am with you. I can coordinate whatever of our defense units can arrive in time." He turned and spoke to the officer who nodded and headed for his staff car.

CHAPTER 19

I N MOMENTS MAAURO RETURNED WITH OLIVIA. MAAURO held a container of light anti-tank weapons and her armspac. The LAWs weren't as powerful as the missiles in the crab-robots, but they were what we had.

I looked at Maauro and her large boxy weapon. "Three humans, the cargo and you may strain the mule."

"I will ride atop a crab-robot, my weight will slow it only slightly and not below the mule's best speed anyway. I could run on my own but I would arrive at the battle site with my heat sinks full. As transports the crabs are more effective than my feet." The three gray and green machines rolled up behind her, their road wheels projecting through the spindly legs that gave them their name. Their 20mm chain guns and missile mounts gave them a comfortingly deadly look. However it was in Maauro with her ability to dominate any computer system she encountered that I pinned most of my hopes.

Pape scrambled into the mule. "We should go by the southernmost bridge, it skirts the city. That's where the relief force is forming up."

"We will not wait for them," Maauro said, climbing atop Crab One. "They can do nothing against this enemy but be targets."

I slid behind the wheel after helping Olivia load the LAWs container. She locked her sniper rifle down, then climbed into the ring behind the small cabin of the mule and pulled the charging handle on the LMG mounted over us, its slender barrel pointed directly ahead.

"Let's go," she yelled. Her blood was clearly up. The one blue eye I could see was wide with excitement and a wolfish grin lit her face. She was, I decided then, crazy.

Pape's face was strained with fear for his wife. Perhaps I was the only one of the four of us afraid for himself. I was determined not to let it stop me or make me falter. I hit the accelerator and the mule slid forward.

I rolled up the mule's windows, the morning was still cool, though the clouds had thickened some. Rain seemed a daily factor of existence here but mercifully not just now. Olivia could duck out of the wind behind the cab. She opened the small window between us so she could hear us.

"How far?" I asked Pape.

"I know the road well," he said looking down at the speedometer, "at this speed, an hour maybe a little more."

I nodded as we raced past lines of men, animals and equipment. Officers and noncoms recognized us and cleared traffic out of our way.

CHAPTER 19

To my surprise, cheering broke out. Seddonese and a few humans waved their hats or shook their weapons as we sped by. We passed south of the city across the southernmost bridge overtaking and passing columns of infantry, then cavalry and finally the motorized transports and armored cars that had started first. They weren't much faster than the cavalry, but did not need to stop. We didn't hold up for them but drove ahead.

Maauro spoke to me over the mule's radio. "According to the Seddonese military traffic, the Destroyer has overwhelmed the small force protecting the town of Chlor and is pursuing the fleeing population which is heading for a valley in that range of hills before us."

I looked up. The hills were well in evidence, stretching across the horizon, low and rounded, they would offer little difficulty to the Destroyer. Pape's paper map showed me that the road went up into the hills and then down into a wide valley before climbing up into the hills then descending to the broad plain where Chlor stood.

Or had, I saw a tower of smoke in the distance being shredded by winds blowing southward. Pape looked up and his face blanched.

"We'll find her," I said.

His eyes were bleak, but he nodded.

I coaxed a little more speed out of the mule. As we started to climb I realized I'd been right to have Maauro on a crab, the mule's small engine, more meant for utility then speed, labored dragging us up the hill. Maauro and the three crabs gradually slid ahead of us. We were alone, the Seddonese military far behind us, and as yet no refugees ahead.

The mule crested the hill, just behind the crabs and we pulled into a scenic overlook to the valley below. On another day it would have been a beautiful view. Today it was a vista to a nightmare.

The road below wound into the valley, for all its width, most if it was forested, the open area by the road was jammed with thousands of fleeing people and some vehicles. We could hear their screams and cries even from here. A pair of artillery pieces from the city's guard were unlimbering to stop the behemoth, or at least draw its fire off the civilians

The source of their terror reared up on the ridge opposite us. I snatched up binocs to get a better view of the towering mass of metal that stood like an armored knight looking down at the pitiful, fleeing mass. I saw a madman's dream brought to life, a humanoid shape, but distorted: a barrel-shaped body with legs and arms too short and thick, the head, large as an aircar, was crested, as if wearing a medieval helmet of some sort. A snarling face of metal glared out at the world.

It was a figure out of a child's nightmare and I couldn't help but cringe back as the giant machine surveyed the scene. From under the crested helm, a beam of light shot out, striking the fleeing Seddonese on the valley floor. Dirt fountained and moments later the crash of the explosion reached us.

The artillery began cracking out rounds. These detonated against the Destroyer to no evident effect, but the same weapon in the monster's shoulder flashed and chattered in response. The crew of the nearer piece fell about the primitive weapon.

Civilians ran now, trampling each other, flinging aside their burdens and abandoning carts as panic whipped them. The beam flashed again and more civilians died.

Maauro raced back to the mule, snatching her armspac out of the back of the mule's cargo bay. "I will take the crab-robots and try to stop the machine."

"We'll help," I said, opening the door to the mule.

"No," Maauro said. "All you have is a light machine gun and the LAWS. It would be suicidal to get close enough to use either. Get the people out of the valley and across the bridges before they're blown."

Before we could begin to argue with her, she sped off, kicking up dust and stones. The crab-robots deployed: two to the right and one following far more slowly in the wake of the speeding android.

"God damn it," I shouted. "Wait, Maauro."

"No point," Olivia said, from the ring where she held onto the LMG. She had it aimed down the valley at the Destroyer for all we were well out of range. The monstrous form, blued by the distance, continued firing down into the fleeing crowd. "We can't catch her. Even the crab-robots can't keep up with her. We'll do more good following her orders."

I looked at Maauro, already disappearing into the woods on the other side of the stream that she easily leapt. I cursed, but Olivia was right, catching Maauro was impossible.

"Wrik," Pape banged a fist down on my shoulder. "We have to get down there!"

I slammed the mule into gear and raced down into the Valley of the Dying.

CHAPTER 20

I *MOVE TO ATTACK FOR ALL THAT THE TACTICAL SITUATION IS APPALLING. The crab-robots cannot maintain station on me, forcing me into a piecemeal frontal attack on an enemy whose power I have not yet assessed. A horde of noncombatants and ineffective Seddonese military are trapped between us on the battlefield. If I await the arrival of the crabs, the reduction of noncombatants will easily exceed 60%.*

The Destroyer detects me and ceases firing into the panicked crowd, even ignoring the fire of the remaining artillery piece which cracks away impotently. I detect with relief that Wrik and Olivia, now far behind me, are following my directions and moving into the valley to get the column moving. I hope Olivia is clever enough not to use the LMG and attract fire.

I leap up into a tree then fling myself into the air, armspac extended in front of me. The bole of the tree snaps behind me as I fire a HEAT missile and my weapon stutters out a dozen AP rounds. I aim for the Destroyer's head where the beam weapon sits. Maximillian, if he is alive, is likely in the armored chest of the massive machine and I will avoid striking that if I can.

I send a wave of virus at the massive machine, but I have not had time to develop any form of interface, or study how the enemy processes data. In essence I am sending a message, but with no surety of its receipt. I hope it will respond in kind as I am sure my quantum brain is superior and it will merely provide me faster access to my enemy's CPU. It does not do so. I detect scanning and ECM. I disrupt its scanning of me and its ECM is useless against my systems. However both allow me to begin to process an interface that will let me to infiltrate its systems. But both means are slow and guarded by anti-virus. I doubt I will be able to infiltrate this unfamiliar system in any useful time frame. It appears today's contest will be with physical weapons.

The Destroyer raises its massive forearms with their armored greaves. The AP rounds sparkle off them, defeated by the depth of the armor. The HEAT round slams in and penetrates, but clearly does not get through the greave. It drops the arms, uncovering the beam weapon in the armored skull, above the giant snarling face some designer gave it to terrify biologicals. The beam licks out.

But I am not new to this game. I have judged my air time and the ground well. I land behind a hillock as the beam raves over my head and blasts part of the hillock. Fragments of rock and super-heated trees flash through the air. A forest fire ignites instantly, just as I hoped.

I speed to the left, keeping below line-of-sight. My enemy has obligingly generated heat, smoke and flying debris that must degrade his sensors. Excellent. Between that and my own ECM, his odds of a hit are very poor at this range. Still, the beam is some form of positron weapon, very powerful. A few seconds exposure even at this distance and I will be slag.

I leap vertically in a spinning motion and fire additional ordnance at my enemy, now only five hundred meters away. Again my fire is ineffective, blocked by the massive greaves.

His return fire fares no better, trailing me by a good margin. Clearly my speed is too much for his targeting sensors.

I order the crab-robot trailing me to take to the road now that it has passed the rear of the refugee column. It speeds down the improved road – its guns and missiles ripple out in an extended volley. Both are heavier than my armament, but it is slower and less durable than I. I want to make sure that's it is not destroyed with its weapons unused.

The Destroyer reacts to this new threat by squatting. Its knees, like its forearms, have armor on them. Between arm and shin greaves it is well protected. From its shoulders, missiles ripple out in response. I order the crab to take evasive action, using its chain gun for defense. I leap upward to fire again, hoping to split the fire of our towering enemy. I use two of my remaining three HEAT rounds.

But my opponent shows skill now. He disregards my fire, though it costs him a hit from a HEAT round on his upper arm and AP hits on his top missile rack. In return, his fire brackets Crab 2. This slows the robot, which, unlike me, can only move in two dimensions. The Crab, impeded by the craters around it, is hit square by the beam. Crab 2 staggers then explodes.

Its sacrifice is not in vain, Crab 2 has bought time for its steel brothers to come down the opposite flank and into range. They open up with chain guns and missiles.

The Destroyer rises, beam and missiles flowing from it, but it staggers under the combined hits from the Crabs and I add in my last HEAT round. Crab 1 is singed by a beam hit and half its systems go off line. I order it to withdraw, firing as best it can.

The Destroyer begins to back away, toward the crest of the hill over which it had marched to the attack. I rejoice. Our enemy is retreating at the moment of his victory. All our heavy ordnance is expended. We have done no major damage, but the Destroyer has been made cautious at our unexpected display of ferocity. I order Crab 3 to move up and cover Crab 1 as it retreats. I consider whether to press the attack, but decide against it. I must cross too much open ground to come to grips with my enemy, now that it is clear my long-distance weaponry is useless. I have still not been able to access his systems with a viral attack and the high-speed maneuvers have caused me to heat up. It is manageable, but if I extend the engagement I risk overheating and losing maneuverability which would be certain destruction.

I turn my attention to the column. Crab 1 has limped up to the rear of the column reaching the rejoicing artillery crew, who should be properly amazed at their survival. Wrik and Olivia are still toward the front, urging the refugees onward. Each holds a LAW rocket. I am so glad they did not intervene.

The armored helmet of the Destroyer vanishes over the hillcrests. Now the terrain favors him. If we pursue we will be sky-lined. I am uncomfortable with this new found caution in me, but perhaps it is the most sensible course of action. Now I too retreat. We must get out of this valley before our enemy decides to reengage.

The stream of refugees reached the foot of the hill below the over-look where we'd begun our descent into the valley. We'd pulled up at a small rise which would protect us from direct fire. Olivia and I unlim-bered the LAWS rockets and hit the ground at the crest of the hill. I put three of the of the single-shot rocket launchers on the moist ground next to me and pulled out my field glasses. Olivia snapped down the bipod of her sniper rifle. She had the other two rocket launchers. I'd placed Pape in the mule's ring mount with the MG. All he had to do was hold down the butterfly trigger, for whatever little good it would do if the Destroyer came on. I doubted we'd last long enough for him to burn out the barrel.

The first refugees, the youngest and strongest, made it to us and collapsed. It was painful to urge the exhausted and traumatized survivors to continue down the other side, but Pape shouted himself hoarse doing so. "Help is just a little further," he yelled in Seddonese. "You've got to get out of the Valley!" People recognized his uniform and started moving.

We watched the battle, what we could see of it. Maauro was a tiny shape even at high magnification. The Destroyer was barely in the valley, still on the far slope. We were well out of range with our weapons and either the Destroyer was too busy with Maauro and the crabs, or it did not regard us as enough of a threat to merit long range fire.

"Mother of God," Olivia said, staring through her scope. "She's hitting it. Look!"

"Dammit," I added as one of the crab-robots exploded. A rain of rockets and chain gun fire from the others slammed into the Destroyer. I spotted Maauro in the air, firing furiously.

"Be careful," I shouted, knowing the foolishness of it.

But the great machine had enough of fighting its darting, tiny enemy. It headed back over the far ridge. Shouts and cheers momentarily drowned moans and screams. More refugees flooded toward us. Some actually turned back, seeking friends and loved ones lost, separated or abandoned in the smoking valley.

"Maauro drove it off, Wrik." Olivia said in disbelief. "God, she's everything you said she was. I saw it and I can't believe it."

"But she didn't hurt it much," I added. "What do we do if it comes back? We're down to one operational crab and a cripple. Most of their armament is used up." I looked at the tube of the LAW rocket in my hands. It seemed a ridiculous thing to oppose the Destroyer with.

"Pape," I shouted. He looked down from the mule's gun at me. "Are there combat engineers in that reinforcement column?"

He stared at me. "Combat Engineers…do you mean sappers?"

"Yes, he does," Olivia snapped, waving at the mob of refugees and ignoring complaints and pleas.

"Yes, surely there will be some."

"When they get here, get them to mining this pass with all they have. If we can bring down this ledge," I gestured to the broad ridge above us, "it shouldn't be able to climb all the loss earth and rock. Either it will have to dig its way through, or march around this range of hills."

"Nice," Olivia said. "Pretty good tactical sense for a flyboy." She turned to Pape. "Have a forward observer team set up so they can see this area, once we blow it, if the Destroyer starts digging we can call down arty on it."

He stared at her. "What?"

She grimaced. "Forgot you guys only developed radio recently, I'll explain about calling for indirect fire when they get here."

"Whatever you say," Pape said, staring at the flooding refugees. I knew he was looking for one face. I hoped to God he would find it.

I could see the refugees parting, some crying out in fear as the two crab-robots, one burned and with part of its upper works torn off, came up the road. Then I saw a welcome sight, Maauro running back toward us. She leapt into the creek between us and a cloud of steam immediately erupted. I knew she was dumping heat as quickly as she could. She emerged on our side, armspac slung across her back, looking none the worse for fighting a machine that outweighed her by nearly a hundred tons.

The refugees looked at her as she climbed out of the creek and easily jogged up to us. Most hadn't seen her fight the Destroyer at the far end of the Valley, or if they had seen her at all, it had been only as a tiny, speeding shape. They seemed to have fastened on the crab-robots as their saviors, patting the scorched machines as they passed them.

"Wrik," Maauro said, as she climbed over a guardrail. "We must expedite our retreat. I was unable to reach the Destroyer's systems by cyberattack. My physical attacks accomplished little more."

I explained my idea of creating a landslide.

She smiled, pleased as ever by my being clever. "Excellent. The enemy is big but needs solid ground."

"Then how they hell did he get through a swamp?" Olivia demanded.

"I would have to examine the area to be sure but several methods occur. It could have used debris or the forests to essentially build a corduroy road. Its nuclear reactor and that beam weapon may have been used to evaporate swamp-water, or it may have detected harder ground and simply picked its way across. Likely all three methods were used. But it determined that a flanking move was worthwhile. That implies two things, first that the enemy is not simply a mindless automata, and second, it does fear massed shellfire from the Seddonese and opted for a surprise attack."

Pape nodded. "We've never been able to concentrate enough guns on it. Either we didn't have enough, or they didn't last long enough to do any good."

"Olivia," I said. "You've got to teach them indirect fire by map and quickly."

She nodded.

Maauro turned toward Pape. "Your voice is almost gone from shouting. What do you wish me to say? I will have the crabs broadcast it over their speakers in an imitation of your voice."

He thought. "Have all military personnel report to me here. We've got to search the valley for wounded. Tell the civilians to keep moving down to the other side of the hill so we can get everyone away from here and blow the valley entrance.

"And," he hesitated, "tell Corra Pape and her family I am here."

Moments later, Pape's voice began blasting out of the crab-robots, startling everyone nearby but getting them moving.

Pape went over to the mule's radio, vastly superior to anything the Seddonese had but he was unable to reach the approaching Seddonese military for some reason and was reduced to sending a mounted rider ahead. The artillery piece, with its lucky crew, gained the ridge and were sited by Olivia. Maauro placed the crab-robots, still blasting their exhortations.

"Enso!" a woman's voice called Pape's first name.

Pape leaped from the mule looking about frantically. A Seddonese female and an older male, learning on each other, came toward us. Pape ran to meet them. "Corra! Father!"

Maauro and I were on his heels. Corra was crying, older man looked in shock. I supported him, while Pape threw his arms around Corra. It seemed that Seddonese processed pain the same way we did. She looked as grief-stricken as any human.

"Thank, God," Pape said, holding the sobbing woman.

I pulled the canteen I belatedly remembered I had and gave it to the older man, who looked at me numbly and said something in Seddonese.

He drank in deep swallows then seemed to focus on the world around him. He spoke again.

"He wants you to give the water to his daughter." Maauro said.

I handed it Pape who held it to Corra's lips. She too drank deeply then said something that drew a sound of anguish from her husband.

"Corra's mother is dead," Maauro translated. "They have not seen her brother. He was fighting with the Army. Many are dead."

I looked at my feet, then up. "Maauro, let's get Olivia and use the mule. Maybe we can help get some wounded out while we're waiting for the Army to show up."

She nodded decisively. We headed for the machine, leaving Pape to console his wife and father-in-law. Pape made as if to join us.

"No," I said. "Keep these people moving. Get those sappers working on blowing this pass. You have plenty to do here."

"Where will you be?" he asked.

"Rescuing anyone we can in the valley," I threw back over my shoulder. "Send stretcher parties as soon as you can."

CHAPTER 21

F I THOUGHT THE SCENE IN THE VALLEY A NIGHTMARE, than descending into it was a journey into the depths of Hell.

The beam fire had done tremendous damage. The trail all the way back to the valley entrance was lined with dead and dying. The injuries of some were horrendous, especially the burns. I quickly lost whatever I had eaten that day. Even Olivia became nauseated when one poor woman's arm came apart as we tried to lift her. The flesh had been cooked off. She died with a shriek I knew would wake me on many nights in the future. I sagged to the ground, retching.

Olivia staggered away, leaned against a tree and screamed "son of a bitch" in a voice that must have torn at her throat. She stood that way for a minute then came back to me, shook me by the shoulder. "Get up, flyboy. We got work." Hours passed in slow horror. The worst were the children, some dead, many beyond any medical help available on this world. After a while I stopped looking at faces.

A flood of Seddonese soldiers came into the valley, some of them cavalry and we gladly turned over this grim duty to them. I made my way back to the mule, fatigue narrowing my vision even more than the smoke from burning trees. We had been lucky in that much, the wet spring had kept the forest from entirely erupting in flames, but the area where Maauro and the crab-robots had fought the Destroyer was burning. I prayed there were no wounded burning to death helpless in those woods. We had no time to fight a forest fire.

Maauro, her face as grim and quiet as I had ever seen it, stopped me. "Wrik, many of these cannot be saved." She gestured at the moaning field of bodies awaiting transport out of the valley. "There's no medical technology present that can do it."

"I know." I stared at the suffering. A few vehicles and horse drawn ambulances were loading the injured. More would be coming, but so was evening.

Olivia paused next to me, her Confed fatigues matted with blood and worse, her eyes hollow. "What are you suggesting?"

"For those who cannot be saved, we...I...should ease their passing."

Olivia lowered her head, her hair hiding both eyes this time.

"We can't, Maauro," I said. "We don't know these people or their religions, we don't know how they would see such an act."

"Can it be viewed as anything other than a mercy?"

"Yes, it could."

"I do not understand, but I will defer to you in this."

CHAPTER 21

"Maauro," Olivia said, not looking up. "You can do more than their medicine can."

Maauro shook her head. "What I can manufacture in myself is utterly inadequate to the need. I could do surgery, but I must prepare myself and the crabs for another battle."

"Perhaps," Olivia said, "perhaps just a few of the children..."

"All beings are networked to those that value them," she replied. "How should I choose the few that I might be able to save? Olivia, you of all people, must understand military necessity. The fastest way to stop the dying is to win the war. I cannot be diverted into palliative measures."

"Yeah," Olivia said.

"She's right," I added.

Olivia glared at me from her human eye. "I said, yes."

"Wrik, Olivia," Maauro added. "Do not take out your anger on each other. You both did well—"

"I did fuck-all," Olivia snapped. "If only I'd had a Tiger VII tank, or a tac nuke. I'd have fried its ass."

"Maybe," I said. "It might be a good idea for you to get the spare radio sets out of the mule, find someone with more brain than braid, and get them up on the prospect of lobbing shells at this thing from long distance and behind cover. I don't care if you have to pound a general's head into a breech, but explain to these guys how to use indirect artillery fire and radio. If the artillery can stay alive, maybe we can slow this thing up.

"Get an aid-station set up at the base of the hill. If they don't know med-evac and triage, teach them quickly."

"All right," she said. "The whole Marine handbook in fifteen minutes and in a combat zone. Anything else?"

"Tell them to abandon anything on this side of the river. They should have the bridges ready to blow. I don't think the Destroyer can swim."

"Yeah, I'll do that. If you hear banging, that will be me slamming some brass hat into a tree." She stalked off.

We loaded the mule with two more wounded who might live and ran it back up to the valley exit.

Seddonese military had finally arrived in force, aiding the exodus of the suffering. A military hospital was set up on the far side of the pass. Pape had set the sappers to work on the ridge above. Olivia grabbed the first senior officer she saw and began a crash course in modern fire control.

After we unloaded the wounded at the field hospital, we returned to the overlook where we'd left the crab-robots and Seddonese field pieces on guard. I got some water and sat, exhausted, by the stone wall guarding the drop off. Maauro and I surveyed the valley below, occupied now only by the dead, the undiscovered wounded and the cavalry searching for them. The sun was setting behind the hills to the west. I had only enough energy left to wonder what would happen if the Destroyer attacked in the darkness.

"God," I finally said, "I would never have believed it, if I hadn't seen it with my own eyes."

"Indeed," Maauro said, sitting next to me, "but I cannot understand why someone would build such machines. Formidable as it doubtless is, the weight and power requirements would seem tactically—"

"Don't think tactics," I said. "Think terror. That thing was designed to spread fear and panic. It's a bad dream come to mechanical life. They doubtless used smaller machines or better-designed ones against the native military. These things were created to terrorize civilians."

"Your analysis is sensible given what we know. Did you find it frightening?"

"Hell, yes," I muttered. "I'll see that monster in dreams from now on."

"Further proof of your thought that it is a terror weapon."

"Well, we've seen it now. Did you gather any useful data?'

"It has complex reactive and multi-layered armor, energy and projectile weapons. It is shielded, but clearly nuclear powered. I do not believe the Destroyer is functioning at its higher levels of awareness. Tactics were very basic. That may be because of its ingestion of the untrained Maximillian into its systems. I have estimated weight and probable maximum speed over ground from the way it moves."

"Why Maximillian?" I wondered as I slowly stood, dusting myself off. The temperature was dropping rapidly in the moist air.

"He is the product of several lines of Engineered humans, most notably Shasti Rainhell, whose capabilities have never been completely understood. Yet we know her genetic code was so strong that even the Evolvers could not convert her to their use. Perhaps something in that code triggered the robot, some analogue with its original creators. While it is possible that it could have used any being caught inside it when it reactivated, I think that unlikely. Maximillian was very unfortunate to have been present."

"Do you think the poor bastard is aware in that thing?" I said as I stared at the returning cavalry leaving the miserable valley with the fading of the light.

"I do not know, but share your fear for him. If aware, it seems Maximillian is unable to control its imperative to destroy all life it encounters on this world, unless he has been driven mad as well. We have seen such things before."

I remembered a space station where the Guild had recreated an Infestor brain and the horrors that had overwhelmed the crew until we destroyed it.

Maauro seemed to divine my thoughts. "We may have to face the prospect that Maximillian cannot be recovered, as with those

CHAPTER 21

contaminated by the Infestors, there may not be enough of his original persona for him to survive, even if we could somehow free him."

"Do you really want to report to Shasti Rainhell that we found her grandchild and then had to kill him? I don't fear much in your company, but Rainhell would make the top of that list."

"A formidable woman with a long tally of dead enemies," Maauro agreed. "Not to be casually undertaken as an enemy. Nor do I wish to be the death of a young being whose only crime may have been curiosity. Yet, we may have no choice if we want to save the remaining people of this world and ourselves."

I sighed. "It seems we are not fated for easy days."

"I was not made for easy days," she replied. "Perhaps this will change some day and I will want to turn my back on what we do. Maybe I will change and come to value peace, at least peace for me. Violence and terror will continue. I will just no longer be a part of it."

She tilted her head to look up at me. "And what of you, Wrik? You could have remained on Star Central and had easier days than these."

"I don't know, Maauro," I said, as we started back toward the mule. I sealed my coat against the evening wind. "Now that I'm here, all I can think of is getting home alive, back to Jaelle, to warmth and light. I wonder why in God's name I came. But it's equally true that I was restless back at Star Central, that I knew I wanted to do this, that it gave me a purpose and a direction."

The wind slapped at me as if mocking my conceits.

"We're here now," I concluded. "All we can do is our best."

"Yes," she replied. "Let us get back to the others."

Olivia declined a ride in the mule. We left her nose-to-nose with some Seddonese officers wearing artillery badges. Pape was nowhere to be found, doubtless off with what remained of his family. Maauro and I put three wounded and an attendant in the back of the mule. A dull rumble made us turn around. Above, we saw the ridge shake and then tumble into the cleft of road that we'd sped down earlier. The way was now closed and I felt less fear about the Destroyer catching the extended column of Seddonese on this side of the river.

As the pall of smoke and dust spiraled up into the afterglow we headed back for the city, rolling alongside the column of refugees and military until we came to the defended bridges. We passed over and returned to *Stardust* after discharging our wounded.

I found Dusko working on the *Sinner II's* engine. He looked me over, shook his head and said there was food in the galley to microwave. The mere thought made my stomach clench. Maauro went into the hold to hook up her powertap to the engines to restore herself and then commence repair work on the crabs. I fell face down on my bunk. I was lucky. I slept for five hours before waking up screaming.

CHAPTER 22

FOUND OLIVIA IN THE MORNING, FACE DOWN ON HER BUNK in her underwear. I grabbed her clothes, which stank as badly as my own had and threw everything in the laundry hoping the machines could get the smell of burnt flesh off them. I tried to face breakfast, but could only manage a bagel and coffee.

A noise made me turn. Dusko walked in with his usual witch's brew of Dua-Denlenn coffee. "The *Sinner's* engine is fixed."

"Good," I said.

"It was bad out there?"

"I don't even have words."

He nodded. "Should I fix something for Olivia?"

"I don't know. She's got an iron stomach but...I'd wait."

"Maauro didn't kill the thing."

"No. She slapped it around some. Made it cautious. But, well, you saw the crabs."

"Yeah she's outside working on Number 1 now, trying to get it into some sort of fighting order. She's got Number 3 reloaded, sent it down to the riverside. Told me to tell you that the Seddonese are pulling everything back across the river and getting the bridges ready to blow."

"Good."

"Will that work?"

"Maybe. It came through the swamp and that was supposed to be impossible. If it is obliging enough to be on a bridge while we blow it..."

He sipped his drink. "I don't want to be the one to say it aloud, but it looks like you are going to make me."

I leaned back and looked up.

"Has the time come to head back for the Confederacy? Run and get help?"

I wiped a hand across my eyes.

"I know you don't think much of me—" Dusko began.

"No. That's not it," I said. "I've been wondering the same thing. I couldn't say it aloud because I've had too much experience with cutting and running. I'm sure the others have thought about it too, particularly Maauro. She's too logical not to."

"Well?" Dusko pursued.

"It could come to it. Thing is, would anybody be alive when we got back?"

"Some would."

"And how many not?"

"If we fight and lose here, it will be more. Maybe all."

"Yeah," I said. I finished my coffee. "We're not ready to give up on Maximillian until Maauro gives up. Then it's a question of, can we destroy it? If we lose, I want to preserve *Stardust* for whoever is left, most likely you, to go for help."

"Me?" The Dua-Denlenn's face was a study in surprise.

"Olivia can fly the *Sinner,* but not the *Stardust.* If the thing gets Maauro, then it will have gotten me too—"

"She won't like the sound of that."

"You won't repeat it."

After a second, he nodded.

"I'm not looking for death," I said, "but it will be she and I trying for Maximillian. We'll likely live or die together."

"She won't permit it."

"I told her once and I'll repeat it now, I can't be preserved just to be preserved. If my life has any meaning, I have to...well I have to face things. No running away. Not again, ever."

He shrugged. "I wasn't arguing."

"Anyway, you have the best chance of surviving. If Maauro and I are gone, it will fall to Olivia to use the *Sinner* and the crabs. If that fails, grab the surviving kids from the expedition and get back to Star Central. Come back with Rainhell and enough firepower to do the job."

"OK," he said and turned to leave, then stopped. "You've changed."

I put down the coffee mug. "Yeah. You too."

"Not so much, Human."

"Enough."

"People who knew us from before would laugh."

"Sure would."

He nodded and ducked out the hatchway.

I found enough appetite to have some more breakfast. Olivia came in an hour later. Looking at her, hair perfect, cleaned up, even her ship coverall creased and immaculate, it was hard to credit yesterday's filth and death. Maybe it was just her way of dealing with it.

"Dusko said he'd rustle you up something," I offered.

"Yeah," she replied. "Ran into him. Told him to hold it for dinner. Nothing will taste good this morning. Toast and coffee, maybe juice that's all."

"Sit," I said. "I can manage that much." It took only a few minutes.

I slid the plate and mug in front of her and then followed with juice. She gave a wan smile. "Not the first time," she began. "But the first time with so many civvies."

I nodded. "Same for me."

"God," she said.

"I always wonder where he is at moments like that." I poured more coffee for myself. "The priests never seem to have a good answer for that one."

"What the hell do we do now?"

"Depends on Maauro," I said. "We can't blast the thing down. Even if you can get the Seddonese military to work out indirect fire, I don't know that they have any weapons big enough to do the job. Maybe with a lot of massed guns…"

"Be tough," she said. "I think a lot will depend on how many missiles that thing has in it. It had to have used about twenty in this engagement. It's not Maauro, surely it can't be making them? But if it has any missiles, well it's a good battle computer, it will counter-battery anything the Seddonese fire at it. Missiles airbursting over their artillery will make short work of them, game over again."

I relayed some of what Dusko and I had said. Olivia gave a bitter laugh. "Great plan. So after Maauro, you and I are killed, he runs for help? Nice of him to volunteer. Bastard."

"Not his fault," I said. "If you could fly *Stardust,* I'd put him in the *Sinner.*"

"Nah," she said. "He wouldn't press the attack like I will. Dusko's too much about Dusko."

"I'm going to check in with Maauro," I said.

"I'll check in the Seddonese high command in a bit. If General Romus will back me up, I can get these artillery guys to follow my lead. I can't blame them for being confused by adding a new doctrine in wartime, but the side that adapts wins. The others die."

I smiled "Cheerful as always."

That drew a real laugh out of her. "Let me know if the Princess of Death comes up with something new. I want to see her put that thing's head on a wall."

"I'll do it." I dropped the dishes in the machine and headed out.

CHAPTER 23

A STAFF CAR PULLED UP AS I CLIMBED DOWN THE LADder to the ground. Pape got out of the ornate vehicle and walked over to us. His usual energy was absent today and his face had a haunted look. He walked up to where Maauro and I were working on crab 3 in the shadow of the *Stardust*. We hadn't seen the young special forces operative since the evening before in the valley. I doubted he'd slept any more than we had.

"Hey Enso," I said, putting aside my tools and welding mask. "I'm sorry about your mother." I stuck out my hand.

He took it firmly. "I have you and Maauro to thank that I didn't lose everything." He looked at her seated up on the crab, where she'd been welding with the plasma torch in her right hand. "Thank you, Maauro. If there is anything I can ever do for you, just tell me."

She looked at him for a second. "I am pleased to have you as a new member of my network."

He looked at me.

I smiled. "That means you're officially a friend now."

He faced her and bowed. "I'm honored."

"Any word on your brother-in-law?" I asked.

Enso nodded, relief on his face. "He's alive though pretty badly banged up. What was left of his unit took the long way around. They made it to the river in the early morning hours. A lot of people did. We're keeping the bridges up in the hope more will, or that we can catch the thing on one."

"Good," I said.

"I do not believe the Destroyer will try to cross a bridge that is mined," Maauro said while adjusting the 20mm gun on the crab. "It has decent sensors. But if it tries to come across, it will do so very quickly. The Engineers must be alert at all times, especially at night."

Pape nodded solemnly. "They know it. They have triple wired everything. There are even men ready to run out and set them off manually if nothing else works, even knowing they will go up with the bridges."

"Any word on the Destroyer?" I asked.

"We still have scouts on the other side of the river. They haven't seen anything yet. Since the sappers closed the pass with the landslide, either it's still digging through or going around. Either way, we should have today, maybe tomorrow. Assuming it comes on. Maauro seemed to have given it something to think about."

Maauro shook her glossy black hair, the afternoon light bounced off it. "It will have analyzed the battle by now and realized our firepower is inadequate to penetrate its armor at normal combat ranges. My hope is that it did not realize I was sending waves of virus at it—"

"Virus?" Pape asked.

"Computerized instruction by radio for it to obey me," she amended. "It simply did not receive them, or they came through as gibberish. But I have gathered some information from its attempts to target me with sensors. I believe that in a second attack I will be more successful. Plus, I plan to attack at close-range where my speed and plasma torch may be decisive."

"Close range!" Pape said. The expression on his face could only be described as appalled. "It's more than a hundred times your size."

"Size is only one factor," Maauro said, waving a finger at him. "Bigger is not always better."

He simply stared.

"I don't like the odds that much either," I said, "which is why I will be there with her when we fight next."

Maauro put her tools back in her toolbox. "We have not discussed this."

"Because we don't need to. You'll need my help."

"A fragile bag of fluids and meat?" she snapped. "What help could you be?"

"What help could I have been at the Artifact?" I said, outraged, "or are you forgetting whose plan it was to tip it out of space? Who saved your butt on the asteroid?"

Maauro hopped down from atop the crab. "That was different. I malfunctioned."

"I think outside the box."

"You come with me and I won't be able to find enough of you to put in a box!" Maauro was standing a foot away, glaring up at me.

"Now, now," Pape said, raising his hands,

We looked at each other, then at him, then at each other.

"Oh, Wrik," Maauro said, "we're having a fight."

Pape burst out laughing. We glared at him, after a few seconds he managed to stop, wiping his eyes.

"Maauro," he managed. "I don't know much about you Galactics, but I don't believe you're going to leave him behind without chaining him up."

"Don't give her ideas," I muttered.

He looked up at the ship. "Is Olivia awake? I wanted to take her down to the general staff. We are trying to reorganize our surviving artillery to be more effective. The general staff listened to her but so much of what she said is so new…we need her."

"I left her in the galley," I said. "Go up to the hatch, turn right. You'll see her.

He nodded and smiled, walking off with a wave.

CHAPTER 23

Maauro and I returned to hooking up the replacement fire-control module in the crab.

An idea hit me as we worked and I turned back to Maauro. "Is there any way you could tinker together some simple form of airbot to send across the river to check on the Destroyer?"

She handed me the tool I needed before I asked for it. "I could modify a jetpack with a remote and a camera. It would do little more than pick up its location."

"That would be enough. How long to design it?"

She smiled at me. "Already done. You forget my brain is segmentable. Most of it is occupied analyzing the battle with the Destroyer and preparing viral attacks. It took only a moment to design so simple a device. It will take about twenty minutes to make it."

I crossed my arms. "How much of your brain do you use to talk to me?"

"Wouldn't you be happier not knowing?" she asked, then closed a panel on the crab with a snick and tossed the tool in her bag.

I sighed. "Probably."

Twenty minutes later we had the device. Maauro and I drove down to the river. The city on the other side of the bridges had never been completely settled and other than scouts and the occasional refugee, was now abandoned. On its far side, somewhere, was the Destroyer. We stepped out of the mule. Seddonese soldiers lined trenches on either side of the bridge and watched us curiously. Maauro quickly fixed wings on the modified jetbelt.

"Without having to lift the weight of a human it should have decent enough range and endurance for our purpose," she said. "I can segment enough brain power to fly it remotely and use thermals to increase its endurance."

I nodded.

Maauro sprinted forward, accelerating to easily 60 kph, to cries of astonishment from the soldiers. She threw the winged belt with its cargo of camera and servos. The little engine lit and the jetbelt spiraled into the sky.

"Let us go to the command post," she said. "They will want to see this intelligence."

We rode back to the CP. Given how primitive Seddonese radios were, it stood close to the river bank, connected to outposts by more reliable communications wire and field phones. Olivia had used up our supply of spare radios on the Seddonese military and put the survivors of Bexlaw's team on making more.

We walked into the CP, set up in what had been a school auditorium in the small town on this side of the river, to find Olivia talking to twenty high-ranking officers as she tried to update a 19th century military into something that might impede their robotic enemy. I told Olivia about the airbot.

"How will we see what it sees?" Romus asked.

Maauro's eyes glimmered and suddenly there was a holographic image of the city on the far side of the river. The collected officers gasped at the image, which was crisp and clear despite the daylight in the room.

"This projection," she said, "is in real-time. I can zoom in on targets on the ground as needed. We will proceed to the valley to see if our enemy is located there."

The room remained silent as the refurbished jetbelt with its camera zipped westward. In only a few minutes it reached the site of the massacre.

"No sign that it tried to dig through what the sappers did," Olivia said.

I turned to Pape. "Which is the shortest way around the mountains?"

He rubbed his face. "South is shorter but again it is swampier that way. North there are low rolling hills."

"North then," Maauro decided. She looked at Pape. "Is it possible that it could try to cross at some other location than here?"

"Not for sixty miles," Enso said. "There are cliffs on this side of the river. Above that, it could ford anywhere though. We have forces at each of those crossings to warn us if it tries to."

"I think it unlikely it will do so," Maauro said. "That would give us several days respite and it surely realizes that wherever it can go, I can get their faster. I believe it will come on directly trying to draw me into direct battle again as well as to engage large elements of your forces which it has destroyed with impunity before. Also if it appears on this side of the river we can withdraw across the bridges into the city, thus no advantage gained by circling us."

"So it will come around the hills and then enter the city," Romus said.

Maauro's reply was cut off when, at the edge of the hologram, the Destroyer stumped into view. The monstrous machine was walking northward, it ponderous steps eating up the ground. The Seddonese sat paralyzed, like mice before a snake. I realized that they had never before had a means of seeing their enemy live, in motion, without death swinging at them.

As it now swung at the airbot. The giant head turned.

"Maauro, dodge," Olivia yelled.

"The airbot is evading at its maximum capability," Maauro countered calmly, "I am compensating for the evasive action so the images remain stable."

The beam lanced from the Destroyer's head and everyone but Maauro ducked. The hologram vanished.

"Unfortunate," Maauro said. "I was maneuvering nape of the earth behind a hill. It simply fired through the hill, the debris cloud got our scanner. No matter. We know it went north. It will not be able to reach the city before sunrise tomorrow. We must engage it then."

CHAPTER 24

OUR LAST NIGHT, IF IT WAS TO BE THAT, WOULD BE SPENT in comfort. We were billeted in what had been an apartment in a reclaimed town north of the river. It had electric lights and running water and was not threatened by any of the vast towers that made up the ancient city to the south across the river. No matter how good the Seddonese had been as builders, I did not fancy sleeping under an eight-hundred year-old tower that hadn't been maintained.

We ate in the officer's mess, a busy, if subdued, place filled with officers coming and going. Attendants in formal dress quietly served us. We had a table in a corner, guarded by Pape's personal attendant. The food was good.

"Rest, Wrik, Olivia," Maauro said after dinner. "I will do final checks on all our equipment. Dusko, please follow me." The Dua-Denlenn rose. He never questioned Maauro's orders though I wondered what she needed him for.

Olivia looked at the slender android's departing back, then she turned to me. "Big day tomorrow."

"Yes."

"Possibly the last day for some, or all of us. If you don't get that monster, Dusko, I and what's left of their military will have to try for it."

"I'll wish you luck now," I said, looking out the window at the westering sun. It was early spring and the night would likely be cold. Too many of the trees hadn't leafed out yet and the landscape still looked barren to me. "If you go into action that means we failed. I doubt we'll be coming back if we do."

"Anyone you want me to tell if that's the case?" Olivia said in an even tone.

I looked down at my dinner. "There's a letter to Jaelle in my cabin on *Stardust*. That's all."

"I don't know much about you, Wrik, but I doubt that's all the people in your life."

"It's all the people in Wrik Trigardt's life," I said, coming as close as I ever had to acknowledging to anyone but Maauro that this wasn't my real name. "There was another life before, but that person was already dead and buried. So, no. There is no one else to tell anything to."

Olivia's face was pensive. "If you live, you should do something about that."

"If I live, I may."

"You know the humans here make a pretty decent bottle of liquor," she added.

CHAPTER 24

I shook my head. "Mission in the morning."

"It's long hours till morning," she said. "Come with me."

I followed Olivia out of the ad hoc mess hall. We went up to the next floor past the guards who were assigned to us VIPS, perhaps to make sure we didn't bug out and flee for the Confederacy.

Olivia opened the door to her room and waved me in. I followed. The setting sun had warmed it up and the room was pleasant. The futon-like bed sat in the middle. Olivia went over to a table and picked up a bottle and two tumblers. She poured for us both. The drink was good but I did little more than moisten my lips with it. Olivia took a solid draw.

"You picked a curious time to embrace moderation," she said.

"I've drank enough for one lifetime already, I suspect." I said, taking another small sip. "This is good. But maybe less good then a last sunset, a last view of stars—"

"A last night," she interrupted, "with another human being?" She gave me a frank look, downed her drink and stood, sliding her jacket off, then her shirt.

She wore a dark bra under it, contrasting with the paleness of her skin, with its faint suggestion of honey. Olivia waited.

I put the drink aside and walked up to her and took her in my arms. She was only a little shorter and barely had to tip her head back for me to kiss her.

The taste of her burned on my lips in a way that made my senses swim. I was a little shocked at what moved me and made me grasp her tight. There was rightness to our mouths on each other, to the taste of her lips and her tongue against mine.

I reached for the strap of her bra and unhooked it, freeing her firm breasts. She pulled my shirt off me and we tumbled onto the futon, shedding clothes. Olivia's body, limmed by the sunlight, was a taut as a bowstring and I ran my hands over the smooth sleekness of her. Her breasts were soft against my face with the nipples quickening to my tongue.

She wrapped her hand around my hardness and grinned. "Good, hard and long, just as I like it." Olivia ran her tongue over my body, causing me to arch, but she slowed us down, kissing and teasing.

"I do like it on top," she said after a few minutes, when it was obvious we couldn't hold off any longer. She pushed me onto my back, slid over me and lowered herself onto me, her sleek strong thighs holding me close. Olivia groaned with the pleasure of penetration and I tried to feel every sense of her: the scent of her body, the silkiness of her hair in my hand, the bounciness of the breast in my other hand. Her mouth tasted like wine.

Sex had always been fun but this time there was something new. As we built toward a climax with each other I realized how we'd been made for each other by nature, male and female of the same species. I hadn't felt this before with my first fumblings with girls on Retief in my teens, or the rare pros I'd been with in spaceports. Even with Jaelle, who had made sex and exploring each other a fun and guiltless game, there had not been this sense of fitting together so perfectly. I finally could hold back no longer and climaxed inside her, holding her close and saying her name over and over.

She too was breathing hard and held me as tight as I did her. "God," she finally said. "Worth waiting for."

I flopped back on the bed, my hands still stroking her. "I thought—"

"Too much, as usual," but she smiled to take the sting out. "I liked you from when we first met. This tonight, is just us tonight. We may both be dead tomorrow. If we aren't… well, we will see. But we have tonight and that will be enough for now."

I nodded. Now wasn't the time for complications, or even for guilt. For all I knew Jaelle was in another life as well. My time with her seemed dreamlike in a way, but I ruthlessly shut the door on that thought.

"If that letter has to get delivered," Olivia said. "I'll have Dusko do it."

I nodded.

"You're still hard," she said, rocking her hips to make sure that I stayed that way. "Maybe you'd like to be on top this time."

We made love again, more slowly and again I had this feeling as I rode her body that I was on the edge of knowing something… what I didn't know… but some great truth. Or maybe it was lust, pheromones, fear and delusion. The sense of being one with some truth departed on the wings of the second climax.

This time Olivia brought me a drink and refilled her own. I was face down and she sat on me so she could dig her strong hands in my back, massaging muscles I hadn't known were tense. I don't know when I fell asleep, I wasn't aware of the transition but Olivia was gently shaking my shoulder.

"Wrik," she whispered. "It's 0100; I let you sleep as long as I could."

I rolled up, a bit muzzy and looked at her as if I could freeze her sleep-tousled hair in my mind.

"Come on," she said, "showers big enough for two and there'll be plenty of hot water at this time."

Neither of us felt much like talking. We just enjoyed the sluicing of hot water over our bodies. I watched how it ran down her body, envying it the journey. We slipped next door to my room so I could grab fresh clothes. People were moving about; no military encampment is ever still.

I closed the door to my room as she did hers and we looked at each other.

"It was good," Olivia said, "it had been way too long for me. If I have to go today, that's what I wanted to take with me."

I nodded, tongue-tied and unable to match her frankness. "Thank you." I finally managed. "I'd never quite… it hadn't been like…"

She smiled a gentle smile I hadn't seen before. "This moment is just for us. Whatever comes or doesn't come after today, let's be sure we both keep this memory somewhere safe."

I nodded, wishing I could somehow express myself better, but Olivia started forward and I followed her.

Wrik and Olivia appear at the command trailer. Dusko is still with the Sinner *making adjustments on the balky engine. Pape and the general staff have huddled over a table looking down at maps by an electric light powered by a noisy generator outside. I am aware of more troops moving down to the river and the steady stream of refugees fleeing north. Children cry in the distance, upset at the cold and the early hours.*

I notice how close Wrik and Olivia stand. That and the way they look at each other suggest to me that there relationship has reached a sexual stage, a common biological reaction to the nearness of death. I wonder what it will entail for our future, if we have one, then dismiss the thought. We will be occupied enough this day.

I wave Wrik over. He comes and places a hand on my shoulder, his usual wan smile on his face. "Good morning, Maauro."

"Good morning, Wrik. I have something for you." I hand Wrik a pill. "This is a refined version of the mental communication web we used on Cimer. It will not last as long, nor have the range, which is safer for you. I am reluctant to use these save for short periods and with as much time between exposures as is possible. Still it will be safer than using radio communications near the Destroyer."

He nods, as always trusting my judgment.

"It will deploy almost immediately in your body proceeding to the same implant site as before," I assure him.

"What about the others?"

I shake my head. "Dusko finds communicating with these painful, both physically and emotionally. As for Olivia, she is not Jaelle. While she serves with us, she is essentially networked to Candace, not us."

"You don't trust her?"

"I do, but only to a certain point."

He nods. I do not mention that I am reluctant to allow Olivia access to my mind in any event. I remember how much leaked across from Jaelle, how I experienced the sensuality and sexuality of her biological body along with her emotions. I am not sure that I wish to share this experience with Olivia.

Beyond that I do not know how much will cross back. Jaelle did not mention it, and I suspect that she kept anything she learned of me to herself. I know that Wrik only felt what I sent to him. It is possible that, because I think of myself as female, the wavelength between me and other females is clearer. I only know that the mind link is difficult to predict.

"I also have this for you," I hand him a packet of clothes.

"It looks like my normal ship clothes?" he says.

"They are based on them. These are specially made to diffuse your heat signature and render you as opaque to sensory attention as is possible, essentially an electronic cloak. You should have the biological signature of a small animal with these."

"Good," he replies. "I feel like a small animal, about mouse-sized."

We attend the briefing with the senior staff; this is only a form of ritual for me. All details of the plan are in my memory. Still the biologicals feel the need to rehearse and rehearse. General Romus goes over the details. Olivia will take us to the main bridge across the river where the Seddonese military is dug in, prepared, with the river before them, to make a stand. If Wrik and I are not successful, they'll have to. Olivia and Dusko will use the Sinner II *and the remaining crab-robots to try and bring down the Destroyer. He wishes us luck and the staff scatters to their various commands.*

Enso Pape stops Wrik to say goodbye. With him is his wife Corra, the small Seddonese female. He and Wrik have become friends since the valley battle. The fact that the other man is in a successful relationship with an alien obviously compels his attention.

Olivia, I notice, spotted the three of them and decided to slip out the back of the trailer. I have noted that she avoids emotional displays if she can. Whatever passed earlier in the evening is compartmented away for now, with a battle looming. It strikes me as ironic that she and I share this characteristic.

"Wrik," a voice calls me out of my brooding thoughts. I turn to see Enso Pape and his wife Corra, no longer the hollow-eyed, exhausted refugee, but dressed in simple, clean clothes that flatter her slender figure. Unlike most, her eyes are not purple but golden with small black pupils.

Enso smiles at me. "We didn't have time for proper introductions before, but you remember my wife, Corra."

"Of course, I'm glad to see you again."

"As I am," she says. "I did not have a chance to thank either of you for saving us in that valley." A shadow slips over her attractive face at the memory.

I smiled at her, figuring she was used to human smiles. "We were glad we could help."

"And today you will again risk your life for us," she added. "We will be in your debt forever if you can stop the Destroyer."

A sense of another familiar presence came over me and I realized that the telepathic link with Maauro had become active. I sent her the message to come over. She walked up to us. "Here is the person who really saved you."

"Maauro," I added. "You know Corra, Enso's wife."

"Yes. I am pleased you survived," Maauro said, offering her hand, an unusual gesture for her. Corra, to her credit, didn't hesitate to take it.

"I saw you," Corra said, her voice awed. "Leaping through the trees, dodging the terrible beam and missiles, firing back, it was…I lack the words. You are no bigger than I, yet you fought the Destroyer and made it back away, something our combined military had not been able to do. It's like you descended from Heaven to protect us."

Maauro gave a shy smile. "I cannot claim any connection with heaven. My Creators made me for war. It appears to be my chief talent."

"I want to thank you," Corra said. "All of you, for all my people. We have had no hope until you arrived."

"We will do our best," Maauro promised.

Corra reached forward and hugged Maauro, then me. Enso looked a bit embarrassed. "I wish I was coming with you."

"And I wish I was going alone," Maauro said, looking at me.

I shook my head decisively. "I'm with you and that's that."

"Looks like we both have stubborn ones," Corra said to Maauro.

Her comment landed right on the axis of several huge questions and stopped any argument in its tracks.

Enso thumped me on the back. "See you for chow in the evening. The food will be crap."

I laughed. "Great. Something to live for."

He stuck a hand out to Maauro, who shook it.

Behind us the mule, driven by Olivia, pulled up. She tapped her com.

"Time to go," Maauro said. We left the command trailer and hopped into the mule. Olivia pulled away without comment, her eyes on the road. It was only a few minute's drive from the command post to the trenches around the last bridge.

We pull up next to a brace of artillery pieces. The bridge before us was an immense structure dating from before the Great War. It had been maintained and rebuilt by the revitalized Seddonese, but they could not have put the structure up. The smaller bridges were of recent make and more easily replaced. This gargantuan structure would be impossible to replace, so the thin hope of victory and the possibility of more escapees coming up from the south had preserved it. But Engineers had wired enough explosive to drop a span of the causeway on this side, greater than the Destroyer could step across.

We stepped out of the mule. Olivia joined us in contemplation of the giant bridge. The sky was cloudy and the city unlit. The whole scene presented a ghostly aspect.

"I'm not big on goodbyes," Olivia said. "You call and I'll be over the river as soon as Dusko can drop me in."

I nodded, unable to come up with anything to say.

Olivia stepped up and kissed me on the lips. She turned to Maauro and stuck out a hand. "Good luck. If anyone can do this. It's you."

Maauro shook Olivia's hand. "I will do my best."

Olivia slipped behind the mule's wheel and headed back to the command post.

CHAPTER 25

MAAURO AND I FACED THE VAST BRIDGE OVER THE DARK, racing water. I hoped the combat engineers were careful with their safeties. Beyond lay Palmat, as it had been called by the thousands of pioneers who'd moved into its vast towers and skyways, before the evacuation pulled them out. These buildings had not been touched in the original war and civilization had collapsed more slowly and less severely here.

We started forward at a brisk walk, weapons ready for all that our enemy was nowhere near. Yet Seddon had held too many unpleasant surprises already. I had the feeling of being a child sneaking into somewhere we shouldn't be. The wind rustled about us, the river waters rolled under us, stars blinked down from above. Our boots made little sound on the roadway surface. The original surface was smooth but cracks and patches marred its finish. Here and there a metal patch covered greater damage.

The whole scene seemed surreal and I felt that sense of distance creep in, as if I was dreaming.

Focus, I said to myself.

"Are you all right, Wrik?" Maauro asked.

"Yeah," I said, licking my lips and suddenly thirsty.

"That thought was so strong that you projected it at me across the link," she said with an apologetic air.

"Sorry," I said. "Just feeling a little, I don't know, disconnected from reality." I hefted my weapon, its weight, the smell of lubricants and metal should have persuaded me of dire truth.

"Does that ever happen to you?" I asked impulsively, my eyes scanning the far shore. We were coming up on the area where the causeway became a suspension bridge. Good, I'd feel less exposed.

"I don't think so, Wrik. I am not sure I really understand the question, but to the extent I do, probably not. Such a state would probably indicate extreme damage to something like me."

"Someone like you," I corrected automatically.

Maauro turned her head and gave me that smile she reserved for special moments between us.

"Whatever happens," I added. "I want you to take care of yourself. You owe me that."

"And whatever happens," she returned, her face gone dead serious, "I want you to not expose yourself unless I call for you. You cannot help me if it comes to open battle with the Destroyer. If my cyber-attacks and physical attacks fail, do not intervene. Promise me this."

"I promise," I said. On the side opposite her, I crossed my fingers in a childish gesture and hoped none of what I was thinking made it across the link to her.

She nodded, then after a moment's hesitation said. "I am glad that you had time with Olivia before this."

I was startled by the change in topic. "You took Dusko with you to leave us alone together?"

"Yes. If this ends in failure, it seemed fitting that your last night should be with one of your own kind."

We walked on for a few more steps around a mound of rusted metal that might have been a car once.

"Maauro."

"Yes?"

"If this is my last night, then I am spending it as I want to, by your side."

It was her turn to walk on silently for a bit.

"Thank you, Wrik," came across the link.

We walked side by side into the dead city, shoulders almost touching.

Once across the bridge, we climbed steadily up the lower levels of the aerial roads until we were fifty meters off the ground. Though these were often filled with debris falling from the greater heights, they ran through the whole city and would keep us above the level of our enemy, yet not so far that it would be difficult to engage it.

At points, Maauro had me hop on her back and she sped along the better-preserved highways so we could cover more ground than with me on foot. I felt slightly ridiculous riding on her, my leg wrapped around her tiny waist, but couldn't argue with the speed she made even over debris-choked roads.

After an hour the sun broke through the clouds, partially dispelling the gloom and rain of the last few days. The city heights had a washed clean look, but many of the streets below were a noisome mess of mud and standing ponds. I was glad we were well above that level and whatever animal life laired in the shadows of the ground level.

Maauro pulled up and I slid off her back. Her armspac had been webbed to her chest and she quickly freed it from the webbing.

I took the safety off my triple-auto-carbine. "What?" I whispered.

"Vibration and noise," she said, "from a heavy tread. Our enemy is ahead at least several kilometers."

I looked ahead. The elevated highway we stood on ran straight for several hundred meters, then curved out of sight between towering buildings. We were in a heavily built-up area of the city. Tall buildings surrounded us, multiple highways crisscrossed above and below us. Sunlight refracted off buildings, but the sun was still low and long shadows lay in the heart of the city. I licked my lips and flicked the safety off my weapon.

"Wait or move in?" I asked.

"Move in," Maauro said. "I cannot predict its pattern."

We moved forward. I consciously switched to the telepathic channel between us. Who knew how good the sensors were in the Destroyer?

"Our friend doesn't seem to know much about armor tactics," I sent mentally. "Why is he wandering about a built up area like this?"

"Difficult to say," Maauro returned. "It may be that because Maximillian is not professional military. Or, it may be that its imperative to seek out Seddonese life and destroy it, causes it to hunt through the city. Remember that my own tactical sense was sometimes compromised by my original imperative to seek out and destroy Infestors."

"Yeah, I remember," I returned with a rueful note. When Maauro had been ruled by her M-7 combat programs, she'd pitch into direct combat with anything touched by the Infestors regardless of the odds.

We stalked forward, not taking to cover yet, as the enemy machine must still be far ahead. I was looking forward so intently, dreading the sight of the crested head of the Destroyer that I damn near went sprawling over some debris in the road. Maauro gave me a reproachful look. But she did not take the chance to urge me to remain behind in cover while she attacked alone. I resolved not to give her any further excuse to bring it up.

We paused at a branch in the road. One level went wide to the left. The other dropped to the rooftop level of an apartment complex that had a pool filled with rainwater and verandas all about a central tower that stretched skyward.

"Luxury apartments," I sent, "lots of open space and connections to other rooftops."

"Yes," Maauro sent back. "Let's transfer to the building rooftops." She motioned me over and I again climbed onto her back. Maauro ran forward and leapt the three meter gap from road to the rooftop. We separated quickly. The landing had made a significant amount of noise, but no beams or rockets slashed down at us and we resumed our stalk, Maauro in the lead. All I could hear was wind and occasionally running water, but she seemed to have no doubt of where she was going.

"It occurs," she sent to me, either picking up my thought or divining it, "that there is a major street running north and south in the center of the city. Such would appeal to our adversary, allowing him to traverse the island in search of prey and yet be in a relatively open area. His appreciation for armor tactics may be more sophisticated than we thought."

"We will enter a building south of its approach," she added. "There we will spring our ambush. I will attack from inside a building. You will observe from a higher position with a good avenue of retreat and you will remember your promise to me. If we become separated, I have marked two rally points on your hand comp. Proceed to the one I designate."

"Understood," I returned, doing my best not to think about crossed fingers.

CHAPTER 26

WE REACH THE SOUTHERN END OF THE BROAD STREET RUNNING *down from the north. I survey the area. There is a park in front of us. But from here, the streets south to the bridge are much narrower, favoring my attack. The broad way forks at the park, but a tower has fallen in the adjacent street, taking down a skyway and that road is effectively blocked. Unless my enemy retraces his steps to go down a road thousands of meters away, he must come this way. In the narrow streets, the advantage is mine.*

"Wrik," I send. "I want you to remain in this triangular building. It allows for a good path of retreat south to the bridge through the skyways. I will cross and attack out of that building." I point at a glassed building where much of the glass is intact, at least above the first and second stories.

Wrik nods, his face pale. He cradles his weapon. He leans forward and kisses me on the mouth. "Good luck to us both. Remember, we will save Maximillian if we can. But I will not trade you for him. Understood?"

I nod. Leaving him atop the building, I quickly make my way down, having to drop the last story as the staircase at that level has collapsed. I walk across the street, keeping in cover, more intent on not making noise than on speed. I know where my enemy is by the vibration of his enormous steps. He cannot see me. He cannot detect me by sensors, so only sound can give me away. The wind gusts unevenly, lifting my long, black hair. I have removed my yellow hair ribbon and secured it within my body.

My sensors tell me the Destroyer is around the corner about eight hundred meters north, coming slowly toward the park. Despite the use of alloys and ceramics, it is extremely heavy and must gauge each step carefully.

I enter the building opposite the triangular structure where I left Wrik and climb the stairwell to a floor well above street level. How I wish I could have persuaded Wrik not to come, or to turn back. I had seriously considered stunning him and leaving him somewhere, but the city is full of wildlife dangers and I cannot leave him unconscious in it.

Beyond that, the thought of using a weapon, even a non-lethal one on him, brings back memories of my previous existence as M-7, when we were on the Infestor Artifact. I came within a hair's breadth of killing him before I could break free of my programmed compulsions. The memory is my bitterest one and it would have made it impossible for me to carry out my threat even with a stunner.

But enough of emotional distractions, I am now five stories up in what was once a department store. Wrik is one-hundred-forty meters away and above on the rooftop where I left him. My own scanners are set to penetrate the electronic cloak I built into his clothes. I frown. I had asked him to retreat further and he had nodded, his way of indicating an apparent agreement that he had no intention of carrying out.

I lay down my armspac; the HEAT rounds and AP have proven ineffective and are not likely to do better even at close range. I must depend on my plasma torch, my physical strength and my ability to penetrate its cybernetic defenses if I can disrupt it physically.

I remain still. The glass six meters in front of me blocks any infrared signature off me. Deep radar would not tell me from any other metal in this built area. So long as I make no noise my enemy should not be able to detect me.

I gather myself as a shadow falls on the street. Then I see the massive shoulder of my enemy.

I attack, accelerating to my max speed in the confined space and unleashing a torrent of cybernetic viral attacks as I lunge out of the building, exploding the glass panels in front of me. I am in the air, my original right arm blazes with the plasma torch. I fire a quick blast of depleted uranium flechettes from my left hand to add to the confusion. One ancient war machine to another, I send it as much destruction as I can.

My enemy staggers and lurches, crashing into the building opposite the one from which I leapt and in which Wrik is hiding. My cyber-attacks are aimed at its mobility and sensors first. But my elation is short-lived. Against a purely computerized system I would have triumphed immediately, but just as the Destroyer's systems fail under the blows of my cyber-attacks, they reset. The biological brain within the Destroyer is not vulnerable to my cyber-assault. It acts as the final redoubt for the Destroyer. From within Maximillian's genetically enhanced brain, where I cannot strike, comes the reboot codes. My enemy is degraded in performance, but his systems are rebooting almost as fast as I disrupt them. Worse still, the time interval is closing. The Destroyer is cybernetically ducking and covering, faster every millisecond.

I land on the enemy's shoulder 1.76545 seconds after plunging out of the shattered window. My armor-piercing flechettes sparkle and bounce off the enemy's giant face and his beam weapon, but do little damage. The giant head turns toward me with its fearsome mask. I see its huge arms beginning to move. I strike with my plasma torch. Ceramic and alloy begin to melt and part under the torch, but not quickly enough. The arms move slowly, to my senses, but not slowly enough that I can keep the torch in the one spot. I backflip away as a giant hand slams onto its own shoulder with a tremendous clangor. The beam weapon lashes out and the building I leapt from explodes in flame and debris.

I am behind the turning head but it continues in its three hundred sixty-five degree turn, trying to lock onto me. Glass, metal and masonry fly about the street as the deadly beam rips into buildings. The Destroyer throws itself backwards into a building trying to crush me. I evade these clumsy attacks easily, leaping about the Destroyer's upper body at high speed, jabbing and slashing with my plasma torch. My enemy, I realize with rueful admiration, is well made and designed. He is slow, but I cannot remain in one place long enough to physically penetrate his armor to vital points.

The Destroyer adds chain gun fire from weapons in the giant head and rockets ripple from shoulder packs. The missiles zip past me, one nearly striking my middle as I twist in mid-air to avoid the attack. My plasma torch melts the chain guns as I lengthen it into a sword shape. I leap away as the beam weapon fires back. Fragments and flame wash over us both continuously as we struggle.

A giant fist swings at me. I leap toward it, grab it and use it to swing myself at the enormous face keeping close to its body. My speed would make me a blur to Wrik's human vision. I make a sudden change of direction as more rockets ripple out.

"Wrik," I shout into the telepathic link. "Withdraw. The collateral destruction in the area is increasing exponentially." He does not reply though I sense he is still alive across our link. My enemy has not realized that I am not alone and must not. I can only hope that Wrik remains sensibly hidden.

I reach the head again and physically attack the joins and seams of the beam gun unit. The weapon tube can endure the heat of my plasma but if I can reach the inner mechanism and tear it apart...

A hand reaches for me, again I backflip but my enemy, by chance or design, changes direction and the immense hand grazes me. The blow shocks me, but I invert and strike with my plasma torch, penetrating a joint and shearing off part of the hand. Still I've been slowed and a rocket hits me in the mid-section. It is too close to have armed and does not explode. Yet it flings me away from my enemy and I crash into a 3rd floor balcony. Danger. I am too far away from the Destroyer and vulnerable to being targeted.

I scramble to my feet as the beam gun tracks toward me. The great arms sweep up to narrow my options so I cannot escape the beam.

A blast of concentrated fire strikes the Destroyer's head. Mini-grenades, AP bullets and particle beams crash into the armored face. Wrik has fired his weapon on cyclic emptying all its firepower in seconds. The Destroyer's cyber-systems are still battling my viruses and it is relying heavily on Maximillian's brain, which, with its biological reflexes, causes the giant machine to flinch, raising the left arm to protect its face. Wrik uses the delay to fire the LAW shoulder-launched rocket he carried. The round hits the Destroyer's face and again it flinches.

I leap back into action, moving to the right and striking with my plasma torch as I race up the right arm. The enemy must choose between returning Wrik's ineffective fire, or dealing with my direct attack. It chooses me.

"Wrik," I demand. "Break off and escape. I will rendezvous with you at Rally Point 2 by the bridge."

"No," he shouts to me. "Not unless you do. It's too big. Run!"

I take his advice but not as he wishes it. I spray the face with flechettes to attract its attention, then leap away and dash around the corner. If Wrik will not withdraw from the battle zone, I will move the zone away from him.

"Wrik respond,"

I immediately hear heavy breathing. "Here," he sends, "running like a gazelle, no indication it's pursuing me."

"Maximize your speed and withdraw to Rally Point. Wrik, you promised me you wouldn't fire!"

"Withdraw my ass. I'm heading across the rooftop to the street you're in. I've still got my triple-auto."

I realize Wrik is sensing my location from the link. He is above me to the left; the Destroyer is on the other side of the city block—

The building next to me explodes. The Destroyer has used his beam gun, set on a wide aperture to core it out. The beam grazes me, throwing me to the ground. It takes .0465 seconds for me to shake off the blow and begin to climb to my feet. The Destroyer, in that instant, fires all its remaining rockets through the hole it has blown through the building and charges behind them.

None of the missiles strike me directly, but the concussions disorient me and I cannot move. As I shrug them off and rise, an immense blow knocks me sprawling into a large area of muddy ground from a broken water pipe. The Destroyer is standing over me and its giant foot comes down before I can do more than brace my arms and feet against it.

I staggered to my feet, my ears ringing, blood flowing down my dust-covered face. I couldn't hear anything physically, but I sensed Maauro. She was in trouble. I reached the roof's edge, the section next to me had totally collapsed and I'd missed falling into it by meters.

Below I saw horror. The Destroyer, torn and smoking, but still moving, stood over Maauro, a foot raised. She lay in the mud and she raised her arms to ward it off. Maauro defeated. Something I'd never imagined. My weapon was gone and useless anyway. I had nothing.

Except my mind.

It came to me in an instant, our last chance. I didn't even know if she could do it.

"Maauro," I screamed, "project a hologram of Shasti Rainhell. Say what I tell you!"

"Yes," she sent back, her mental voice calm as if she wasn't under the Destroyer's massive foot.

"Do it now!" I demanded.

I do what Wrik orders without question though I do not understand what he plans. I glare up at the massive machine, trying crushing me. Fortunately I am in mud and he is mostly pushing me deep into the ground. I project my voice in Shasti Rainhell's voice.

In an instant, Shasti Rainhell was standing in the street next to the monster's foot. She was as we last saw her. Her black and silver hair shone, and her green eyes blazed in the pale face. "Grandson!" she shouted in an amplified voice. "Maximillian, it's me. I've come for you. I've come to bring you home. Stop this now!"

The Destroyer reels back, its arms in front of the giant face as if to ward off a blow.

I look up at the towering Destroyer, gathering my feet under me and amazed by the success of Wrik's tactic. I launch all my cybernetic attacks into my enemy. His defenses are scrambled, ineffective, the biological reboot it had before is not working. I am now conscious of Maximillian as a separate entity in the machine, as if the boy has suddenly awakened to his grandmother's call. I sense pain, bewilderment and an overwhelming grief and loneliness.

I must press my advantage. "Max," I shout in Shasti's voice. "Come out Maximillian. Come back with me, Max. Come home!"

The Destroyer thrashes, smashing the building behind it. The machine fires its weapons randomly, in sputtering bursts, even the beam weapon flashes as if damaged. My cyber-attacks gain ground. The Destroyer is on its own, trying desperately to put Maximillian back into comatose servitude. I cannot be careful but rip through systems tearing apart linkages, severing programs.

"Maximillian," I implore in Shasti's voice. "Grandson. Come out. Please. Do it for me."

A giant hand reaches out but not to strike. It is a gesture of desperation. An anguished howl bursts from the great gray shape. Across the telepathic link from Wrik I feel a flood of sympathy and pain. He recognizes the agony in that cry.

From deep inside the Destroyer, a last cry rips from its speakers. "Grandma," a young voice screams. "Help me!"

CHAPTER 26

The Destroyer topples backwards into the street as I slam into its CPU, severing its self-destruct and auto-repair circuits. I savage all, save one maintenance program, which I trigger. The massive chest plate of the Destroyer slowly grinds open.

CHAPTER 27

I **STARE AT THE DOWNED MACHINE, ITS CHEST PLATE OPEN-**ing. I couldn't believe it worked.

"Maauro," I shouted both mentally and aloud. "Are you all right?"

"Yes, Wrik. My damages are minor. Are you?"

"Same, bruises and cuts. Is it dead?"

"It is. Let us hope it has not taken the boy with it. I have called for Olivia and the *Sinner*.

"Good. I'm coming down."

By the time I negotiated the staircases of the damaged building and reached the street I could hear *Sinner II's* engines. But I only had eyes for Maauro, her exterior was chipped and scratched as I had never seen it before. Fortunately her face looked undamaged, then I realized that she'd probably concentrated on repairing it to lessen my concern. I put my arms around her and hoed her close despite the waves of heat beating from her body.

"God damn it," I managed, trying to keep my voice level and failing. "I thought he had you. I thought you were going to die."

She was stroking my back with her original right hand which she used whenever she touched me. "I was. This time it was you who saved me, dearest friend."

"Not bad for a fragile bag of blood and bone." I managed.

"You are the very definition of the unexpected, Wrik. A valuable quality that will cause me to overlook your blatant lies to me about staying in cover and not firing."

I laughed. "Well, if you are going to throw every little thing back in my face ..."

Engines whined and *Sinner* went into hover above us. The bomb bay opened and Olivia drifted down on a jetbelt, her sniper rifle cradled in her arms. She landed next to Maauro and me, her eyes on the fallen monster. She had a large duffel bag across her shoulders, the aid kit.

Olivia turned to both of us and whistled at Maauro. "Wow, he did a number on you. Are you going to be ok?"

"The damage is largely superficial," she replied. "All is within my repair parameters when I can spare the energy."

Olivia tapped her mike. "Dusko, return to the base and let everyone know what's happening. Come back with the mule and a stretcher."

"Roger that," he said. The fighter slewed about and headed for the river.

She turned to me and started unpacking the aid kit.

"I'm ok," I said in surprise.

"Yeah," she said. "Not so much." She made me sit and poured most of her canteen over my face, apparently I was covered in dirt and blood. Antiseptic spray and wound seal finished it up. My body armor was dented and scratched but it seemed nothing had penetrated. I felt too many bruises to bother identifying individual ones.

"Come on," I said, impatiently after she fixed the worst of it. "Let's look inside. We've come a long way and through a lot to see this young man."

Maauro led as we approached the fallen Colossus. She leapt up onto its chest and Olivia and I followed more slowly, climbing up the Destroyer. Its body was pitted and scarred, gouged and burnt. A tremendous heat scorched our exposed skin and we had to be careful to avoid the places Maauro struck with her plasma torch on its upper body.

We approached the cavity in the chest. Maauro leaned in and began pulling metal and plastic out. In a few moments we saw a clearplast container with a human form dimly visible in it. Maximillian.

Maauro lifted the heavy plastic cover off the young man. I was almost physically struck by the smell of him.

"Is he dead?" I managed.

"No," Maauro said, slowly pulling leads and attachments off the emaciated body. The fragments of clothing Maximillian still wore were filthy and I could see pressure sores all over him. I had to fight nausea.

"Let's get him out of the cold," Olivia said.

I realized she was right, the wind was kicking up again. The only heat came from the scorched Destroyer. Above us clouds were piling up, probably another damn rainstorm on the way.

"I will need hot water and clean clothes," Maauro said. "I'll manufacture bandages in my body. Bring the aid kit. Doubtless I will need to make more but it will be a start."

She reached down and severed some belts holding him in. Tubing covered his penis and rectum and I simply didn't want to think about any of that.

I was grateful to run and get the aid kit. Olivia and Maauro moved the emaciated boy into a building. Maauro used her plasma torch to heat some metal so it emitted a comforting warmth. She bent some more metal into two cauldrons, one which she filled with water from a pool. She stuck a hand in it and in seconds had purified the water by running it through her into the second cauldron.

"Please go outside," Maauro said, taking the aid kit from me. "I will do the wound cleaning. This process will be unpleasant."

"I can handle it," I said.

"There is no need," she replied. "Leave it to me. Ignore any cries, there will be some pain as he is too weak to anesthetize."

Olivia, her face strained and as grim, nodded. "Yeah, all yours, I wasn't cut out for nursing."

We walked out but Olivia kept going and I followed until we were about a hundred meters away. We could hear sounds, but the distance was too great for them to be intelligible.

Olivia shivered.

I started to take off my coat, but she stopped me with a gesture and a wan smile. "Wasn't from the cold. I was just thinking of that poor bastard sealed in there month after month, rotting."

"Try not to," I said.

Olivia reached into her backpack and came up with a small flask. "Don't usually condone drinking on duty. Today's an exception. Denlenn brandy." She took a long sip and shuddered after, then handed it to me.

I also took a long draw of the fiery liquid. Somehow it seemed to hold the smell of death further away and I was grateful. I handed it back to her and she replaced it. We stood watching the weak sun drift toward afternoon over the ruined city, each of us lost in our thoughts.

"Wrik, Olivia." Maauro called. "You may return now."

We walked back, reluctant to face the wreck of Maximillian, but Maauro had worked some wonders. His clothes were gone, destroyed or recycled in her. He now wore a light, tan, one-piece covering, with what looked like fleece booties. Bottles hung over him from stands she'd made from bits of metal, dripping fluids and nutrients into the depleted body. Maauro had used everything in the aid kit it seemed, then consumed some of the material around her for her internal factories. The litter he lay on kept him off the ground. While a smell of disinfectant and illness still clung to the area, it was not the appalling stench of decay.

"I have used the most powerful antibiotics I dared," she said. "I have wound seal and synth flesh on all the decubitus ulcers. Had he not been young and strong, he wouldn't have survived. I amputated some toes and fingers that could not be saved."

"Is he aware?" I asked, swallowing hard.

"He seemed conscious, but not aware, when I extracted him. Like a weak animal. He passed out quickly when I tended his wounds. I would like to move him back to the ship as soon as we can. Additional surgery might be necessary and the cleaner and more sterile the environment the better.

"First however I am going to hook up to the Destroyer and drain its power supply. I have been using power at a prodigious rate."

"Glad somebody's got an appetite," Olivia muttered as Maauro ducked out. I moved to follow her then stopped looking at Olivia and Maximillian.

She gazed at me. "Go. I'll watch the boy."

"You sure?"

"Wrik I don't think you could stop yourself from following her if you wanted to and you know what? You don't want to."

I decided not to answer her. For one thing, she was right.

CHAPTER 28

AFTER SEVERAL WEEKS OF CELEBRATION AND RECOVERY, we lifted off for Confed space. *Stardust* was crowded: Elgee the Morok had recovered enough to travel, she and Fitaz, the Frokossi survivor of Bexlaw returned with us. The human, Tomas, remained with a girl he'd met on Seddon. We also carried Parisha, now an accredited Seddonese diplomat. Our last passenger was the wounded and silent Maximillian.

The crowding led to Olivia and I doubling up. Maauro also gave up her cabin, spending her time on the bridge or in the engine room. She was a good nurse for Maximillian, who exhibited little sign of awareness beyond being able to eat and drink. Nursing him would have been grim and wearying for anyone but Maauro, who talked to him all the time while trying to restore his body with physical therapy.

One night I heard singing. I slowly made my way to the sickbay. Olivia and Maauro were there. Olivia was singing. Not well, but they were old songs, soft and gentle. She was teaching them to Maauro, who wanted to be able to sing lullabies to the shattered boy. I walked away, and wondered how anyone could ever doubt Maauro was a living being.

When we returned to Velstus it was to find the Confederate Battle Cruiser *Seydlitz* stationed at the exit jump point and not a trace of the ISM. *Seydlitz's* captain refueled us and immediately dispatched two automated courier drones, one to Earth and one to Star Central. Then he used his engines and grapples to boost our speed and get us to the next warp point. We were bound for Star Central with Maximillian. The battlecruiser was destined for Earth, bearing the other survivors of the Bexlaw expedition and the Seddonese ambassador.

There was another leave-taking as well

Olivia had packed her gear upon receiving orders from the *Seydlitz*. She called me to her quarters.

"I didn't expect it to be like this," I said.

She smiled, a little sadly, I thought. "It's the way of the service, isn't it?"

"And that's ok with you?"

"This is the life I choose, the one I want. Don't feel bad, Wrik. You're not missing anything with me. I told you I have places to go and things to do. Playing house was never in the cards. Didn't work that well for me the first time and he was a Marine, not a man of shadows and mysteries. Do I even know your real name, yet?"

I looked away.

CHAPTER 28

"Wrik, I have something to say to you. I think it's a bit of wisdom worth sharing. I hope it is."

I turned back to her.

"You're consort to an alien, and you're something I can't even name with an android. I don't doubt the truth or the depth of your feelings for either. But I know you'll never be able to fully commit to anyone, until you stop running from whatever you're fleeing. Until you return to your home, reclaim your real name and face down whatever it was that made you leave."

I could only barely breathe.

Olivia walked up to me and kissed me on the lips. "We'll see each other again. We're not done yet."

"Olivia," I said. "Stay alive."

She smiled and slipped past me out the hatch.

I turned off the light and stood in the darkened room for twenty long minutes.

So it was that seventeen galactic standard months after we had left Earth, *Stardust* returned to the orbit of Star Central. Our trip in from the warp point had been a silent one, save for one micro-squeak transmission to Shasti Rainhell, who we hoped would be waiting for us. It warned her that we were bringing her grandson back, but all was not well.

I did not call Jaelle and asked Dusko and Maauro to hold off communicating with anyone until after we had landed and turned Maximillian over to his grandmother. After more than a year and half of real-time, I didn't want my first sight of Jaelle and her children to be by a screen. This I needed to be face-to-face for. Both honored my request and neither seemed to see it as unusual.

A reply to our microburst came back as quickly as light could return it. Rainhell was waiting for us. She would meet us in the early morning hours at the landing pad by Lost Planet. She'd handle all security and urged us to remain radio silent until she had her grandson back. Maauro shot back an acknowledgement and we assumed orbit unheralded or acknowledged by any other than the automatic traffic control.

We separated the *Sinner II* from *Stardust* to prepare for landing. Dusko said he would land separately later.

"Why?" I asked.

"You can deal with Rainhell and returning the damaged goods," he replied.

"There will be no trouble," Maauro said, "only thanks offered."

He shrugged. "Thanks mean little to me. I will accept having a favor owed to me by a powerful leader. And I'm less sure of her than you are. In any event there are pleasures and people I wish to see and messes," he glanced sidelong at me, "that will not be improved by my presence."

I nodded. "Okay, land later in the day. We'll see you when we see you. Stay out of trouble."

He grunted and headed for the *Sinner*. I'm sure he was as tired of our company as I was of his.

The ALS brought us down long after everyone at Lost Planet would have gone home, on a moonless night. We rode down on our impellers, lighting up the area. I could see vehicles waiting for us. I killed the engines with an odd feeling. So much had happened in the seventeen months, yet returning to Star Central made it feel as if we had never left. As if the intervening year and half with our voyage into lost worlds had never happened.

Stardust itself felt strange and empty to me. Olivia and the rescued had gone on to Earth. Dusko's moody presence banished, the ship held just Maauro, me, and the barely responsive Maximillian. I don't know what sort of homecoming I'd envisioned but it wasn't this funereal, silent return.

"Are you all right?" Maauro asked when I didn't rise from my seat.

I looked up at her. I'd come on this voyage because I couldn't bear to be parted from her. Even now I could not put a proper name to what she was to me: friend, loved one, all but lover. "I feel," I said slowly. "Like the ghost at a party. Or maybe more like a man trying to sneak back into his old life."

"With all its complications."

"Yes," I said, surprised. *Why should I be,* I thought, *who do I talk to? Who knows every secret and concern I have but Maauro?* And on this voyage she too had learned and changed and grown.

"Out there is Jaelle, who I love but haven't seen for a year and half. In that time she'll have had children if she could. I don't know where their father is or how I will have to deal with him. But the big question is, 'What does Jaelle feel now?" What does she want? It was always a challenge to make this work before. Can we do it now with all that has happened?"

"Those answers," Maauro said, gazing at the vehicles now moving slowly toward us, "await you out there. They cannot be found on this deck or divined by me."

I drew a deep and shaky breath. It wouldn't get easier or clearer sitting here. I stood.

Maauro put her hand on my arm. "Whatever awaits either of us when we leave this deck, know that you and I are permanent in this existence. Know it and always rely on it."

I raised my hand and stroked her cheek. "I know it. I hope you know the same is true with me. The bond between us may trouble others, maybe us too at times, but it is and will be." I wanted to say, "I love you."

I'd said it before and easily enough but with Jaelle so near and my emotions so raw and mixed it seemed somehow too much. Maybe she felt it too, so we used words that added up to the same thing, but didn't carry such a freight of confusion.

"It will be strange for a while," I added.

She smiled. "When isn't it strange? We are male and female. I no longer think of my femininity as an affectation. When, sometime, somewhere, I became a living being, I became a female living being. Yet nothing can change the fact that we are on different sides of an abyss. You are biological life of flesh and blood and I am silicon, ceramic and metal. There is no present way across, there may never be. Perhaps there should never be. Love for us may always remain a thing of shared time and experience with little physical expression."

"Now," I said. "You waited until now, to start this conversation."

To my astonishment, Maauro laughed. The first time I'd ever heard her do so. My God, was she growing and changing before my very eyes; becoming more human by the second?

"See," she said. "I really am female."

"I never doubted it," I returned. *Unfortunately, neither had Jaelle,* I thought to myself.

"What I meant to say," I continued carefully, "is that I will be occupied with Jaelle and all the changes in our life, but I don't want you to think that I'll forget about you."

She shook her long, black hair, confined by its yellow silk ribbon. "Such a thought would never occur to me. Besides, I may use the time to find myself a handsome boy robot."

"He'd be lucky," I replied ruefully, "and I, no doubt would be both jealous as hell and sure he wasn't good enough for you."

"Then all is as it should be," she said. The smile faded on her face. "Come let us finish our last duty of this voyage."

We walked down to the cabin where Maximillian lay. Despite our best efforts the boy was still painfully thin.

"I have him lightly sedated," Maauro said, "for fear of the stress. This is a normal but deep sleep." We loaded him in a gurney and took him down to the midships hatch. Maauro confirmed the gantry was outside with its elevator. I opened the hatch and enjoyed the scent of fresh air, even at the edge of a spaceport. There was a small park opposite our office, lit only by its outside lights. Beyond lay the city and the spaceport glowing with a million lights. From the park wafted the scent of green and growing things that dispelled the sick room smell in the airlock.

We rolled the gurney on the gantry elevator and it lowered us the few meters to the ground. A cool wind cut through the unwalled elevator. I zipped my jacket and checked the fleece blanket on the silent boy.

As the cage rolled back, we could see several large aircars and something too big to be an ambulance. I suspected Rainhell had a mobile trauma unit with surgeons on standby. Her retinue of guards and staff halted at her upraised hand. She strode toward us, not running, but no normal human could have matched the speed and length of her stride.

She reached us and knelt before the stretcher, her face tight with grief. "Maximillian, baby, it's grandmother. I've come to take you home."

"He's deeply asleep," Maauro said.

Rainhell raised her eyes to me, brilliant with unexpressed rage and tears. "Give me all the worst now."

"Maximillian was stuck inside an alien war machine, functioning as part of his CPU for over a year as it rampaged across a planet. The thing was out of a nightmare, a humanform robot over thirty meters tall. It didn't...it didn't take care of him well. Physically he has lost four fingers and most of his toes. Mentally, well he has been able to follow simple commands but little more. He hasn't spoken."

Her mouth became a grim slit in the perfect face.

"There is some reason for hope," Maauro ventured. "I can find no sign of structural damage to his brain. This silence may be a reflection of emotional trauma. Perhaps in time, with care and rest, he may recover more of his identity."

"He will have all of that," she swore, "the best of anything that can be done." She kissed her grandson on both his closed eyes. "Grandmother is here. Don't worry. Nothing will touch you now. Mother and Father are coming. I've sent a warship for them. You'll see them soon."

Did I imagine it, or was the boy's expression more peaceful, more relaxed?

"You're the one who saved him," I blurted out.

"What?" she seemed to focus on me with difficulty.

"We'd failed," I said. "Physical attacks, cybernetic attacks, nothing could break the Destroyer's grip on him. It was about to crush Maauro when we summoned up your image in a hologram. You told Maximillian that you loved him and had come to take him home. He woke, cried out, 'Grandmother, help me.' That broke the link, and Maauro finished the Destroyer off and got him out."

Rainhell rose, her face hidden under her long hair. She put a fever-warm hand on my shoulder. I could feel her body trembling, almost shaking as she fought for composure, struggling with rage and grief. Her grip on my shoulder was beyond a strong man's.

A single strangled sob escaped her. I wanted to put my arms around her, but knew I couldn't. So I just stood there and endured her grip in mute sympathy.

"Thank you," she whispered. The grip eased and she patted my shoulder in apology. There would be bruises tomorrow. I couldn't have cared less.

She wiped a hand across her face. If there had been tears, I hadn't seen them. She gestured and a team of medics and security raced over, surrounding the boy and bearing his litter off to the waiting trauma vehicle.

Shasti turned back to me. "You have someone waiting for you, young man. She's at home with her three kits; all four are in good health. They have been watched over nonstop since you left."

"All four?" I ventured.

"Yes," she replied. "The father, a diplomat from a respectable family, left for his homeworld three months ago when the contract ended. He has no plans to return."

Now it was my turn to be silent and grateful. I nodded.

"Bexlaw?" she asked.

"Dead."

"Good, that saves me doing it. There are others who will pay dearly for this."

"Another day soon," I said, "we should talk. There's a contact. There may be a way around wholesale bloodletting."

She looked at me, a shadow of something in her eyes. Finally she nodded. "I will listen."

"I can handle everything from here, Wrik," Maauro said. "You should go. I will see you when I see you."

I walked over, took her small face in my hands and kissed her. She held onto me with her careful right arm for a few seconds.

I turned to face Rainhell.

"I will remember you always, Captain Trigardt."

"As I will you, Captain Rainhell."

She gestured to a man standing by one of the aircars. He opened the door. I started for the vehicle. I slid into the seat, bound for home and maybe now, finally ready.

I watch Wrik vanish into the aircar with a mix of emotions, not all of which I can put a name to. I turn back to Rainhell with some relief, glad to have something else to focus on.

"From this point," the tall human growls, "I will have no greater priority than restoring my grandson and undoing the damage to our family. But first I must make a few minutes for you. Take it as a sign of your importance to me and the enormity of the debt I owe you that I do so just now."

I nod, unsure of what to say.

"Maauro," Rainhell says, "walk with me a while?"

We head away from the ship. Not toward the waiting cars, but toward the small park across the street. I occasionally go there to contemplate a tiny waterfall in a shaded spot. Shasti heads toward it as if she knows that.

CHAPTER 28

"We are, I think, very similar in many respects," Shasti says, to my surprise. "We're both artificial in origin. I was made of biological materials, but those materials were the assemblage of millions of strands of altered DNA. I had no actual parents. Even among the Engineered I'm unique in that.

"In a way we are both the dreams of our Creators, for all that their dreams sometimes wrapped us in nightmares. Do you understand what I mean?"

"I believe so," I respond. "It's difficult. For all the eons since my creation, most of them were spent alone on a rock in space, barely aware, with no thoughts worthy of consideration. Only the seven years before my stranding and the six since I awoke in your time have had any meaning. So I am young and inexperienced in some ways."

"Would you then be guided by me, who has seen much of life and love, Little One?"

I look up at her in surprise. "I will listen to all you say."

"Wrik does not quite realize this, or wish to admit it if he does, but his time with Jaelle is coming to an end. They will remain consorts and friends, I judge, but the passion between them is ebbing away."

"You are certain of this?" I ask, alarmed, unsettled and confused all at once.

"I loved a Nekoan once. I loved her all of her life, but it returned to the friendship it was before we crossed that line together. Nekoans love passionately, but not long: biology, custom, however one explains it. That's their nature. There is no forever with them."

"I have feared this break in my network," I say. "Feared its coming, feared I'm the cause of it."

"You are, in part," Shasti returns. "Wrik could not stay behind if you left. He simply could not. Jaelle will not be able to forget that, even if she forgives it. Beyond that, even if Jaelle was a human, this might have happened. They're at different places in life, wanting different things. The fact that she's Nekoan and a little older, brought it on sooner. As I said, I don't see them separating, but she is a practical being. She'll turn more and more to her kits, her legacy for them in the company she's building and the matrilineal line of her family. The fact that Wrik is human and can never wholly occupy the place a Nekoan male would for her, will make them orbit farther and farther from each other."

The wind stirs our long hair, insects chirp in the dimness of the night. Overhead clouds scud across the star-lit sky. It would rain in the morning and keep the temperature down to something Wrik would find pleasant.

"You mean to tell me more than this," I say, gazing up at the sky.

"Yes. There are powerful feelings between you and Wrik. I sensed this even from the first. Love, I would say. Not the common sort, not even deep friendship, but the sort that is rare to find in this existence."

I turn to her, staring into her jade-green eyes. If I had a heart it would be hammering. I do not know if I fear more that she will continue, or that she will not.

"You don't deny it," Shasti says with a small smile.

I sit by the rocks, overlooking the waterfall. After a moment she sits next to me.

"There is..." *I begin, then hesitate.* "How can I say what is between us? I could say love, but I have learned that there are more shades to that word than exist in the spectrum. Do I mean the same thing by it that you do? That he does?"

"Love," *Shasti muses.* "It took me a long time to recognize it as the rare and precious gift it is. Never to be scorned or taken lightly; whichever of its many forms it takes."

Sadness steals through me. "I believe I'm capable of it. Perhaps I'm the only machine ever to feel so. I have emotions, though they seem pale and weak things to what you biologicals feel. The powerful emotions I have felt, have all been in my context with Wrik: my desire to protect him, to spend time with him, even to simply hear his voice. Yet I am incapable of physical love."

Shasti shakes her head slowly. "Maauro, a being that could overcome all you have done can solve that too. You may have to be very brave, Maauro and stake your claim for something you want. Don't wait until a door closes before realizing that it is there."

"Did you once wait too long?" *I ask.*

"Yes," *Shasti replies.* "I was very, very lucky. That one door closed, but others opened for me. Still I wonder.... Well, never mind that."

Two birds fly down to the small pond and skim the water before settling. We sit in silence for minutes, letting the beauty of the place settle what the conversation has stirred up.

"Time for me to go," *Shasti says.*

I stand and walk beside her as we head out of the small park.

"It's said that I have a long memory for harms done me and mine," *Shasti says.* "I also have a long memory for those who have done me a kindness, as you have. In the hard times that are coming, and I believe we both see them on the horizon, remember me should you ever need help."

"I will," *I say.*

We reach the edge of the park. The aircars, with their guards and attendants, stand waiting across the street.

Shasti turns and smiles down at me. "I hope we meet again."

"Thank you, Shasti," *I say.* "I promise to think long and well on all you have told me."

CHAPTER 28

To my surprise she leans down and kisses me on the cheek, then straightens and walks briskly off, her black and silver hair a banner in the breeze.

THE END

www.ingramcontent.com/pod-product-compliance
Lightning Source LLC
Chambersburg PA
CBHW060640260626
47161CB00008B/2926